Luisa Buehler

The Reenactor:
A Staged Death

Book Seven

A Grace Marsden Mystery

Publishing

The Reenactor: A Staged Death
A Grace Marsden Mystery Book Six
An Echelon Press Book

First Echelon Press paperback printing / June 2011

Cover Art © Nathalie Moore
Award winning Graphic Artist

Echelon Press
9055 G Thamesmeade Road
Laurel, MD 20723
www.echelonpress.com

ISBN: 978-159080-593-0
1-59080-593-3
eBook 978-159080-594-7

PRINTED IN THE UNITED STATES OF AMERICA

10 9 8 7 6 5 4 3 2 1

Other Books by
Luisa Buehler

The Grace Marsden Mystery series

The Inn Keeper: A Registered Death (*Book Six*)

The Lighthouse Keeper: A Beckoning Death (*Book Five*)

The Scout Master: A Prepared Death (*Book Four*)

The Station Master: A Scheduled Death (*Book Three*)

The Lion Tamer: A Caged Death (*Book Two*)

The Rosary Bride: A Cloistered Death (*Book One*)

Missing
Featuring
"Harry's Fall from Grace"

eBooks

Tuscan Tall and Too Close for Comfort

To Gerry and Kit, for your patience and love.
I dreamed the dream and you encouraged me.
I love you guys!

I want to thank so many people who made not only this book, but the series possible and plausible. Heartfelt thanks to Karen Syed, my publisher, for believing in my abilities as a writer and in Gracie's appeal as a character.

Many thanks to Kat Thompson and Mary Welk for their editing expertise. They worked diligently to help me write only what you wanted to read.

For this book I want to thank Barbara Pardol, genealogist extraordinaire, who found an appropriate family tree on whose branches I could hang murder and betrayal.

Many thanks to Peter Kiefert, Quartermaster with the 10th Illinois Volunteer Infantry. He provided much needed clarification of terms and procedures and a great suggestion that I've shamelessly claimed as my own.

If errors occur in either genealogy or reenactment issues they are my errors alone for not knowing what I didn't know and therefore didn't ask.

Thank you to local merchants in Lisle and Downers Grove who became involved in the writing of this book in an unusual way. Mark Stutz the owner of Joyful's Café and his manager DeAndria Heath hosted a coffee tasting where attendees could vote on Grace's new flavor du jour, *Highland Grog*. Randy Russell owner of Wine Expressions hosted a wine tasting party where we chose Harry's newest wine, *Luchador*, a tasty Shiraz.

Thank you to the fellow writers who traveled through this series with me providing support, friendship, and more than the occasional rescue from a plot quagmire.

Finally, a heartfelt thank you to all of you who have read the series and enjoyed getting to know Grace and her chums and who have followed her adventures with eager engagement in her life; perhaps thankful she is not your neighbor.

I have been privileged to write for you and I bid you goodbye in this series. Please join me in saying, "Goodnight, Gracie."

Chapter One

When the bullet thudded into the tree behind me I was as surprised as the shooter. I touched my face where the sudden air current had skimmed my jaw. A second after full realization reached my brain my knees went wobbly.

The Confederate soldier scrambled over the hummock he'd crouched behind and ran toward me. A foot race ensued between Johnny Reb, two Union privates, and one angry Englishman.

Harry reached me first and pulled me into his arms away from my near fatal location. His forehead twisted in deep furrows above blue eyes filled with relief. He tucked my head against his chest. I felt his heart hammering against his ribcage.

His voice carried clearly over my head. "Who the blazes is in charge!"

Only half the field remained in my line of vision. The errant shooter stood head down, panting from his dash to the tree line, his weapon held loosely at his side. He lifted his chin. "I'm sorry. I didn't see you." He looked at each of the other reenactors and back at me. His gaze swung to the tree and back to his buddies. "I didn't expect anyone to be here, I mean a civilian."

A tall man dressed in a Confederate uniform rushed into the circle, turning immediately to the shooter. "Pete, what happened? Why did you fire into the trees? The target was the haystack."

"The haystack!" Harry's body shook with anger. "The

bloody haystack? It's ten yards off." Harry flung out his arm indicating the direction opposite my previous perch.

Pete's commanding officer met Harry's outburst with a calm voice. "I'm sorry." He looked at me. "I'm happy you're okay. This side of the field never figured in our plan." He faced Harry. "Please accept my apology, I'll find out what happened." He put out his hand. "Kurt Clements."

Harry reluctantly grasped the outstretched hand. "Harry Marsden. My wife, Grace."

Our circle grew as news of the accident spread throughout the encampment. I knew which set of feet would be rushing at me in varying degrees of ability and agility.

"Harry, they said a woman was shot."

My brother Marty reached us first. My dad clocked in three steps behind him. Not bad for a baby boomer with a pasta paunch.

Harry pivoted toward them, bringing me round to their view. "I've got her, Mike. She's fine." Harry looked past Marty and spoke directly to my dad. "No one is shot; bad report." He loosened his hold on me in a seamless transfer to my dad's bear hug and stepped closer to the tree.

"Honey, we heard a woman in a dark green jacket had been shot. We couldn't find you." He hugged me harder.

"I'm okay, Dad. I'm okay."

He slowly released me.

Marty tapped me on my head. "Way to go, Sis. You got the whole camp streaming this way." My younger brother's pronouncement wasn't far off the mark. Of the over one hundred participants at this re-enactment, more than half either milled around, craning their necks for a better view, or made their way across the field.

A man with bars on his blue uniform pushed through the outer edge of people. He came directly to me. "I'm Jack

Shewman, the organizer for this encampment." He nodded briefly at Kurt Clements. "I set up in the other field for this afternoon's battle. I came as soon as I heard." He removed his wide brimmed hat and blotted the sweat on his forehead with his sleeve. "Thank God you weren't hurt."

"She could have been killed. What's the matter with you people? Don't you teach these bozos how to shoot before you give them a loaded weapon?" My father's voice rang with anger.

The captain stood his ground, fingering the brim of his hat while he waited for my dad to stop. When he heard the pause he spoke. "Mister?" He waited.

"Morelli, I'm her dad."

Jack Shewman nodded once. "Mr. Morelli, this is unfortunate. A scare like the one your daughter experienced is nerve-wracking but she was never in mortal danger. We use blanks, special wadding, not lead balls."

Apparently, he thought his statement settled it. Apparently it didn't.

"Wadding, you say, Mister Shewman?" I heard the lowered pitch in Harry's voice. "Then I would suggest, Mister Shewman, you don't know your arse from a wad to wipe it with."

Everyone turned to stare at my husband who stood at the front of the tree I'd stood before earlier. He tipped his open palm forward to reveal a piece of metal the size of a kid's gumball.

Chapter Two

"Holy man," burst from the mouth of one of the confederate soldiers who'd joined their friend. "Holy crap, Pete, why'd you load live ammo?" Pete's face turned cherry red. "Man, you could have killed her." The reenactor shook Pete by the shoulder. Harry stepped quickly toward him and grabbed the musket slipping from Pete's hand. He looked relieved to be rid of it.

Shewman gaped at Harry's hand and reached out for the lead ball. "I'd better take charge of that." Harry ignored the request and slipped the metal into his pocket. He handed the musket to Clements, and nodded toward Shewman. "Someone had better call the police."

Someone had called the police, but the not in the usual manner. The standing joke, when someone falls ill, is to call out, "Is there a doctor in the house?" Apparently, law enforcement personnel enjoy battle re-enactments. When the call went up for a cop, within minutes, four law officers rushed to the scene: three reenactors, one Confederate, two Union, and one "plainclothes", in other words, an attendee just like me.

None of the four, three FBI agents and Ric Kramer, a River Forest police inspector, had jurisdiction. Ric came to watch his fiancée, Marisol Nunez, participate in the encampment along with two of her FBI buddies. And as always, he was there watching over me.

Chapter Three

Many people who knew Ric, and knew me, would have bet the farm we'd be the couple preparing for nuptials. Could have happened once, a while back when life had played havoc with my marriage.

I'd turned to Ric for help. He'd been around ever since, for the most part waiting to see if my marriage would survive, for some of the time doing his best to destroy it.

When I couldn't get information on Harry's rescue mission to South America, I had turned to him again in a bizarre repeat of a decade old scenario.

In a place deep in your heart you know the answers. We rarely listen to the heart, having been taught from infancy to *think about your feelings*. An oxymoron–if you *think* about it.

Those convoluted thoughts clouded my feelings, stopped up my emotions like a quickly sealed top jammed onto an over-full thermos; the tiny bubbles forming and bursting around the rim signaling the end result.

Harry had been in South America too long. His mission of mercy to rescue Hannah and Lily, noble at the outset, had evolved into a race with time to stabilize Lily for a flight to the U.S., and to find his sister, who'd either wandered off or been kidnapped from the crash site. Time loomed large like the ticking of a stately grandfather clock, or a bomb.

Harry's safety in that country under the current regime would be measured in hours, and it had been days. Days of silence twisting at my heart. Years before I'd used my intellect to believe the reports of my husband's death. In my heart I'd felt his life continued, but I let others, people who loved me, shepherd me through letting go, believing what they thought to be true, agonizing through a memorial service, feeling it a sham because in my heart…

Not this time. I picked up the phone and dialed the number I'd never forgotten.

The phone rang until the telltale shift in tone signaled the answering machine would pick up. I hung up quickly. This message couldn't be communicated to a machine. It had to be spoken directly to him; in person, face to face, like before.

How could I talk to him if I couldn't find him? How could he help me keep Harry safe, bring him home if I didn't ask him, again?

"Grace, I'm ready." Will's voice pulled me from my thoughts. He stood at the door to the garage, a maroon backpack dangling from one shoulder. Harry's son shifted his weight and crossed his arms, striking the classic pose of 'man waiting for woman'. He stood in miniature exactly as Harry had stood at the same door, waiting for me to grab my purse and rush through the door he would open and hold for me.

Harry and Lily shared custody of Will. For the last seven days I'd been in charge of Will. Lily's emergency transport to the United States had brought her as far as Grady Memorial Hospital in Atlanta. She remained there until she stabilized enough to travel to Chicago. She'd already had one life-saving surgery to repair a ruptured spleen.

I stared at Will and retrieved my purse from the

counter. He opened the door and went through to the garage, leaving the door standing wide open behind him.

Seated in the car, Will pressed the button to raise the window. He snapped into his seat belt. His pack sat on the floor between his feet. A cardboard tube stuck out the top, zippered in to the side.

The trip to his school takes ten minutes. Conversation would be limited to my asking questions about after school activities and pick up times.

I knew Will worried about his mom and dad but with the attitude of an almost teen he didn't show it. Maybe at his age he couldn't imagine losing both of his parents, especially the dad he'd just discovered. Harry and Will had lost years and had been happily trying to build a foundation for the years they would add together.

I pressed my lips closed to squelch any errant sigh or sob. I wanted to hug him and tell him his life wouldn't shatter. Our relationship lacked warmth and trust. Will, with childlike logic, felt convinced if his dad divorced me, his mother would take my place in Harry's life and the three of them would live happily ever after. I wondered if now he prayed they just lived.

"What's in the tube?"

Will stared straight ahead. It wasn't uncommon for him not to answer me. If his dad were here he'd tell him to "mind me" or at least not "sass" me.

If his dad were here I'd be sitting at home enjoying a fourth cup of coffee while I tossed off a wave to them.

"It's a map," he said quietly, still focused out the window.

Had anyone else, like my dad or my brother, Marty, or even my dad's girlfriend, Jan, asked, he would have expounded.

"A map of...?" I waited, hoping for a smallest kernel of conversation.

"You don't have to pick me up today. I'm taking the bus with Frank. We're going to work on our knots for the Webelos Roundup."

Will's troop offered to host Cub Scouts at a local campground tomorrow, the purpose being to attract young scouts to their troop. Getting new boys was competitive.

I knew better than to suggest I might be able to help him learn his knots. I grew up with four brothers, all Eagle Scouts. As a kid I exhibited my OCD tendencies by twirling my hair until clumps of it would pull out. My mother insisted my brothers teach me how to tie knots and braid lanyards to keep my hair intact. She also cut my hair into a pixie style; hard to twirl stubby hair.

"Should I pick you up at Frank's? Is his address in the scout directory?"

Will rolled his eyes. "It's called the Family Handbook."

We'd pulled up to the drop-off entrance. He'd be out of the car in a flash. "Will, I need to know when to pick you up. Maybe we'll stop for dinner at KFC or–"

"I'm eating with Frank and his parents." He looked at me while his hand reached for the door. His glance slid away. With the door open and his backpack in hand he spoke over his shoulder. "I'm spending the night, too, so we can leave for the campground early."

"Will, wait a minute."

The door slammed and his back straightened as he slung the pack over his shoulders. I noticed the bulge in the bottom compartment, no doubt his Boy Scout pants and class B uniform shirt.

Damn, snookered again by this kid. I banged the steering wheel and regretted the outburst as I spotted Mrs.

Nordlund, the principal, waving me on to allow the next car to deposit their student.

Sheesh, what would she think of me?

I left the school lot as directed and headed home, planning only two stops: the cleaners and Joyful's Café. *How could I run mindless errands? How could I look forward to a steaming cup of Highland Grog and a short sit-down at the café?* I wasn't unfeeling, well maybe numb, on automatic. This is what anxiety felt like to me. I remembered from before, not knowing if Harry still lived tied me in knots, prompting me to tie knots until my finger tips bled. The memory tugged at my hands and I stroked the lanyard extending from the keys in the ignition. I flipped on my directional signal with more force than I intended. Harry always cautioned me, "Someday whilst making a right turn you'll flip the bloody lever into your passenger's lap." My eyes slid to the empty spot. Silly.

I'd done the dry cleaner two-step, pick up and drop off, at Leo's cleaners on Main Street. Two or three more trips and I'd have the family's dry cleaning on track again. I could never bring myself to carry in a huge bundle of clothing for cleaning. I liked small neat manageable orders. It made no sense to wrinkle things even more by wrapping them in a bundle of sleeves and pants' legs in order to make one trip to the cleaners. My dad called it a "lazy man's load". I glanced behind me to make sure I'd hung the burgundy pantsuit on the hook. On occasion I'd end up talking to the person behind the counter and leave without my cleaning. Not today. The freshly pressed suit would go directly into the garment bag for next winter season.

Joyful's Café had several tall round top tables and the more traditional square top standard height tables. If I were meeting people for a chat I'd sit at the lower table. Today, I carried my Highland Grog to the round top in the corner. With my back to the wall I could stare out the window not seeing, but looking deep in thought, rather than sinking into depression.

I ordered a large because I wanted to sit longer than twenty-five sips. I liked counting, always did. As a kid I made people nuts by telling them things like how many steps they had in their house or how many flowers bloomed in a pot or how many sips it took to drink the school-size carton of milk at lunch time. The large size coffee took thirty seven sips; at least another half hour of sitting.

My staring eyes missed him completely.

Chapter Four

The scrape of the chair interrupted my inward vision. His voice scrambled my brain.

"I thought you might be here." Ric Kramer stood next to me, so close the scent of Grey Flannel tempted my nose to inhale deeply. He placed a plate with a raspberry swirl pastry on it next to my coffee. "I thought you might be hungry; I know it's your favorite."

Because of the tall chair I could look directly into his eyes; dark eyes filled with concern. The same concern I'd seen in those eyes the first time I'd turned to him for help. He'd brought me food then too.

He sat in the chair across from me and placed his coffee opposite mine on the smooth wood. Ric Kramer had always been the most handsome man I'd ever met. I'd known him since college when I met my best friend, his sister, Karen. Even after an explosion almost killed him and left him with multiple surgeries and months of rehab, he stilled turned heads.

My side vision caught sight of two women bouncing interested glances off his back. He had that effect on my gender.

I looked at the pastry and pushed the plate towards him. "I'm not hungry," adding as an afterthought, "And it's not my favorite."

"I know." His grin lit up the tiny corner of my heart he still owned. "It's mine." Ric pulled the plate securely behind his coffee in case I changed my mind. He lifted the pastry to his mouth and sank his teeth into half of it. "Hmmm, the best." He munched easily like two friends meeting for a friendly chat. Only his eyes never left my face or lost their look of concern.

"How did you know I would be here? I called but…" I shrugged the rest of the statement.

"I have caller ID. I saw it when I got out of the shower." He took another bite and chewed slowly, then sipped his coffee. "I figured you'd want to think and I knew you took Will to school so I took a chance you'd be here." He smiled and folded his arms across his chest. "And here you are."

Anyone who knows me knows Joyful's been my favorite coffee shop since we moved to Pine Marsh. It felt far more interesting and cozy than the local chain. I looked at his smug expression and posture and attempted to mirror it, but my shoulders hunched and my hands stayed around the large cup, drawing warmth from the hot liquid.

Ric popped out of his pose and placed his hands over mine. I felt a gentle pressure. I knew I had to look up. His dark eyes showed no impatience. I kept my voice low so as not to be overheard.

"He can't stay there any longer. Please, call someone. Someone down there who can make him come home."

My vision clouded with tears. I fought the blink that would send them rolling down my cheeks. Instead I willed the tears to return to their origin. Physiology had never been my strength. I closed my eyes and felt the wetness on my skin.

"Gracie, I can't *make* him come home. He won't leave until he knows about Hannah. You know he won't." Ric rubbed the tops of my wrists trying to calm me.

I only nodded; I couldn't trust my voice.

"We have information from another source on the ground, but no one has been able to determine if this guy's story is reliable." Ric's hands tightened around my wrists.

This couldn't be good news. My stomach churned and the coffee I'd enjoyed felt dangerously close to betraying me. I forced the words out. "I want to know."

Ric slipped my hands from around the cup and held them gently. He looked at me as if gauging how much he should tell me.

"Please tell me what you heard. I deserve to know." The noise in my head peaked and I heard the words as though spoken by someone else. Maybe my brain wanted to filter his answer or maybe my brain preferred to shutdown.

Ric's voice had no problem cutting through the gauze in my head. "This man, one of the first responders to the crash, claims to have seen Hannah after that night. He says he saw her in a fishing village, miles away from where the plane went down. He told others and Harry he had been there on business and saw her at the boat dock talking to a fisherman who had directed her to a boat."

There had to be more to this story. On the surface it wasn't a bad thing. It meant she was alive. Why didn't it sound like a good thing?

"What aren't you telling me?"

Ric looked hard into my eyes and I felt riveted to his stare like I couldn't look away in case something unfolded in his dark eyes.

"The boat they directed her to, if the story is true, belongs to a local drug lord."

There was more, I could sense it through his hands, see it in his eyes. I continued to stare, waiting for what I began to fear.

"He's the son of the man Harry killed when his

assignment went haywire."

The assignment which should not have even been his. He'd retired from British Intelligence when we married, but they had coaxed him back one last time. It had almost been the end of him. He'd been presumed dead for almost a year.

My heart lurched against my chest and my blood drained from my head. I saw the panic in Ric's eyes, then nothing.

Chapter Five

His firm grip kept me from toppling off the chair and smacking the floor. I slumped forward into my Highland Grog. Luckily I'd taken the coffee in a Styrofoam cup not one of their heavy ceramic mugs.

My brain began to clear quickly, just not fast enough to prevent the collision. Ric's dilemma, let go of my hands and protect his clothes or hang onto me and watch the flood of hot liquid land in his lap.

In a move worthy of a 10 on any gymnastic scorecard he stood, tucked back from the dripping coffee and kept me stable by lifting his arms and mine in an awkward arch. The children's rhyme of "London Bridges Falling Down" ran through my mind. The fog lifted and the horror of what Ric had told me tightened around my heart.

Deandrea, the café's manager, rushed to the table with napkins. Ric sidestepped the pool on the floor and slipped his arm around me, guiding me off the high stool and towards a low table in the corner. I sat where he pointed. I shivered and wrapped my arms across my chest, gripping tightly to hold myself together...or so it felt. Deandrea looped my purse over the chair back and returned with a mug of coffee.

"You okay? Looks like you could use this."

"Sorry about the mess," I mumbled.

"Shoot, happens a lot." She turned her dark eyes on Ric. "How about you, sir? You need a refill?"

Ric shook his head. "Not for me thank you." He pulled

folded money out of his pocket. Deandrea waved him off and smiled at me. "No need."

"Thank you. That's nice of you."

"No problem, I just wrung out the napkins into her mug." She grinned and walked away. Her humor eased the awkwardness.

"Do you want me to drive you home?" Ric's forehead furrowed and his eyes searched mine for assurance I wasn't going to tumble again.

"No, I'm good. You caught me off guard." I stopped and looked hard at him. "You like doing that, don't you?"

"Doing what? Why are you getting all steamed up?"

"You like dropping news on me. You never sugar-coat it do you? You always hit me between the eyes so you can be there to pick up the pieces, to steady me," I waved a hand at our previous table, "to guide me through it."

I wrapped both hands around the mug to keep them from shaking. The heat radiated through the ceramic.

"Grace, what's wrong with you? I don't take any pleasure in *dropping* news on you, but I've always been honest with you. I thought that's what you wanted…the truth."

My eyes filled with tears and when I stared down at my hands the tears rolled down my cheeks, sliding around my chin to form a dripping point. Ric's handkerchief gently dabbed at my face, attempting to dry my eyes. I released my grip on the mug and took the handkerchief.

"I can't go through this again. He survived once. I'm afraid he won't make it back a second time." There, I'd said it. I knew Harry had to rush to South America when the plane carrying his sister and his son's mother crashed in the jungle. He'd found Lily and gotten her the medical attention she needed and a medivac flight to Florida. He hadn't found his sister. I knew he'd stay there, in danger, until he found her. "When did you find out all of this, I mean, when did Harry find out. Is he already on the coast?" It felt better to be asking questions.

"Harry would have found out a day and a half ago. I'm sure he's on his way to the fishing village; could already be there."

My eyes felt dry as though no tears had ever formed or ever would. The sand paper feeling when I blinked hurt, a good sign. It meant I wasn't numb. I needed to stay alert and focused. "It could be over. We could be sitting here and he could be…" I wouldn't say it, couldn't bear to hear it out loud, especially by me.

"Grace, look at me." Ric waited until I dragged my eyes to his face. "You know how I feel about Harry; hell, everyone does. I may not like him, but I understand his kind."

I lifted my chin prepared to defend Harry. Ric talked over my gesture. "He knows how to take care of himself, he's been trained to do that, and he can be ruthless if it means survival, his or someone he loves. That's what I mean by his kind; survival training never goes away no matter how much you force it behind your *normal* life. If anyone can find Hannah and bring her back, it is your husband."

I wanted to believe. My God, how I wanted to believe.

Chapter Six

Ric had been right. Within days we'd had news that a small fishing boat carrying two Brits had landed on the backside of Curaçao in the Netherland Antilles. One person suffered from dehydration and sunburn, but the other had sustained a gunshot wound. That's all we knew for three more agonizing days until John Langstrom, a friend of Harry's from his old life, called me and left a heartening but bizarre message.

"Mrs. Marsden, this is John Langstrom. I've known your chap for twenty years. Fine man, good friend. I'm ringing to let you know he's with me and he's safe. He's sent his sister on to her mum in Arundel, but he'll be staying on with me a bit longer. We've a small adventure ahead."

That had been the message. No word from Harry. He knew I'd cry myself sick begging him to come home; he knew he couldn't say no if he heard my voice. At least that's what he said when he stood in front of me one week later. It had been Hannah who'd been shot when they'd stolen the boat.

Both Marsden siblings had sailed since childhood. Harry's experience in special services for the British, and even Hannah's time with Girl Guides, made setting a course and staying true an easy task. The difficulty had been in keeping Hannah hydrated and comfortable. Harry had used his clothes; cutting the legs of his trousers and splitting them open, to create a shade screen for his sister. He'd wrapped her skimpy camisole around his head to afford him some protection from the grilling sun. His body, unaccustomed to the Southern Hemisphere sunburned and blistered.

The fishermen who'd rushed to help pull the craft ashore expressed concern over his shriveled skin until he made them understand about Hannah. They gently lifted her from the bottom of the small craft and carried her to one of their homes.

He'd told us he'd been frantic to get help. "Doctor, *rapidamente!"* Harry pulled money from his pocket. The universal language worked. A doctor had been summoned and, to Harry's relief, he really was a medical man. He examined her wound, raising his eyes briefly to meet Harry's gaze. "She's lost a lot of blood, but we need to get the bullet out to avoid further infection. I'm a general practitioner; this type of wound is beyond me."

Harry said he'd felt the most helpless since he arrived at the crash site and began tracking his sister. To bring her to safety only to lose her now was not acceptable. He'd swung his gaze from person to person asking, "Who helps you when someone in your village is shot?" Harry had explained to us he'd felt fairly certain gunshot wounds weren't commonplace, but weren't unheard of in this coastal village so close to drug lords and cartels.

No one had answered. They shuffled away lowering their gazes, but not before Harry saw the fear in some eyes and the pity in others. He'd planned to approach those who'd shown compassion to get his answers. The doctor came up with a plan.

"There is a clinic in *Ranje*, a larger town up the coast," he'd explained. "I can dress the wound and give her what doses of antibiotics I can spare until we can get her there. I have a vehicle, but I am afraid to move her. The road is not good and part of it loops into the interior where it is not safe."

The next two days had been hell for Harry. To the credit of the doctor he agreed without hesitation to drive. One of the men whose eyes had shown compassion lined the back of the open vehicle with reeds and blankets to create a nest for Hannah. Harry sat with his back to the cab so he could cradle his sister's head in his lap. He rode with the doctor's borrowed pistol in one hand and a water bottle laced with laudanum to keep Hannah hydrated and pain free.

The journey had been uneventful; time being more their enemy than any other factor. Harry stayed with Hannah throughout her surgery and recovery. He had answered questions from the local police, had contacted the closest British Consulate, had paid for medical supplies to be sent back to the doctor, and had made arrangements for his and his sister's flight to Heathrow. There he relinquished his guardianship to their parents who had begged him to come home with them. Harry had hugged them and fussed a bit over Hannah before disappearing into the crowd and the busy airport. Two weeks later he returned to the States and me.

Chapter Seven

When he walked through the doors from his flight it was déjà vu all over again as he limped toward me and I gripped my dad's arm. The back of Harry's left knee had become badly infected and the damaged tissue had been removed. He would heal easily, but his skewed pace reminded of the earlier time and more serious injuries.

My family couldn't mark any event without food and his homecoming proved no exception. My father cooked Harry's favorites. Actually, they were my dad's favorites, but no one ever disputed his choices. He made three cheese lasagna, stuffed artichokes, stuffed peppers, eggplant parmesan, and Chicken Marsala.

We celebrated Harry's homecoming at our house, in the backyard. Lily had recovered sufficiently to attend, and Will had been glued to one parent or the other, jumping up to refill a beverage or to remove a plate. He carried two cups of tea to his parents, Lily seated in one of the nicely padded lawn chairs and Harry propped on the glider so he could put up his leg. Will scampered between the two of them thrilled to have them back. He reminded his mom when she needed to take her medication.

I wondered how long Will would be at their beck and call. I mean after all at twelve I figured the thrill of having his parents back would wear off soon and he'd get lippy and difficult again. He'd never stopped being lippy and difficult with me, but I remained *persona non grata* to Will.

I turned my thoughts to happier ones involving my dad

and his lady friend. They planned a late June wedding, to be held in my backyard. This was a second marriage for my dad and a third for Jan. Neither wanted a fancy wedding. My older brother, Joseph, the family priest, would be tying the knot if he could get permission to return from his post in Rome.

Jan sat next to me. Her short blonde, curly hair framed her heart-shaped face. I could see how my father had fallen for this attractive woman. She patted the top of my knee. "Do you think I could convince your dad we should have Tommy Bahama wedding finery and have margaritas and guacamole?"

"You're joking, right?" I stared into her blue eyes waiting for an answer.

"Absolutely!" Jan tapped my knee, her throaty laugh swirling around my confused head. "Sorry, Grace, it just popped into my head. Of course I'm joking. I've been working with Mitch Trerra, the wedding planner I met at the last encampment, on some of the details. He is really good and several people in Naperville recommended him, but Mike rolls his eyes at most of Mitch's suggestions. Pashminas in big baskets at the entrance to the backyard hit the deepest nerve. "We gotta have blankets for them in case they don't think to bring a light jacket," she mimicked. Her gaze shifted to the group of people sitting near Harry. "Plans for our nuptials are in the air even as we speak." Her chuckle sounded forced. "Think I'll visit April and Cash. Can I give them some treats?"

Jan loved my horses. She'd never ridden until she met April Showers, my Tennessee Walker.

"Oh, they'd love that. I know they'd like to be out here with us. I have baby carrots and apples in the mud room."

"Should I cut the apples?"

"Yep. April likes quarters but Cash will eat halves."

I knew my dad and Harry had talked about the flowers for the wedding. My dad, Mr. Romance, wanted an archway covered with roses, daisies, and clouds of baby's breath. Jan's daughters, Judi and Anne would be carrying bouquets of sea green hydrangeas, roses, and succulents. Jan would carry a simple bouquet of her favorite flower, green cymbidium orchids. They'd also discussed menus, since both my dad and my husband did more of the cooking than Jan or me. Harry voted for High Tea, my dad wanted to cater surf and turf. I wondered if either of them had asked Jan.

They'd left the guest list to me since I kept in touch with, or at least had current addresses on, most of our relatives. Jan hadn't given me her list yet. I had offered to use my calligraphy pens and hand address the invitations. Jan's daughter, Anne, had ideas for the invitation. She used the newest scrap booking techniques. Our meeting next week would firm up our plan and the list.

I watched Jan's light step as she walked toward the barn. Her petite frame and easy stride reminded me I should lay off the guacamole if I wanted to fit easily into my bridesmaid dress and glide across the flagstone path Harry planned to lay in the yard for the occasion.

Will stood at my side, polite because some people sat within earshot. "My mom is tired. She wants to know if she can lie down inside. She can use my bed."

I glanced at Lily. "Of course she can, but she might prefer the couch so she doesn't have to take the stairs. And it's 'lie' not 'lay'," popped out automatically.

Will's eyes narrowed and through compressed lips he hissed, "What*ever*. You're not my teacher, you're not my mom…you're nobody."

My face paled; I felt the blood drain. I looked away to avoid those cornflower blue eyes, flashing with anger and dislike.

"Will," Harry called out in a low tone.

Will walked to his dad's side. The conversation started low, too low for me to hear, but the body language looked loud and clear. Harry had seen my reaction and must have asked his son what he'd said to me. Will's head dipped and he stared at his shoe tops. He shook his head once, nodded once, and nodded again. One 'no' and two 'yes'; I could only imagine the questions that had solicited the head movements.

Will avoided looking at me and walked to his mother's side. Lily's pale hair swung toward her chin as she leaned forward to push herself out of the deep cushioned chair. Will offered his arm to steady her. She moved slowly, taking the shortest path to the back door. Lily, with Will doting on her, passed behind my chair. My stepson still avoided contact, but his mother slowed her steps even more and nodded her head. "Thank you, Grace. Being around people is more tiring than I imagined, not at all like being alone all day." She moved on before I could comment. I didn't know how to answer or if I needed to bother.

Chapter Eight

The usual suspects, Harry's nickname for my family's core party people, stayed to take charge of clean-up. We never left anyone's home after they hosted a party until it gleamed in pre-party order.

I still get teased about the time one of my friend's mothers came upon me washing her kitchen floor after a party she had for a bunch of us from Regina. I explained I'd seen the mess we'd made and wanted to make sure it looked like it had pre-party. We'd promised Tracy, her daughter, we'd clean up. Tracy's mom had shrieked with delight saying, "That *is* how it looked before the party!"

Gertrude carried in the floral patterned tablecloths and napkins from the patio tables.

"Thanks, Gertrude. Just put them on the stairs and I'll bring them up later."

Will rattled the short stack of dishes he carried when he pushed past Gertrude and put them, none too gently, on the counter. He stopped and looked up. "Sorry," he muttered.

"Sorry, because you are almost pushing me over or sorry because you almost break dishes?" Gertrude's usually soft voice carried a firm edge.

He squirmed and stared at his shoes as if he'd spot the answer written on the criss-crossed laces or smudged in the dirty toe.

Gertrude extended the pile of linens to him. "Take *dese* upstairs for your mama."

My eyes widened at the title. I wished I could have held my surprise inside.

Will's arms automatically closed around the bundle pushed at him. I waited for the flinch I saw on his face to translate to some nasty remark about how I wasn't his *mama*. His eyes narrowed, but he made no comment. He rushed to the stairs and took them two at a time.

"Thanks, Will," I said to his back. His shoulders stiffened.

"*Und* put them in the basket nice," Gertrude added.

Will had turned the corner by then. Would he use the excuse he didn't hear her to explain why the linens would be tossed at the basket with most of them scattered on the floor around the target?

Gertrude shook her head. "*Ach*, boys. My *brudder* had same face when we must do what mama say." She smiled at me and took my hand between hers. "*Den dey* grow up and have bigger face."

"Walter, they're giggling. Can't be good, old man." Harry's stage whisper to his friend, and Gertrude's intended, made us laugh harder.

"I am carrying *tings* like I'm told. You bring *nothink mit* you but one bottle." Walter carefully placed the nested bowls and platters on the counter next to Will's load.

Harry grinned and lifted the bottle higher. The way he leaned on his cane gave him a bon vivant look rather than an invalid.

"This bottle is full. I thought the kitchen help should have wine while they, ah, we worked."

My dad walked in leading a parade of people carrying stuff. He too hoisted a bottle. I laughed and inclined my head toward Harry.

"We need two bottles with this crew." My dad

surveyed the room. "Maybe three."

"Mike, you uncork, I'll get the glasses." My husband handed glasses to Walter who placed them on the island counter.

I knew Will would have taken the back stairs to avoid passing us, but the laughter must have caught his attention. He would tolerate me in a large group, plus he didn't want to miss any of the fun. He stood in the door way. My dad noticed him first. "Hey, Will come over here."

Will quickly went to his side where Dad engulfed him in a one-armed hug. My dad tousled Will's blond hair, a familiarity I'd never even attempt. Will pushed into the gesture like a cat looking for more attention.

That thought brought a real cat to mind. I hadn't seen Elmo and his siblings, Trey and Patch, for awhile. Elmo preferred living in the house, but his brothers loved the barn. I'd go search them out after we cleaned up.

"Okay, Will here's how we do this. You'll be partying with us for years to come so you're the new generation. The Morelli Family and Friends Party Rules are easy. One, you always bring some dish to share–"

"Or two or three," my brother Marty called out.

My father grinned and continued. "Two, you always make sure Granddad's wine glass is full."

Hoots from my brother, Cousin Nick, and niece, Kate filled the room.

"Okay, can't blame a guy. Two, you always keep the food moving from table to table or one end of the table to the other or from inside to outside. In other words…" He paused and raised one hand extending his index finger and flicking his wrist.

"Keep the food front and center," we all shouted. Will laughed at what I'm sure he thought to be crazy behavior.

"And finally, three, you always leave the place in better shape than before the party."

Dad grinned at Will. "Remember, you're the next generation. It will fall to you to teach Connor and Claire, who, by the way, I can't believe have slept through most of the party. Karen, what'd you put in their milk?"

He turned to Harry. "Better check your whiskey."

I left them laughing and organizing the clean up to go search out my kitties. It wasn't like them not to be curling between legs, hoping for treats or, at the very least, cuddles.

Chapter Nine

No sign of them on the patio. Whoever had picked up outside must have scoured the area for fallen morsels unless the trio of felines had already eaten the leftovers and skedaddled.

I headed for the barn to check in on April and Cash. The door stood partially open. I moved the door a bit to slip inside. Six pairs of eyes, three feline, two equine, and one human, looked at me in various stages of reproach. In my mind, I heard April and Cash snorting, "Sure, now she comes in to see us." Followed by several meows telling me, "We looked and looked for snacks and nothing."

"I hope you don't mind, Gracie." Jan gestured at the stalls. "I needed some time away and they seemed to like my company."

Jan sat on the floor, leaning back against the sawhorse holding April's saddle. Elmo snuggled in her lap. Trey and Patch lay in a bundle off her right hip. Elmo lifted his orange body and stretched in preparation to walk off her lap. I sat down cross-legged and welcomed the furry fellow onto my lap. *Definitely coming back as a cat who belonged to a sucker like me.*

Jan's hands left empty by Elmo's departure twisted at a tissue in her hands.

"Something bothering you?"

Jan stopped fidgeting and stared at her hands. She raised her face fully to look at me. Her blue eyes, subdued and a hint of puffiness, answered my question.

"What's wrong?" My throat suddenly dry at the thought my dad's fiancée might be getting cold feet, I swallowed hard. "Jan, you can talk to me, really."

"I know I can Grace. You were the last of Mike's kids to accept our relationship. You're an honest person, painfully honest sometimes." Jan smiled and reached out to pat my hand.

Elmo licked the tops of her fingers. We laughed at his conciliatory gesture. "He says he'll listen too."

Jan took a deep breath, lifting her shoulders and holding in the breath for a few extra beats. She released the breath and lowered her shoulders. "First of all, there is no doubt I love your dad. I knew from the second time we met he was a 'keeper'. It would have been love at first sight, but I wasn't wearing my contacts the first time we met. We met at your house, remember?"

"I remember. You certainly flirted with him like you saw right through him. Lonely widower, nice guy with a great daughter."

Jan grinned and held up her hands. "Morelli's have no amount of humility do they?" She became quiet. "This wedding is developing, make that, exploding into something I never intended."

"You don't want to marry my dad?" My voice caught in my throat and I reached for the scrap of yarn I almost always carried with me. My fingers needed to braid, to twist and tie so my brain could settle down and comprehend how I could help my dad survive the biggest sorrow of his life since my mom died.

Jan reached forward again this time with both hands to cover my fingers and yarn. Elmo squirmed out from under the arc like a kid playing 'London Bridges'. "Oh, Gracie, of course I want to marry your dad. I love the palooka. I don't want the circus he wants. He thinks I want a big wedding because I never had one. I know he wants a big wedding because he and your mom never had one. I didn't have a big wedding because I didn't want one. My mother was disappointed all I wanted consisted of a trip to the JP and a small cocktail party at the house." She stopped and seemed to recall a distant memory. "Of course she did pay for a lovely honeymoon in the Bahamas."

I breathed a sigh of relief. "That's all that's bothering you?" I leaned forward and hugged her. "I can fix that. We can fix it right now. C'mon." I released her and stood up, brushing the bits of straw from my clothes.

Jan took a little longer to unbend and stand. "Should look at my driver's license before I do the Pocahontas Squat," she muttered.

We bid good-bye to the gang and closed up the barn.

Harry and my dad walked toward us.

"I told Mike when I can't locate you indoors I check the barn. See Mike, she's like Elmo, an inside cat with occasional cravings for barn visits."

I didn't know if I like the comparison or the laughter, but I kept quiet knowing this could be Jan's chance to talk to my dad, if she would take it. She seemed prepared to let the opportunity pass. Not on my watch. This had to be settled before my dad and Harry arranged for pergolas and ponds and waterfalls for the greatest show on earth.

"Dad, Jan has something to say to you, about the wedding plans."

Jan's eyes narrowed and I feared a reproach.

"What is it, honey? Did you think more about the Koi pond idea?"

My dad stepped closer and I saw a brief look of relief fill her eyes. Her shoulders relaxed and she took my dad's hand. "Not exactly."

They moved away from us. Harry started to follow and I placed a hand on his arm. "They need to talk."

An arched eyebrow asked the question.

"Everything's fine," I answered. "Now about this inside cat with barn privileges…"

Harry put his arm around my shoulders and lowered his lips to my ear whispering, "Once everyone leaves let's meet in the barn."

He was on the mend.

Chapter Ten

Two and a half months and life had almost returned to normal. Harry's leg healed well, as evidenced by his sprint across the field.

My dad and Jan's wedding, only two weeks away, and the circus atmosphere seemed under control–mostly.

Lily had temporarily moved back to Pine Marsh. She lived two doors away from us in the house she had owned two years ago and had sold to Hannah after Lily had decided to buy a brownstone closer to Chicago.

Every week brought some development in Hannah's recovery. Harry spoke with his parents or Hannah daily. His parents expressed their concern for their daughter's fragile mental condition. She'd become a recluse, staying in her room during visits from family and friends, turning down invitations to outings, and ignoring her old firm's attempts to re-employ her. The family, every one of us in turn, had pitched in to help Karen raise the twins. Karen had signed a contract to teach again at Trinity High School. She didn't want to give up teaching, but two eighteen-month-old babies were a handful. The schedule to care for Connor could have taught the military a thing about troop movement. Claire remained with Karen, only Connor moved from A to B to C.

We each had our weekly schedule posted along with back up phone numbers. I'd given up asking Karen why we couldn't shift the kids so each of them had family time and Mommy time. On that point she remained firm and mute.

* * *

Walter and Gertrude had Connor Care today. Jan had convinced my dad to join her at the re-enactment and Dad had asked Marty and me to join him, and I asked Harry who had asked Will. Nothing in my family resembled a quick *do you wanna go with.*

Because of the near accident, the living history program had been delayed for thirty minutes during which time law enforcement checked every weapon for live ammo.

Mr. Shewman, I refused to address him as an officer, kicked at a tuft of grass outside the battalion tent where we'd gathered. "Who'd do something like this and why? If news of this leaks out, it could damage the integrity of these encampments. Hundreds of people would be discouraged from attending."

"Cut the box office woes, Shewman," my dad growled. "How about the *integrity* of my daughter's life? I hope the news jumps all over this."

I slipped my arm around my dad's waist. He calmed down a little and returned the hug. Until an officer from the Sheriff's Department arrived Ric Kramer had the loosest jurisdiction. He and Harry had joined Kurt Clements, Pete Corvo, the shooter, and the other members of the patrol at their bivouac.

A young boy wearing the ubiquitous uniform pants tucked into worn leather boots and top half of "long johns", poked his head around the tent flap. His kepi cap perched back on his head revealed curly red hair.

"Mr. Clements wants to see you and the civilians," he said and nodded toward me and my dad, "over at the supply tent. They found two weapons loaded with *minié* rounds."

The boy about-faced and hurried back, possibly to get a front row seat for the showdown; one authority figure throwing down on the other. The entire encampment must know what I only sensed. Jack Shewman and Kurt Clements didn't play well together.

Chapter Eleven

"These men say the muskets stood at the ready for the afternoon living history program. I thought the rule of thumb in your re-enactments encouraged loading the weapons in front of the spectators to show them the process," Harry said.

"It's a point of safety too," Marisol added. "At least it's supposed to be. Each person loads his own weapon right before firing. You know exactly what's in there; it's like checking a weapon to see if it's loaded, only in reverse."

The obvious question rose among us like a bad smell. The reenactors looked at each other, like kids on a playground when someone let's go with a killer fart.

I looked for Marty to catch his eye, and realized he hadn't followed us. The shooting had pulled him away from his reason for attending. He'd brought his metal detector with him, intending to sweep the battlefield for treasure. I'd told him this wasn't a battlefield but a farm the reenactors used. He'd said, "All the better. If there's nothing old maybe I'll find new stuff these people lost."

Shewman cleared his throat and attempted to clear the air. "This afternoon's program is running tight because of the extra presentation." His lips twitched like he'd tasted something sour. "I told the men to load their muskets and leave them in the tent until the event. Two men on the sideline would demonstrate the loading process, but let the patrol take position and fire during the demo, like an overlay."

"That's not how we do it," Kurt Clements said. "Safety is our number one priority."

"Really, I thought getting sponsor money ranked up there." Shewman's lips pulled in full sneer. "If you hadn't agreed to this extra presentation by the Daughters of the Confederacy we wouldn't be in a time crunch."

Ric's voice cut into the fray. "I don't care about your programs or your cut. I want to know who loaded three weapons with live ammo, because that's the guy who's going down."

"You." He pointed to Pete. "Who gave you the gun and the new target and why didn't you check it."

The tips of Pete's short dark hair gleamed with sweat. He shifted from foot to foot–*left, right, left, right, left, right.* I found myself picking up the cadence, but I shifted only in my head. Watching him execute a pattern transferred into my brain. It felt comforting.

He stopped abruptly and I twitched. Harry spotted my movement and worked his way to my side. He leaned close. "Are you okay? Do you want to leave?"

"I'm good; just drifted."

He nodded and slipped his arm around my shoulders. Harry understood my verbal shorthand.

Pete's voice sounded stronger; he'd had time to recover. "Like I said, the lieutenant…"

"Which lieutenant," Clements interrupted.

"I never saw him before; thought he just joined up with the 10th. He walked up to me and handed me the gun. He said, 'Corporal, do me the honor of firing this musket. The sightline is troublesome and I'm told you are perhaps the best shot in the battalion.'

"I recognized the flintlock as a .54 caliber barrel with a flatblade sight stud. It's a sweet piece of power.

"Then he says, 'Fire toward yonder oak.'"

"Wait a minute. He said, *troublesome and yonder*?" Clements shook his head. "Who talks like that?"

Pete shrugged. "I didn't think anything of it. Some of those guys use the old time expressions to keep in character. Like I said, I never saw him before. He must have just started."

"Why would you say that, Pete?"

"Cause he was so pale. We've been on a half dozen encampments. Even with sun block and a hat you get sun. Can't help it. Especially your hands." Pete held out his for scrutiny.

I glanced at the faces and hands of the other reenactors and they looked tanner than most people would be by Memorial Day weekend.

"Okay, so he's pale. Can you describe him?" Ric demanded.

"He's about his height and build," Pete pointed at Harry, "with dark eyes. Couldn't see his hair cause of his hat. He carried his gloves folded in his belt and he had a sword and a side-arm. On second thought, I don't think he just started. His uniform looked too worn and broken in. Course he could have bought it from someone. And it had yellow stripes, means cavalry," he added I think for our benefit, "and we're infantry. See," he pointed to blue chevron on his uniform. Pete stopped and scratched his head.

"Anything else about him?" Ric encouraged.

Pete shook his head, then looked up.

"What?"

"Well, two things. His tunic had a blood stain practically over his heart. At least it looked like an old blood stain. I guess that's why I thought it was an old uniform."

"What's the other thing?" I spoke before I realized I wanted to.

Pete swung his gaze to me. "His eyes. I don't know but they looked scared and sad at the same time. I know this sounds crazy, but I've seen that look. I'm a veterinary assistant and his eyes looked like the eyes of the animals I euthanize."

I shivered and noticed uncomfortable glances from everyone. Ric shook it off first. "We've got old clothes, with the wrong color stripe, on a six foot tall man with sad eyes. Great. I'm looking forward to turning this over to the Sheriff's guy. Wish I had a little more to give him."

Ric left to wait at the entrance for the Sheriff's police. Shewman rushed to get in step with him. I saw him gesturing toward the main tent, turning almost sideways as he walked to get in Ric's face. Annoying Ric Kramer was never a good idea.

"What's he blowing about, do you suppose? He's not going to get on with Kramer at this rate."

"My thought exactly." I took Harry's hand and started walking. "I'm not keen on staying for the afternoon skirmish. I know Josephine is here doing a quilt-making demonstration and talk about the symbols of the Underground Railroad. I'm meeting Jan at Josephine's tent for that. It's at 12:00. Let's visit with her before we get lunch."

I turned to include my dad. "We could try Walter Peyton's Roundhouse. You said you've never been. Neither have I, but Barb raves about it and Will's troop went there on an outing and a tour of the brewery."

Harry looked over his shoulder. "Where is Will?"

My dad hooked a thumb over his should toward the tree line. "He went off with Marty to search for treasure."

"We'll get one of those contraptions for Will and they can cover twice as much ground."

"Oh, you can't buy it for him. He's going to get it as a prize for selling popcorn," Dad explained. "That's how Marty got his. It's probably the same kind."

"I understand. I don't buy the metal detector; I buy enough popcorn so he can win it."

"No, you don't do that. You buy some popcorn, but he goes out and sells the majority. You've got to learn the ropes." Dad grinned.

"Sure, like you never helped one of the boys get over the top."

"Gracie, honey, I had four boys who all sold popcorn at the same time. I couldn't buy much."

"Okay, you show him the ropes; I'll get Marty and Will. I'm going to be hungry in an hour, most assuredly starving by 1:30."

"Mike, tell me the truth. Could she really out eat her brothers? I am continually amazed at her ability to consume food."

"All of them except the *baby*." He pointed toward the trees. "He could pack away as much as two of them. Peg always planned dinner for eight not seven. But Gracie came in a close second."

"I heard that," I shouted over my shoulder without turning around. I smiled to myself. True–I'd never met a meal I didn't like–except liver and tripe. I'd felt self-conscious on dates and ordered minimally, knowing when I got home I could raid the refrigerator if Marty hadn't cleaned it out. My thoughts turned inward and my eyes downward. I practically walked into the oak tree.

"Whoa, Gracie. Watch where you're going." Marty's voice came from above me. I lifted my head and shielded my eyes to peer up into the leafy canopy. I spotted him about thirty feet off the ground perched securely on a sturdy branch.

"Please tell me Will's not up there." I swallowed hard and forced more air into my lungs.

"Relax, Sis. He's in the cemetery searching the ground. He really likes walking the grid. He's going to be good, maybe as good as you."

Marty referred to the pattern of sweeping used to insure all the ground is equally covered. I took to his pattern immediately and had more patience and persistence than anyone except Marty. He loved his new hobby, for me it soothed my obsessive compulsive jitters. Once I started a pattern I *had* to finish.

"The cemetery?"

"Yeah, on the other side of the fence. It's an old one, I think some military graves from the Civil War."

"You let him go over the fence and wander around unsupervised?"

"Grace, you need to lighten up. Will is almost thirteen. He'll be in high school next year. Time to loosen those apron strings."

"Loosen them, I haven't even put on the apron. I just got him last year and he doesn't care what I think anyway." I tilted my head back to see my brother's face. "I can't talk to you this way; come down."

"No can do. I'm looking for zincers and they're easier to spot from up here. I'm marking the grid with their locations."

My brother had many strange interests. Monuments made of zinc had been one of his interests for at least ten years. I did accompany him a few times to local cemeteries to record and photograph the zincers. Harry began to share the interest and the treks became far flung. I backed out of the road trips after the three of us spent the night sleeping in the Jeep so we could "shoot" the zincers in the 5 a.m. fog.

Call me silly, but if I'm going to be up at dawn, it will be from my warm bed, with a thermos of hot coffee, for a peaceful ride atop April Showers.

"We're heading over to Walter Peyton's Roundhouse at 1:30. In the meantime some of us are checking out Josephine's tent and her quilt making demo. I'll get Will." I stomped across the distance from the oak to the fence. I inhaled, preparing to shout, but Will's voice sounded first.

"Hey, Uncle Marty! Over here; I found something." Will waved his arm over his head in a wide arc. "C'mon, hurry!"

I noticed Will wore Marty's "tool" belt; his old belt from Philmont Ranch rigged to carry two leather holsters he'd made at camp. He carried a garden trowel in one and a small garden hand spade in the other. Other items like plastic bags and vials of cleaning solution hung from the belt in old purple cloth bags from Dad's Crown Royal days.

A few strands of wire at intervals strung from posts set about fifteen feet apart created the barrier. I could see where Will must have stepped down on one strand and ducked under the other. I wasn't much taller than him. I'd follow his lead.

Marty arrived next to me in an amazingly short time. "Here, Sis, duck under." He used his walking stick to hold up one strand and he stepped down on the other. His face gleamed with excitement. Everyone who knew Marty expected this expression. A veritable Peter Pan, the boy who never wanted to grow up. His exuberance caused problems in his younger years: detentions, totaling the family car, under-age drinking, and cow tipping his freshman year at Eastern Illinois University.

We reached Will's side in minutes. He'd walked the grid and scored in the lower far quadrant.

"What have you got?"

"Constant, strong beeps. There's something big under there. Maybe gold?"

Will's face gleamed with the same excitement; his expression the child version of my brother.

"Don't know about gold, but you've got something."

"I think it is gold. Couldn't it be?" His eyes swung toward me. "Couldn't it be?"

I hated when he asked me a question, which as an adult I felt I should answer truthfully. Gold in an old cemetery adjacent to a farm. Not likely. His eyes searched mine.

"Could be. Why not? Would be awesome."

His smile reached his eyes and I felt warmed by it. I'd sold out, so what. "Yeah, awesome. I think it really is gold."

"You know little buddy you might be right but Houston, we've got a problem."

"Houston?" His voice squeaked and he quickly cleared his throat to mask his adolescent voice change.

I'd have to make sure I rented *Apollo 13* for him.

Marty waved off the question. "You're on top of a grave, Will. Whatever it is we can't dig up a grave."

Relief flooded through me. I'd seen the marker and for a moment thought I'd have to argue Marty and Will off the idea of grave robbing. Sometimes I underestimate my little brother.

"Unless…" I heard the excitement packed into one word. Will's head snapped around to face Marty, his eyes lifted in hope to my brother's face.

"Unless," Marty continued, "we only dig down a few inches. This signal is so strong I bet it's not down six feet."

"Yes!"

"No!"

They both looked at me in surprise.

"What, it's only a few inches."

"Marty, it's somebody's grave." I leaned closer to the weather worn granite block. "It's the final resting place of Lieutenant James H. Blackmore. You can't dig in like you're digging up tulip bulbs."

"Oh, bother," Will said. His tone sounded so reminiscent of Harry.

"I think you mean, oh brother!" Marty rolled his eyes at me.

"No, he means exactly what he said. It's what Harry always says when *he* can't be bothered by following rules."

Will's grin told me I'd scored points for connecting him to his dad.

"Look, Grace. Why don't you go back and let them know we'll be along in a minute. Better yet, tell them we'll meet you there. I drove myself so Dad could take Jan to Farm and Fleet afterwards."

My eyebrows rose at the name of the large retail outlet for feed, seed, and tractors.

"Don't ask. He's thinking Iowa and Field of Dreams."

"Why'd you rent it? You know how he gets about growing things." I wagged my finger at my brother. "Next time rent *Under the Tuscan Sun*. I'd rather visit Tuscany than Iowa."

Will giggled. "I'm tellin' Grandpa."

"Way to go, Sis. I bet if you go tell everyone we'll meet them he'll conveniently forget this conversation." Marty's light tone implied he considered this fun and not blackmail. Apparently Will understood.

"What conversation?" His face went wide-eyed and

poker serious. A hint of a tug at the corner of his mouth said otherwise. *Another 'so Harry' characteristic; will I ever resist discovering the similarities and making the comparisons. I remember how Mom would comment how one of the boys so mimicked my dad. Is it okay for me to feel a bit like a mom to Will?*

"Geez, Grace, I'm kidding. It's not like you're making a life or death decision here."

I caught a movement from the corner of my eye. One of the reenactors walked toward us from the tree line. Probably coming to tell us we were out of bounds. He carried a wooden ammo box but no weapon. His pale face bobbed above his blue tunic. He approached the fence. *Would he leave the box on the ground, and pull it under? Would he duck under or grab the post and vault over? I didn't expect option number three–he walked through it.*

I stepped in front of Will to shield him. I didn't know from what, it seemed the right thing to do. I sensed Marty next to me, but I never took my eyes off the soldier walking toward me. His dark eyes held my gaze across the distance. He broke eye contact and looked at the box under his arm then at the grave. I knew in my heart his earthly remains lay in the grave.

Marty tugged my arm. "Grace. Gracie, what's wrong?" He moved in front of me and blocked my view. "Grace," he said softly, "look at *me*."

He'd guessed. Since we'd been in Canada together last year he'd come to understand my peculiarities.

I shifted my eyes to his concerned face. I could sense when the soldier disappeared. A peek over Marty's shoulder confirmed it. The heaviness I'd felt before I saw him had lifted.

"I'm good. Thanks."

"What's going on? Are we digging or not?" Will had sat down on the grave.

"Will, move off the grave. Show some respect," Marty said.

We'd been taught to not walk, step, or sit on graves from an early age. Each of us had accompanied our parents to Queen of Heaven and Mount Carmel cemeteries to tend to the graves of our dearly departed. When you come from a local Chicago Italian family you have a lot of dearly departed. We even have two empty graves with markers commemorating their deaths in Italy. My brothers and I called them our dearly *deported.*

Will stood and moved off the grave. "We're going to maybe dig up the top of his grave, but I can't sit on it?"

He had a point. Suddenly I realized the soldier's point. I grabbed Marty's hands. Marty jumped.

"What's wrong?" His voice squeaked with surprise.

"We should dig in and find that box."

"What box? What are you talking about?" He stopped and stared at me. "What kind of box?"

"A box with gold?" Will's voice, solemn and soft, reminded me of church.

"I'll tell Dad and Harry you'll meet us at the restaurant. You have over an hour. Don't be too long and be respectful."

"Absolutely!" Marty and Will nodded quickly.

"And tamp the grass down again, don't leave a mess," I added.

I scanned the fence line and saw where a small gate marked the entrance about 100 yards away. I chose to use a more conventional path for my exit. Besides, I didn't want to risk confronting the soldier's spirit.

If I'd learned anything about spirits since the first time

I felt the spirit of my aunt guide me to her killer, I'd learned the spirit stays close to where they died. I didn't think there had been any battles this far north, so most likely the spirit I saw stayed near the grave with the tantalizing "beeps".

I checked the name on the arched gate. *Eternal Peace Gardens.* My shoulders twitched. *Not for everyone*.

Harry met me at the entrance. "What are you doing in the cemetery? Don't tell me there's a Morelli in there?" His smiled slipped when he saw my face. I missed slapping a "happy face" on by a few seconds. No matter, anyone who knows me knows how to tell if I'm lying. My peculiar physiology causes my usually lavender eyes to turn a deeper shade when I'm lying or frightened. Something about the adrenaline produced.

"Marty and Will are finishing their grid. They'll meet us at the restaurant. They don't care about the quilt demo." I hoped a partial truth would keep my eyes pale.

"Why so glum? Wouldn't the boys let you sweep?" Harry's eyes held some skepticism and I knew we'd probably have this conversation later. "I volunteered to come seek you three out. Something like herding cats, Jan said." He put his arm around my shoulders. "Well, at least I've one to show for my efforts."

We walked to the line of tents in quiet companionship. Harry knew I would tell him everything when I was ready. I always did.

Chapter Twelve

We heard the infectious laugh before we found her tent. Josephine's laugh worked like a beacon to those who needed a smile.

We moved to her tent like a gaggle of geese marching across a field to a pan of bread. Jan greeted her first. "So this is where you hang out when you're not terrorizing youngsters in your classes." Josephine opened her arms wide to include Jan and my dad in a massive hug.

"You came. I'm so pleased." She released the first wave and waggled her fingers at us to step up. Harry moved closer to her and when I followed him Josephine placed one hand out in a 'halt' motion. "Excuse me child, but I need to be huggin' this hunk of man solo–if you know what I'm a sayin'."

Josephine slipped into her 'disguise' vocabulary, which would fool anyone. When we first met her we never suspected she held two Masters and a doctorate. One of her life goals, to record family oral histories and any written accounts of the years the Underground Railroad operated in our country became easier to achieve if she could blend into small towns or tight communities. If people knew her academic background they wouldn't talk to her as readily.

Her other passion was quilting. She produced beautiful quilts depicting the various symbols attributed to the Underground Railroad.

"Oh, Josephine, this is lovely," Jan said. She held up the corner of the current work for us to see. "I don't recall this pattern. What's it called?"

"You don't recall it because I only found it two months ago." Josephine's eyes gleamed with excitement. "I've been waiting for you to stop by so I could show it off." She patted her tight, curly hair in place. In the short time I'd known her I'd come to realize the patting was a "tell", a giveaway that she had a story to share and she was getting herself ready.

Josephine's dark skin glowed with perspiration and I wondered how hot she must feel under the layers of Civil War era clothing. The day had turned warmer than predicted and her outfit looked heavier than summer wear. Josephine's niece, Julia, researched costumes and accoutrement for several reenactor groups, giving them tips on the authenticity of period clothing found in old trunks in someone's great-grandmother's attic.

"It's getting hot out here." My dad shrugged out of his jacket and tugged his collar to one side. Harry must have felt thought the same.

"How about iced tea?" I saw a beverage tent near the entrance," Harry offered.

"I'll go with you," Dad said.

I think they wanted out of the quilt tent. Jan and I nodded yes. Josephine offered a caution.

"Make sure you order the War of Rebellion sweet tea and not the War of Northern Aggression sweetened tea. There is a difference." Her short, snort-like laughter turned a few heads.

"What about you, Josephine? One lump or two?" Harry grinned as he asked her. The one lump or two routine started as a joke between them.

"Why Sir you are most kind, but I already have placed my order with my tent partner," Josephine raised her voice in mock dismay, "who I fear must have abandoned me and left me parched in this wilderness."

We laughed at her drama and realized she raised voice for the benefit of the woman who had entered the tent holding two large clear plastic tumblers. The dark amber colored liquid looked cool and refreshing.

"It's like running a gauntlet out there. As soon as they see you're carrying drinks people lose their manners and their walking patterns. But I spilled nary a drop." The woman handed one tumbler to Josephine and swept a strand of hair from her cheek. I bet she'd been anxious to get the hair off her face the whole time she'd been carrying those glasses. The difference between people with OCD and others is I would have had to try even if it meant spilling the drink.

Harry and my dad waited for the introduction. Josephine smiled at the petite woman flushed from the experience of dodging recalcitrant crowds.

"Everyone, this is my friend, Arlene Jastrzembowski, we call her AJ. She is a fabulous seamstress. If it weren't for her skill with a needle, most of these here reenactors might look as rag tag as their models actually were."

Josephine's eyes gleamed with pride and affection for the smaller woman. "AJ, these are my friends. I may have told you about them, Harry Marsden, the hunky Englishman," she inclined her head toward Harry, "and her, the one who attracts trouble is Grace Marsden." Josephine smiled at me and I couldn't take offense–I mean, I did seem to attract my share of trouble. "This handsome fellow with the gorgeous graying temples is Mike Morelli and this lovely lady, a big reenactor fan and quilting student, is Jan Pauli. They are tying the knot," Josephine mimicked tugging a noose up the side of her neck, "in three weeks."

We laughed at Josephine's apparent view of matrimony. She'd joked recently how her genes weren't compatible with anyone who expected long term vacuuming, cooking, or hanky-panky. We had roared at the 'hanky-panky' comment.

"It's a pleasure to meet all of you. Josephine did share how she met you." Arlene's glance rested on me longer than anywhere else. "The story absolutely fascinated me."

Harry clasped her hand. "Pleasure to meet one of Josephine's friends. Tricky by half to keep her in line."

My dad shook her hand. "Nice to meet you. We're on our own mission. We'll be back."

The tent seemed spacious with the exit of the two guys. "Here, sit here." Arlene lifted a bonnet off the matching chair to the one Josephine's moderate bulk occupied. Arlene wore her hair pulled back into a snood at the nape of her neck. She quickly perched the hat on her head, but not over the snood, whose color matched the ribbons threaded through the brim of the bonnet. "We're supposed to stay in character and costume but it's too hot for the jacket so leastways the bonnet should give folks the idea."

The jacket hung over the back of the chair she'd offered. The deep red worsted wool looked like it would be hot, especially over the long sleeved, high neck blouse Arlene wore. Her skirt, a paisley type pattern of purples, blues, and reds, was accented with a red waistband. The bonnet picked up blue tones with the red ribbons and snood for accent.

"It's a beautiful ensemble. I didn't realize how colorful the clothing of the period could be."

"The reenactors work at their research, so they're costumes aren't," Jan hesitated searching for a word, "*farby.*"

Josephine laughed and nodded. "You are learning."

She translated for my benefit. "Farby is the term we use when something is not an accurate portrayal of the times, like someone wearing modern eyeglasses or sitting in an aluminum folding chair. Most often means the item is too modern, but on occasion someone brings something pre-dating the period. We take our research to heart.

"Arlene made the entire outfit she's wearing," she continued. "Even did the embroidery on the waistband to match the work on the front of her jacket. She made my outfit too."

Josephine's linen jacket, also red, complimented her solid deep blue skirt and the band of multi-colored triangles about four inches high embroidered at the hem.

"Wow," Jan said.

"Double wow," I added.

Arlene laughed and shook her head. "It's nothing. I've been sewing and doing needlepoint since I was a kid. It soothes my nerves at the end of a tough day or week at work. I work for a commodities firm. Cheaper than a shrink."

"Oh, yeah, she loves to sew, but she don't make nothing for you lessen it's got the color red." Josephine's speech pattern indicated how much she liked Arlene. "If I'm lying, I'm dying. You can't get nothin' from her that don't end up red."

The four of us laughed to the point of tears. Dad and Harry returned, double-fisted with drinks.

"This doesn't bode well, Mike. They're having a hen party and we've put our foot in the coop."

Arlene whooped louder at Harry's comment. I could see why she and Josephine would find friendship easy. She was one of those people who put you at ease. Her outburst started another round of laughter.

"Here you are, ladies." My dad handed me and Jan two clear plastic tumblers with the same amber colored liquid as Arlene's glasses held. The opaque plastic tumblers Harry clutched masked the true color of their beverage. Beer, I suspected. Knowing my dad, they'd made a quick detour to the car and the cooler he had in the trunk.

I wanted to try out my new word on the guys. I lifted my glass to indicate a toast. "Lift up our farby drink ware, in a toast to new friendships." We each took the mandatory toast-type sip. Harry and my dad chuckled. I began to explain, "Farby means…" I stopped cold.

They grinned from ear to ear, and finished my sentence, "Far be it from me to tell you that was not around during the Civil War."

Josephine and Arlene whooped with laughter, mostly I'm sure at the stunned look on my and Jan's faces. Jan looked at my dad. "How in heavens name did you know that?"

Dad grinned. "Maybe you talk in your sleep." Jan's cheeks reddened and I felt the same response. Too much information about my dad and Jan for me. I turned to Harry.

"And what's your excuse?"

He grinned and pulled a folded piece of paper from his pocket. "A chap near the refreshment tent offered a survey with categories about things like household items, songs, and clothing of the Civil War era asking if the item was Farb. Mike and I have been de-farbed. See, says so right there. We did quite well, the two of us." Harry held out the paper to show his high mark and the words, "Officially De-Farbed".

"You two run along and visit the sutlers while we ladies have a chat," Josephine instructed.

"Visit who?"

"Sutlers, darling. Merchants who followed along behind the troops selling their wares. Our modern vendors." Harry pointed back toward the area they'd come from.

"But only if they're selling period style goods," added my dad holding up his finger for emphasis.

"Go! You two are insufferable with your new-found knowledge," Jan said.

Harry and Dad grinned and shook their heads. "You know, Mike we try to better ourselves with a tad of learning and this is the thanks we get. They don't care a bob for our minds."

We burst into laughter. "Out, out!"

"How about we meet up at the car park in one hour? Is that enough time to visit?"

I nodded and brushed Harry's cheek with a quick kiss. "Plenty of time. I want to stop at the Bits 'n Bobs tent and that's it."

"We're headed to the cooking demo. The guy is making cobbler." Dad turned to Harry. "I think it's peach. We could make cobbler to go with the wedding cake." Harry nodded solemnly. I could tell by my father's tone he was joking; I glanced at Jan. She grinned and shook her head. We laughed at the expression of mock chagrin on Jan's face.

"You gotta' love him."

"Gee, I bet your wedding planner will be devastated he didn't think of cobbler first," I deadpanned, expecting a laugh.

Josephine sniffed her displeasure at the mention of Mitch Trerra, Jan's wedding planner.

"Am I missing something?" I looked from Jan to Josephine. The moment passed and Josephine waved her hand as if to dismiss the comment.

"He reminds me of students I've had, sweet, too sweet

to your face, but cooking up something behind your back." She waved her hand again. "Don't mind me."

I changed the subject. "Josephine, it's been great seeing you again. Say hello to Julia for me. I thought she might be here today."

"She and her young man decided to go golfing. Guess where they went to play that useless game?" Josephine's wide smile deepened the dimple in her cheek. Her eyebrows lifted and her eyes widened waiting for my guess. She looked positively impish in an over sixty and overly plump kind of way.

"You're joking. Pine Marsh?"

Josephine slapped her ample thigh. "Yessiree indeed. You are here and they are there. She is planning to call ahead for a visit and you expected to see Julia here."

"Are you returning for the afternoon living history? They're firing a cannon," Arlene added.

My knees weakened at the thought of an errant cannonball whizzing past my head. "No, I've had enough living history."

Josephine tilted her head to one side and stared hard at me. She clapped her hands to her mouth, then slowly lowered and opened them palm up offering them to me to take. I slipped my hands onto her pink palms. She wrapped her thumbs over the tops of my hands and rubbed small circles on my skin.

"Don't tell me that was you this morning?"

My purple eyes answered the rhetorical question.

"Oh, no," Arlene said. "You? What a terrible thing to have happen."

"The living history might be delayed. Last I heard the police locked down the weapons and Mr. Carter and Mr. Shewman were trying to figure out the rest."

We said our goodbyes and spent the rest of our time at Bits 'n Bobs picking out cute, age appropriate, "old-fashioned" wooden toys for Claire and Connor. Seems lately I couldn't go anywhere without seeing something for the twins, especially Connor since I saw more of him. I didn't want to be accused of buying his affection or spoiling him, but I couldn't help myself. How could you not spoil a toddler? Harry and I were in it for the gurgles and grins, but I knew it would be difficult to give him back, so to speak, once Hannah healed and came home.

We passed the "authentic" clothing tent and I spotted a toddler size Confederate Cap. Jan spotted the bonnet.

When we approached the car my dad grinned at Harry and snapped his fingers once, and held out his hand. Harry handed over paper money.

"What was that about?" Jan raised an eyebrow.

My dad held up the five dollar bill at both ends and snapped it straight. "This is how fellas make their beer money; in this case betting on their ladies' shopping habits." He kissed the bill. "Better than horses."

Jan plucked the money from his fingers and slipped it into her pocket. "Yes, much better."

The look on his face was priceless. I'd have to ask Harry later what else they bet on. Or maybe not.

Chapter Thirteen

"Where are those two knuckleheads?" Dad turned his head to look at the entrance. We'd been at the restaurant for twenty minutes. Marty's and Will's tardiness dominated the conversation.

"Twisting your head around like an owl won't help them get here faster." Jan patted his hand. She picked up her stein and sipped delicately from the thick rim. Everything about Jan was petite and delicate. I couldn't look that smooth sipping champagne.

"Gracie, tell me again about the hold up?" My dad looked me straight in the eyes and I knew in a few seconds my eye color change would bust me.

"It's about time," Harry said quickly. "You're one beer behind," Harry joked with Marty, "and one root beer for you." He motioned the empty chair between him and me.

"I think we need a pit stop first, right pal?"

Will hesitated then agreed. "Yeah, I'll be right back."

They walked past our table to the restrooms located beyond the bar area.

Marty's fingernails bulged with dirt. He'd brushed what he could from his hands, but he'd need soap and water for those nails. I thought I'd spotted a scratch on the top of his right hand. I didn't know if anyone noticed.

"Good Lord, were they digging for truffles? Did you see Will's hands?"

"Not from this side of the table," answered my dad. "They must have found something and worked it out of the ground."

"But Marty carries those garden tools. Why would they use their hands?" Jan looked at me, which encouraged the other two pairs of eyes to do likewise.

I shrugged hoping to buy some time. They kept looking at me. I couldn't take the scrutiny. "Who knows with those two?" I attempted a light tone. "Maybe they got excited about their find and dug by hand to be careful or respectful."

"Respectful? An odd choice of words, old girl." Harry's term of endearment tickled me.

"Like I said, who knows?" I picked up my beer stein.

"We're thinking you know."

Lager streamed down my chin and pooled on the table.

Dad pointed to my hand on the stein. "Lift and stop before you inhale your beer. You seem nervous."

"Just clumsy," I mumbled and mopped up the puddle before it rolled into my lap.

"Oh, Sis, a waste of the brew. You're cut off." Marty sat down next to my right and Will sat between Harry and me. "If you hadn't gone to artsy-fartsy Regina, you'd know to squeeze out those napkins back into the stein."

"Eeeww." Jan scrunched her nose and mock shuddered.

Will giggled and stared at Marty with the biggest case of hero worship I'd seen since my brothers had found heroes. Harry noticed it too. When he'd first learned of Will's existence, almost two years ago, he'd approached the thought of fatherhood as though Will were an infant, a baby to mold and mentor. The eleven year old he got didn't want to be molded or mentored. I assured Harry no thirteen year old thinks considers their dad a hero. That honor comes later, usually when they're raising their own children.

"Martin."

Dad's use of Marty's full name stopped the giggles and the conversation. Only the music playing in the background seemed oblivious to the reprimand. Billy Joel continued to bang out *Born in the U S of A*.

"Tell us what the two of you have been up to."

"I climbed into the oak to look for zincers in the cemetery next to the field. Will ran the detector on the area."

"Which area?" Harry leaned forward.

Will's eyes shifted from Marty's face to the paper coaster under his mug of root beer.

"Under the tree area. So, I'm in the branches and Gracie comes by looking for us." Marty paused to take a sip of his beer.

I didn't like being in his story. At the mention of my name both Dad and Harry glanced at me as though to confirm Marty's story.

"Will got some strong *beeps* and we investigated."

"Exactly where did you get this strong reading, Will?"

Will's head snapped up and swung from Marty to Harry. His face flamed and he mumbled, "The graveyard."

My dad and Harry exploded at the same time, targeting their sons with lowered voices.

"Marty, you know how I feel…you were raised better than that." Dad shook his head and exhaled a deep short breath.

"We will talk about this when we get home," Harry promised. "I know you weren't raised to dig up graves."

Oow, this could be touchy. Either Will will strike out at Harry with something like, 'like you'd know how I was raised' or he'll turn his dad's anger toward…

"Well she didn't stop us." His childish smirk infuriated me.

Harry looked at me. I opened my mouth to explain, but Will wasn't finished. "She told us what to look for, said we could dig under just a few inches."

Now all eyes stared in various modes from Jan's sympathetic look to Marty's apologetic one. The most hurtful gaze emanated from my dad; the look of disappointment. Forget Will's nasty, ha-ha, got you glare, even Harry's confused look; it had always been my dad's approval I sought. Heck, I was seven years old before I realized his referring to me as his favorite daughter wasn't high praise since I was his only daughter.

My neck and face flushed with heat. In a moment of embarrassment I wished the floor would open and provide me an escape route from the faces around me. The stale smell from the beer soaked napkins reached my nose and I swallowed hard to suppress an unexpected gag. How could it taste so good and smell so bad. My fingers itched to smooth out the rumpled napkins.

"How did you know to tell them what to look for?" Jan's voice, gentle and low, asked a normal question to which I had no normal answer.

I kept my teeth clenched and my head down. My eyes filled with hot tears. I didn't want to cry, especially in front of Will. Didn't want to give him the satisfaction. I had to do something, I couldn't just sit there. My thumbs had been making small circles at the hem of my sweater. I'd completed twenty circles clockwise and had started twenty circles counter-clockwise. As soon as I finished I could look up. No one spoke, only Neil Diamond pushing out *Coming to America*. I heard a chair scrape across the wooden floor.

Done.

I raised my head. Harry stood next to me.

"I think a beer is about all I'm up for right now. Gracie

and I have a dinner party at the Atwater's tonight. Wouldn't do to fill up." He pulled two twenties from his wallet and handed them across to my dad. "This should cover our drinks." Harry stepped behind my chair and pulled it back a bit as I stood. He helped me into my jacket.

Will looked confused and began to stand. Harry addressed Marty. "No sense in Will going hungry. Would it be too much to ask for you to pop him home later?"

"No problem." Marty moved one chair over and clamped Will on the back.

Will looked up at his dad. Did he see a bit of disappointment on his face? I wouldn't wish that sinking feeling on anyone, not even Will.

Chapter Fourteen

We sat in the breakfast nook. I'd made a half pot of Highland Grog. Marty loved the new flavored coffee from Joyful's Café as much as I did. I figured he'd have a coffee when he returned Will.

Harry had put on the kettle and sat now with a mug of black tea laced with lemon and milk. He finished jotting down a tick mark under "junco" indicating he'd spotted one.

I waited. I knew he wanted to ask me about the cemetery. I sipped my coffee and watched him record his bird sightings waiting for him to ask. My dad always told us kids, "He, who speaks first, loses." Mike Morelli, perfected the art of staring quietly at one of his children until the silence made us spill our guts.

I'd picked up the mug with my left hand. I used my opposite sometimes when I wanted to be obstinate. I'd started baby hood left-handed or maybe ambidextrous. Nonna Santa feared her granddaughter would be left-handed; she brought her entire belief system of superstition with her from her village near Naples. She made a point of giving me biscotti or crayons or toys only if I reached with my right hand. If I switched the treat to my left she would take it away. Seems like a cruel thing to do, but she loved me and thought life would be kinder to me as a right-handed person. She'd lived to wonder if maybe her early ministrations had caused my OCD. As an adult I'd assured her the disease wasn't her doing.

I loved patterns; they developed in my head so quickly

and for most occasions. I could lose myself in a pattern and not stress about events happening around me. I couldn't find a pattern; none emerged to sooth my mounting stress.

I watched Harry sip his tea, slip both hands around the mug and stare out at the bird feeders positioned to lure the avian population of Pine Marsh to his sightline.

C'mon, do sips, taps, c'mon. With my mug committed to the wrong hand I couldn't catch a pattern. *Change hands, already. Can't, gotta finish left handed.* I sipped the hot liquid faster hoping to empty the cup before I poured out my story. The call of a cardinal caught my attention and I half turned in my seat to look for the bright red bird. He flew from the feeder into the branches of the River Birch near the corner of the house.

"He's a beauty. Third one today. Course he could be the same one circling back to build up his numbers for my benefit. Hoping to get more seed or another feeder if I think there are more of them nesting in the Marsh. I sometimes feel these feathered fellows keep showing me what they want as if they perched on my shoulder and whispered in my ear."

"That's what it felt like, Harry. Like he wanted me, us, Marty and Will to find his box. He stared at the grave. He was holding the box, but how is that possible if Marty found it…he couldn't have been holding it."

I slammed down my mug sloshing hot liquid over the rim. *That was one way to finish my coffee.*

"Calm down. Start at the beginning or I won't be able to walk this with you." For the second time today someone mopped up my spill. Harry pulled a cloth napkin from the basket on the table and patted up the ring of coffee from around and under my mug. "Refill? I've more serviettes." The corners of his mouth lifted and brought my spirits up with them.

"From the beginning." I inhaled, closed my eyes for a moment then, squared my shoulders, and began. "When they announced the battle would begin in thirty minutes I thought I'd take a look at the demonstrations and exhibits. I wanted to find Josephine and her quilts. I watched a cooking demo, but didn't find Josephine. I kept walking past the last tent toward the tree line."

"Why walk down there, Grace. The exhibits didn't set up down that lane."

I shrugged lightly. "I don't know, I just did. I saw a soldier standing near the oak. Maybe I thought there was something to see. I veered toward the trees."

"Was the soldier there when you reached the trees?"

"No, in fact when I think about it, I think he had been on the cemetery side when I first saw him. I mean, the fence is wire and from that distance I thought he stood on the farm side, but as I walked to the trees–"

"Were you pacing?" Harry referred to my method of marking space. My brothers had taught me how to figure the length of my stride so I could "pace off" distance and be accurate. When you pace off a stretch of ground you walk in as straight a line as possible so as not to skew the distance.

"Yes, that's why I think he was on the cemetery side." "By the time I reached the trees I could see he'd been off to my right, which would put him squarely in the cemetery and close to the grave of Lt. Blackmore. He was nowhere in sight when I got there."

I hunched up my shoulders and exhaled a noisy breath.

"Gracie, could you make out anything about him?"

"No, too far away. All I noticed was his Union uniform."

"Could you see any insignias or stripes on his

uniform?"

I shook my head.

"How about his hat? Did he wear one?"

"He did, but it wasn't the little pillbox type. He wore the kind with the full brim."

"Good, good, we'll move on. Did you hear or see anything once you reached the tree?"

"Nothing. It looked like they were getting ready to start the skirmish, so I stayed there. It was a different perspective from your vantage point. I saw some of the troops behind the haystacks and thought that a clever way to ambush your enemy. No one seemed to notice me."

"Your jacket and trousers provided you with perfect camouflage. I don't think they would have spotted you since the trees weren't their focus. Gracie, didn't you notice when one of the blokes pointed his musket in your direction?"

"I focused on the guys behind the haystacks. The next thing I knew I felt the bullet whiz past my ear." I shivered and Harry's hands covered mine. His expression relived the terror he'd felt until he saw me safe. I pressed my lips together and looked away.

"I heard the guns *pop*, heard the reenactors cry out, and heard the *thud*. It sounded so real, the shooting, the moaning of the wounded soldiers."

I jerked my hands out from under Harry's. His eyes widened in surprise.

"I just remembered. The moaning, it sounded so real. In the split second before I realized what hit the tree I thought how in character these people stayed."

"Yes, they're committed to realism, but what's that to…"

"Harry, I have this awful feeling. Has everyone been accounted for at the encampment?"

The doorbell rang startling me, and I knocked over my mug. Harry handed me another napkin. "That will be Marty and Will." He squeezed my shoulder and kissed the top of my head before he left the kitchen.

I heard them before I saw them. Marty, Will, my dad, Jan, and Ric Kramer. The air preceding them felt charged with excitement. *Why is Ric with them? Something doesn't feel right.* I hurried to put on a fresh pot of coffee and plug in the kettle for those hot water people.

Marty turned the corner first, rushed at me, pinning me against the counter.

"I'm not giving it to him," he hissed in my ear.

"You've no choice," Ric said obviously continuing a conversation. "That is stolen property. Don't you get that?"

"Fellas, fellas, can we sit down and get some perspective on this." My dad's conciliatory request held an edge of concern. Harry and Jan sat down at the nook. Will stood next to his dad.

Ric shook his head. "Mike. There's nothing to get a perspective on. They're grave robbers."

Harry exploded from his chair. "Kramer, don't be a fool! You've no call–"

Ric stepped toward Harry. His emotionless expression, in sharp contrast to Harry's, made me nervous, like a mouse with a bored cat; bored until they pounced.

Dad moved to intercept whatever he thought might happen, but Ric took only the one step.

"You all seem to think you're above the law. You," he said and pointed at Harry, "and especially that one." He jerked a thumb over his shoulder at me.

"Now wait a minute," my dad's voice interrupted. "There is no call to drag Gracie into this."

"Drag her, Mike? She's the drum majorette when it

comes to getting involved where she doesn't belong. She could write the book on interfering, obstructing with investigations, and if it wasn't for the fact I was–" Ric's eyes widened and he glanced quickly at Harry, then back at Dad. The tips of his ears flamed red. He pushed his hair off his forehead, stared at his hand like he'd just seen it. Ric cleared his throat. "Like the trunks, Gracie, you've got four hours. When time's up I get a warrant and once I request a warrant the information goes on record. You don't want that."

Ric walked to the doorway and turned. "I'm actually the nice guy here. The grave you guys vandalized," he looked around the room to include me, Marty, and Will, "enjoys federal designation because the parcel with the war dead is considered federal property, so you are looking at more charges if they catch wind of this. Four hours. I'll let myself out."

"Oh, crap!" Marty faced the room hands out, palms up. "Geez, I never meant for all this to happen." He looked at Harry. "I never meant to get Will involved in a federal crime."

Will's eyes grew to saucer-size and he stepped closer to his dad.

"For God's sake, Marty, there's no federal crime. If there were, he," Harry nodded toward the empty doorway, "wouldn't have been able to stop the FBI from descending on our doorstep."

"He could if he hadn't told them…yet." Jan spoke softly from where she sat.

"He's engaged to one of them. Why wouldn't he tell her, them?" Marty's question hung in the air. Slowly, as though pulled by unseen strings, everyone's heads turned and all eyes focused on me. I felt the heat rise from my neck and slam into my cheeks.

"Why's everyone staring at Grace?" Will sounded genuinely concerned.

Ah, the honesty of a child. Why indeed? Because years earlier when the world thought Harry Marsden had been killed in a South American prison, Ric and I made plans for a future together? Because when three years earlier I became embroiled in a cold case at my college and Inspector Kramer investigated the case and old feelings stirred?

"And what trunks was Uncle Ric talking about?" I saw Harry wince at his son's use of "uncle". When Will became part of our lives he called Hannah and Karen "aunt" so by extension, as Karen's brother, Ric became "uncle". Family titles became one of those "goose-gander" arguments Harry had decided to live with rather than create an issue. I had told him what my dad's parenting advice had been to my brothers with children–*don't sweat the small stuff unless someone's bleeding or they're standing on the roof.*

I fielded the question. "A couple of years ago your dad and I stored two trunks in the carriage house." Will's eyes widened.

"The one in the clubhouse; your aunt's old trunk? The one we can't stand or sit on?" In an attempt to be a nice step-mom I'd let Will turn the out-building into a clubhouse complete with "No Girls Allowed" signage.

I nodded and noticed the smiles from my dad and Jan. "Yes, well there'd been two and your dad and Aunt Karen and I (I always liked to list myself last as though the position would diminish my culpability) decided to investi– ah look in the trunks first before Ric came to take them into custody."

Will burst out laughing. "Take them *into custody*, like they're people?"

"Cute story, Gracie, but we have to hurry if the Inspector is on the up and up." Marty moved toward the door to the garage. "I'm parked in your driveway. I'll be right back." He turned in the doorway and looked at me. "You might want to put an old rag or something on the counter." He pressed the open button and ducked under the overhead before the door rode all the way up.

I followed him into the garage to get an old tablecloth. I knew my brother was excited. He didn't have my telltale eye color change, but Marty did a kind of weight shift from side to side that gave him away if you knew him. If you didn't, you thought he might be an adult with a bladder problem.

I'd barely shaken out the old towel in the garage and spread it out on the counter before he returned. He placed an oilskin-wrapped parcel on the cloth and solemnly lifted the ends away from each other, exposing the wooden box. Marty hadn't struggled to lift the package to the counter height, but he hadn't just lofted it up there either.

"Probably not empty given the way you carried it," Harry said. "Is it locked?"

I shot him a look; it still spooked me how he seemed to read my thoughts. He grinned at me, understanding the look, and mouthed the word, *Druids*, his English answer to the Twilight Zone.

"If you two are finished, I'd like to check this out before you-know-who returns."

Harry smiled and moved away from the counter. He stepped into the garage, and I had an idea of why.

"Uncle Marty, is it locked?"

"Yeah, I gave it a quick tug." He ran his finger over the keyhole. "Anyone got a skeleton key?"

"Maybe the key is taped to the bottom?" Will's voice

sounded hopeful.

My dad moved in closer, lifted one side, and ran his fingers under the box. "Sorry, Will. No cigar."

I glanced at Will to see if Dad euphemism registered with the almost thirteen-year-old. I wasn't surprised to see him nod in acceptance. Will spent a lot of time with my dad, his newly discovered 'grandpa'.

My dad ran his hands along the side of the box feeling the seam where the lid met the rim.

The box wasn't square. It looked about a foot from front to back and maybe a foot and a half from side to side. I could only judge dimensions based on well-known metrics, in this case, Danny's Deli's foot long Italian sub sandwiches. The depth of the box could be a little more than half a foot long.

"This is well made; be a shame to bust the lock." Dad passed his hand over one side pointing to the stenciled words.

"1000 Ball Cartridges musket for rifle CAL .58 1861", Will read clearly. His expression grew dreamy. "Wow, this is from the Civil War."

"Depending on which side of the Mason-Dixon Line you stood you'd have called it 'The War of Northern Aggression' or 'The War of Southern Secession'," Jan explained. She grinned at our surprised expressions. "You know I'm into this stuff."

We did indeed. Jan's interest in Civil War Reenactments is what prompted my dad's interest, which in turn pulled in Marty and me, and I grabbed Harry who brought Will. It's always a chain reaction with the Morelli family. One of us gets involved in something, everyone gets involved.

"Do you know what 4-F stands for in modern day

military terms?" She swung her gaze from face to face.

"Sure, it means you can't serve because of a physical or mental impairment," my brother answered. We pretty much all nodded agreement.

"Do you know where the term came from?"

We looked at Jan, waiting for the explanation.

"If you used a musket you needed to load it with powder and projectile. You've seen the demonstration of how the soldiers take a paper cartridge from their ammo pouch and tear the paper end off, pour the powder, reverse the packet and load the ball."

Jan paused to make sure we followed her.

"Well, if they didn't have their 4 front teeth, they couldn't tear the paper could they? And that, my friends is from whence the term 4-F evolved."

Two heartbeats of silence followed while we absorbed her explanation. Marty's eyes looked skeptical, while my dad's expression shone with pure enjoyment. Harry's arched eyebrow reflected my opinion.

Only Will seemed uninterested in the etymology of the term. His eyes had remained fixated on the over-one-hundred-year-old treasure. Will reached out and reverently stroked the top of the lid, and extended his hand further over the box as if to protect it from harm. "We can't break this."

"We won't have to, if I haven't lost my touch." Harry carried a small pouch, which he placed on the counter next to the box. He untied the leather thong and opened the bag flat. Six thin, narrow metal picks lay in their own leather slips. "One of these should do," Harry mused while touching each tip to determine the one to choose for this task. I thought he did a bit of grandstanding for Will's benefit, whose eyes popped saucer-size for the second time today.

"This one," Harry announced, plucking a pick from its sheath and holding it up to the light for one final inspection. I glanced at Jan and saw the same "Oh for heaven's sake get on with it" expression I tried valiantly to keep off my face. Will and Marty seemed mesmerized and even Dad had that *adventure* look on his face. Definitely a guy thing.

"Whoa, are those burglar tools?" Will's breathless question posed a dilemma for Harry as the expression on his face turned a bit confused.

Harry lowered his hand to the countertop. His cheeks sported a hint of color as I think he realized his dilemma. *Be cool or be law-biding* must have raced through his thoughts. Adults would understand; we knew about his past life in British Intelligence, well we knew as much as he shared; so really, not so much.

"Burglar tools, no, not at all."

"But they look like burglar tools," Will insisted.

"Suppose they do to the untutored eye. These are locksmith picks; very much on the up and up."

"Why do you have them? Were you a locksmith once?"

I grinned behind my hand, pretending to cover a yawn.

Dad interrupted and turned the conversation back to the here and now. "Let's find out about your dad's apprenticeship later, okay, Will? Right now we should get this open."

Will nodded and grinned at Harry. "If you can."

We laughed at Will's taunt and looked expectantly at Harry, who smiled and bent to the task. He carefully inserted the pick of choice into the old keyhole. "This lock is in remarkably good condition. The box either hasn't been in the ground long or it's been protected by the oilskin cloth."

Jan had moved aside to let the guys have a better view.

She idly rubbed an edge of the oilskin between her thumb and fore-finger. The repetitive motion appealed to me and my brain began to insist I follow suit.

I lifted the length of yarn tied to my belt loop and rubbed the coarse strands between my thumb and first two fingers. Jan had already let go and stood waiting for the box to reveal its secrets. She folded her arms across her chest. The thought she might be cold entered my mind, but my own need to develop a pattern and complete it pushed away other thoughts. I noticed Harry had exchanged the pick for another. I rubbed the strands first clockwise, always clockwise first, then counter clockwise. *Ten loops. Nice, slow loops.* The movement lulled my thoughts which caused a sense of watching but not being in the moment.

"Got you now, don't I?" The lid lifted slowly to rest on its back hinges. Everyone surged around the counter to lean in for a look.

Six loops more.

Marty wrinkled his nose. "Uh, smells like grandpa's socks."

Will giggled, looking at my dad for his reaction.

Dad tapped Marty on the back of his head. "You expected roses?"

Three more, Grace. Hurry

Can't hurry or I have to start again.

I caught Harry's glance. He winked. He knew.

"Books and chewing tobacco," Will's voice pleaded for a different outcome. "There's no gold."

Three, there, done!

I rushed to Harry's side. He backed away to let me get a closer look. Had I been expecting gold? Maybe a little.

The place in my brain that loved all things old, mysterious, and musty rejoiced at the sight of the small brown leather journal tucked under the larger items.

My brother, who had the attention span of a gnat, moved and stood in the doorway to the garage. "Hey it's Kramer and his fiancée." He pressed the button to lower the door and jumped back into the kitchen.

"Marty, what's wrong with you? Why did you do that?" His face flushed as he stared at us. "I, uh, I don't know." He shifted quickly side to side and looked down at the box. "He said four hours. It hasn't been two."

The doorbell rang and all eyes swiveled in the direction of the front door. Harry moved first. "I'll let them in. C'mon Will."

Will went with his dad. My dad motioned Marty to the nook. "Sit down and have some coffee. I'm pouring."

"Hmm, seems like a good time for a bathroom break," Jan said and left the room.

I stood looking into the box, left to my own devices. I felt the smooth leather under my fingertips. It slipped quickly from under the tin box of "Ma's Chaw".

Could I keep my eyes from betraying me? No one would suspect the small parcel, about the size of a pocket planner, lay in the pocket of my sweatshirt.

"I'd like to see that." FBI agent Marisol Nunez held out her hand.

Chapter Fifteen

My face flamed. I'm sure my eyes turned the color and size of Concord grapes, but no one noticed.

Harry handed Marisol his birding journal, open to a page where he pointed to an entry. "I remembered you'd mentioned you're a birder of sorts. Right there, Ms. Nunez, is the first sighting of the Rose-breasted Grosbeak." Harry smiled with enthusiasm. He caught my eye, and made contact with Ric Kramer's gaze, which shifted between Marisol and the open box.

"Great sighting. They don't usually migrate north until later. We'll have to compare notes someday when official duty isn't the priority."

Marisol's shift in focus put the room on notice. She turned and walked to the counter. She glanced at the contents of the box and looked up.

"Has anyone touched anything or removed anything?"

"We just got it opened when you two showed up." Marty shoved his hands in his jeans pockets. He gestured with his head toward Ric. "He said we had four hours. Guess we know who calls the shots."

Geez. I can't believe my brother's antagonizing the FBI.

What about you? You're withholding evidence.

At least I'm quiet about it.

"Martin Michael Morelli, I raised you better."

All eyes focused on my father, then my brother. Marty pulled his hands slowly from his pockets and crossed his arms over his chest.

"No crime, no foul. Isn't that what you Yanks say?" Harry moved next to Marisol and pointed to the box. "We spent most of the time trying to unlock it so as not to damage the box."

"Yeah and my dad used his lock picks from when he used to be a locksmith," Will added. "He jiggled and wiggled it and it opened like magic."

Ric stared at Harry. "Yeah, Marsden Magic. I've seen it before, smoke and mirrors and misdirection."

"No, Uncle Ric. He used those pick things. They look like burglar tools like on TV, but they're lock tools."

Harry's face reflected nothing. Of course as far as he knew there was nothing to reflect. He gave me the briefest glance and I thought his eyes flicked over my pocket. I fought the urge to pat my shirt, which I imagined looked like a piglet in a python. My heart raced and I struggled to keep my hands away from my pocket.

I heard the snap of rubber. Marisol had donned latex gloves. She handed Ric a plastic square which he unfolded to the size of a Hefty trash bag. Marisol closed the lid and gently re-wrapped the box in the oilskin. Ric positioned the open bag to receive the package directly from the counter minimizing the chance of losing anything clinging to the oilskin.

Once they secured the item he sealed the top of the bag and lowered it to the floor. Marisol looked at the counter top. She lifted what looked like a wooden tongue depressor from her inside pocket and produced another much smaller plastic bag into which she carefully scraped the entire residue from the counter. She sealed the bag and slipped it inside her pocket.

"I know you meant no harm when you dug up this box, but grave robbing is a real offense and you could be in serious trouble." Marisol looked at Will and Marty. "Not so much you, Will. You're just a kid who most likely fell under the influence of a not so-clear-thinking adult." Will swallowed hard and stared at her. "That adult however..." Marisol spoke softly with no hint of humor in her tone.

Marty flushed under the beads of sweat dotting his forehead. He rubbed both hands over his face.

"Dad, Uncle Ric, you can't let her get Uncle Marty in trouble." Will's frantic plea tugged at my heart.

"Sport, I'd say Uncle Marty got himself in trouble."

Will turned to Harry. "Dad do something." Will moved to stand next to Marty. "It wasn't his fault. She told him to do it." Will lifted his accusatory finger and pointed at me.

So much for tugging at my heart; more like taking aim.

Marisol looked at me. Ric answered. "Grace didn't do any digging. Maybe she knew, maybe she gave implicit consent, but she didn't dig it up."

"Why are you sticking up for her? What about Uncle Marty?"

My brother cleared his throat. "What I did ranks as truly stupid, not the act of a clear thinking adult and I should not have involved Will. Harry, I apologize for setting this crappy example for him."

"Uncle Marty no–"

Marty held up his hand. "I never intended to desecrate, or in any way dishonor, the remains of a war veteran. I would never disrespect a fellow vet no matter how long ago he served." Marty shook his head. "Stupid, but not malicious."

No one spoke until Ric quietly said, "It is your call, and I'll back it up." Marisol tilted her head to look up at Ric. Her dark hair swung away from her high cheekbones. For the record, they looked slightly flushed.

"I'd expect nothing less." She looked back at Marty. Her hair shifted with her movement and framed her face. "I am not arresting you," she paused, "at this time."

The release of breaths and sighs in the room indicated how tense we'd all been.

"I am asking you to come to the FBI office to answer some questions." She turned her back and motioned for Ric to grab the box from the floor. "You can follow us now." Her statement left no wiggle room.

"Ah, sure. Now is good for me."

Marty used smart-ass humor as much of a shield as anything. Always labeled the class clown, but so much of those antics hid his true feelings of inadequacy compared to three older brothers who scored "gold" at all they did.

"I'll drive with you, son." Again a statement not a suggestion or request. Dad turned to Jan. "Hon, are you okay with staying here until I get back with this palooka?"

"Fine by me, if it's no imposition." Jan looked at me.

"No, that's great. I'd love for you to stay."

At this point, still seething over my step-son throwing me under the bus, I didn't want confrontation.

We watched them leave. The pit of my stomach rumbled and I remembered I'd skipped lunch. I knew I should eat something before the dinner party or I'd likely scarp up the appetizers ahead of the other guests.

The aroma of Highland Grog reached my nose about the same time I realized Jan stood at the sink running water into the kettle. Fresh coffee sounded great.

"Jan, you are a treasure." Harry put his arm around her shoulders. "Mike's a lucky bloke. I'll tell him so next time he's round."

"That better be tonight," she said and laughed.

"I'll be back in two shakes for the kettle. Will and I

have a bit of a conversation that's due." He lifted his arm from Jan's shoulders and draped it over Will's thin frame. "Don't we, son?"

"Ah, yeah, I guess."

I knew Harry would take up my cause with Will; a hopeless one since Will would never like me. He believed, with all the power of a kid, in the idea if his dad wasn't married to me his dad would marry his mom and they'd be a family, a real family. I'd overhead him say so to Tracy's son Matthew. In a way, I understood. I'd been the last of Mike Morelli's children to embrace the idea of his re-marrying. I felt his rush to the altar (though my mom had been gone for five years when he met Jan) slammed my mother's memory. A step-mom at my age! I saw how my dad loved her and how her love made him feel. I wouldn't deny him joy. It's different with Will. At his age, it's mainly about what would make him feel joy.

So why should Harry be the bad guy? What does it matter anyway? I did give my implicit consent. I am older; I should know better.

Do you hear yourself? The whiney kid ratted you out. You're his family. You're his dad's wife, period, end of recriminations.

Easy for you to say.

I am you.

Oh, yeah.

My head hurt with too many internal jabs and jousts. Harry could handle this however he wanted. Jan placed a cup of my new favorite flavored coffee in my hands and nodded toward the nook. A plate filled with cheese and crackers and carrot sticks waited for me.

I looked at Jan and felt the tingle of tears at the back of my throat. Maybe I could use a step-mom.

Chapter Sixteen

The look on Harry's face when he joined me in our bedroom to get ready for dinner, told the tale on his talk with Will.

"He's sorry, Gracie. He's a good kid; just got wound up is all. He hated how Marty took the brunt of the hot seat when it had been him pleading and pushing him to dig up the treasure."

Harry put his arms around me and rubbed one hand up and down my back. "He'll come round. We'll be a proper family."

I leaned my cheek against Harry's chest and let him continue the mini-massage. How proper a family did we have to be? Who decided *proper?*

"Hmmm, feels good."

"We could skip the dinner party." He tightened his arms around me. "Barbara will have loads of guests; won't miss us a bit."

I wiggled against his arms so I could look at him. "She would be disappointed if I didn't come, but devastated if you checked out as a no-show."

Harry sighed and loosened his grip. I slipped my arms around him and pressed against him whispering, "We could be fashionably late."

Not exactly loads of people, but our late arrival made us the last of the six couples greeted at the door by our gracious hostess and neighbor, Barbara Atwater.

"Isn't this always the case," she'd teased at the door. "The people with the shortest trip are the last to arrive."

"You know how it is, crossing the expanse of asphalt and lawns in our lovely compound." Harry had planted a peck on Barb's cheeks. "Lost time coming around the Azalea hedge. I wanted to try a vault, but Gracie's no fun."

Barbara took us round to each couple, to make introductions and connections. She was brilliant when it came to plotting dinner parties with the right people. After two intros I knew this would be the artsy-fartsy salon dinner party. After the day I'd had I looked forward to fluff and fandango.

"Grace, Harry, I'd like you to meet Barb and Dave Pardol. Barb is a genealogist. Dave is a photographer with an interesting specialty. He investigates, verifies, and photographs proof of internment for people searching for their families' grave sites."

"Barb, Dave, these are my neighbors, Harry and Grace Marsden. Harry publishes non-fiction books connected to and about the Chicago area. And Grace is a children's books author."

I held my breath when Barb reached the "And Grace", part of the intro, fearing she'd pop in something like, "And Grace solves cold cases."

We'd made it through the "who's who" with minimal chit chat since we'd missed the cocktail hour and dinner waited to be served.

Devin Atwater, our neighbor's son, played the role of server. He'd come home from college for the summer. Barb had been distressed when he'd changed his major again, from architecture to culinary. A six year college career and corresponding tuition loomed large for our friends. I'd wondered when Barb told me, what Will would be like at eighteen age, in college. Heck, I couldn't imagine him in high school, a milestone looming in the near future for us.

Devin's athletic build filled out the ubiquitous uniform of black pants and white shirt perfectly. His dark hair and green eyes turned heads. I marveled at how he'd grown from a pesky little kid, who wanted to hang around the horses every minute, to a stunning young man whom I really liked.

He'd added a black bow tie to his ensemble and carried a folded red cloth napkin over his forearm. I didn't know if the other guests knew Devin's parentage so I refrained from hugging him.

"Thank you young man," I murmured when he filled my water glass.

"It's okay, Mrs. Grace, they know who I am." I was touched when in this circumstance he still easily spoke the title of respect his mom had taught him to use with adults.

I squeezed his hand as he passed my chair. "There's a hug for you later."

Harry and I took seats across from each other with Dave to my right and Barb to Harry's left. The gentleman to my left, a gallery owner, talked enthusiastically with the woman on his left, a sculptress. No doubt, some business might develop between them. I happily chatted with Dave. Anything to do with graveyards had always fascinated me. Growing up in the Hillside area, home to eleven cemeteries, made it difficult not to develop an interest. Growing up in an Italian family who took an active role in tending family plots made it impossible not to develop a personal knowledge of cemeteries. Queen of Heaven and Mount Carmel are directly across the street from my alma mater, Proviso West High School.

I noticed Barb Pardol chatted easily with Harry, asking him at one point how far back he could trace his roots.

He answered her with one of my favorite Marsden stories. "My sister took up with genealogy for a bit. She was over the moon to find there'd been a Marsden in the Beefeaters at London Tower. The discovery lost its pleasure when some records showed our mum's ancestor, Nigel Hornsbooth, hanged for acts against the Crown about the same time my dad's forefather worked the Tower. My sister stopped after she caused a bit of embarrassment in the family. You need to know the revelation is not always what you'd hoped. But you'd know best about that. You must have fascinating stories you could share." Harry leaned, gleamed, and steamed his dinner partner. I mean he has this manner irresistible to most women. He leans a little bit toward you, not too close, but like you're the only person in the room, smiles with his mouth and with his eyes, the gleam, and then the inevitable "steam," as a slight flush creeps up the woman's neck. I have pointed this out to him; he denies it.

"He's done it now. I know her expressions. Barb will talk his ear off. He's opened the floodgates," Dave said smiling with affection.

I chuckled. "He loves learning new things–he'll be fine. Besides," I nodded my head toward the woman to Harry's right, "she seems immersed in her own conversation."

The red-haired woman, the gallery owner's date, talked quietly with her dinner partner, her hand lightly tapping his forearm to punctuate her story. I'd forgotten her profession.

"Barb and I don't have any young kids, so I'm sorry but I don't think I'd know your work."

"I haven't brought out anything new in years. Barbara is generous when she introduces me as an author."

"Did you get tired of writing?"

"Not exactly, I turned a few corners in my life that I

hadn't plotted. I'm beginning to write again. I have a toddler niece and nephew, and they are inspiring me, especially my little guy, Connor. Maybe by the time they can read I'll have a new book." I smiled wondering why I'd shared more with this stranger about my dreams than I had with friends. No "stranger danger". A stranger wouldn't roll their eyes or doubt you, like family could; therefore no danger.

"How did you come to photographing graves?"

"It started with my idea to write a book on zinc monuments in the Midwest."

"No wonder Barbara seated us together. My brother, Marty, roams graveyards looking for those. We were at a Civil War re-enactment in Oswego today and he climbed into an oak tree to have a bird's eye view of the adjacent graveyard to scout out zincers."

"Barb was at the re-enactment today. She mentioned Eternal Rest Gardens, or something like that?"

"That's the one, but there weren't any."

Dave smiled and nodded. "Could you spot zincers before someone told you?" His eyes gleamed with enthusiasm.

"No, I couldn't, but now I spot them everywhere. Like I said my brother is hooked and I went out on a few early mornings with him. What lured you?"

Dave filled soup and entrée courses with the how, the why, and the wherefore of the metal grave markers. I didn't mind. We headed into the library, for coffee and dessert, still discussing zincers.

Our hostess touched my arm as I walked around the end of the table. "Grace, can I talk to you for a minute?" She paused, "in the kitchen." She took my elbow, nodded at Dave, and smiled me away from yet another zincer story.

I followed Barb into her beautifully appointed kitchen.

Our kitchen had lots of wood and warm colors; like pictures I'd seen of the Tuscan countryside. Barb's kitchen reminded me of a country manor kitchen on steroids. Stainless steel gleamed from every stark white wall. The classic black and white checkerboard floor gave you a sense of the nineteen twenties and thirties, a theme helped along by the framed black and white photos of small town vignettes, like an outdoor market, an outside café, and a view of the local picture show's marquee, *Gone with the Wind*.

I leaned against the black granite counter top between the side-by-side fridge and the prep top. "The party is lovely, Barb. Do you need some help?" Devin had already wheeled out the dessert, crème brulee. I heard the soft hum of her dishwasher. There didn't seem to be much left to handle except the fragile stuff.

"No, It's all under control. Well, Devin's got it covered. I wanted to talk to you about this morning."

"This morning? I don't understand."

"Barb Pardol told me when she arrived, she had been at Oswego today for the 10th Regiment's mock battle, and a woman from Naperville was shot during the reenactment." Barb's eyes gleamed. "Didn't you tell me during our walk this morning you planned to go to the re-enactment?"

Barb and I try to walk every morning at six. We meet at the point where our yards flow into the crushed pecan shell path stretching behind the three homes on our side of the compound. Our route winds through the woods along the ninth hole of the Pine Marsh Golf Course and back along the interior loop closer to the yards.

"First of all, no one was shot. Shot at, well not really at, but not shot." I thought enough said on that topic would be best.

"What's second?"

"What?"

"What's second? You said 'first of all', which implies there is at least a second." Barb waited expectantly.

I hadn't realized I'd said, "First of all." Did I subconsciously want to tell her more?

"Grace, your eyes are purple." Barb's voice rose in pitch. She grabbed my hands. "What aren't you telling me?"

I inclined my head toward the door. "Shouldn't you be seeing to your guests?"

"Their bellies are full and the cognac is flowing. They don't even know I'm gone." She let go of my hands, perhaps realizing I needed them to express myself. "Besides," she added, "I saved you from Zincer Man, an accomplishment worth something, right?"

I grinned. "Boy, you're good."

She shrugged and crossed her arms against her chest. "Of course, with your eyes it's a cakewalk."

Tell me something I don't know, I thought. "Okay, one, no one was shot nor was that ever the intention. Two, the person wasn't from Naperville. Three, she was from Pine Marsh." I waited for the sequence to register.

Barb's hand flew to cover her gasp. "Why is it always you?"

I didn't think her question a fair assessment, but I didn't respond. It seemed rhetorical.

Before Barb could comment further Harry walked into the kitchen. "I thought I'd find the two of you in here having a catch-up chat." He smiled. I could almost hear Barb's brain shifting away from me and toward Harry. She adored everything English, including my husband, but in a good way.

Harry draped one arm around each of our shoulders and pulled us close. "My two favorite Pine Marsh mischief makers–is the plot afoot?" he laid on his English accent for Barb's benefit.

She had the decency not to squirm with delight under my husband's arm, although I knew she wanted to.

"Ladies, I came to suggest a change of topic might be in order."

I thought he meant my conversation with Barb, which he couldn't know about unless he'd been listening at the other side of the door. Not his style; mine maybe, but not Harry's.

"The cordials being served aren't enough to keep the atmosphere, shall we say, civil."

"Oh, dear." Barb's eyes widened then narrowed in concentration. "It's the blowhard with the gallery, isn't it?" Barb's hand clenched at her sides. "I knew he wouldn't play nice."

Harry and I laughed at her euphemism, but I'd rarely seen her so upset.

"If you thought he'd be a pain, why'd you invite him?"

The phone rang and Barb looked grateful to avoid answering the question. She grabbed the receiver on the second ring, listened, mumbled, "Okay," and hung up.

"That was Will. Ric and Marisol are there looking for you," Barb emphasized *you.* "Ric didn't want to barge in here, although given the circumstances, it could only help."

"Barb, did Will say Ric wanted to see me, only me?"

"Yeah, and he sounded really happy about it."

Chapter Seventeen

"Kramer, couldn't this have waited for morning?" Harry leaned against the counter. He'd removed his jacket and loosened his tie.

"You could have stayed at your party. I needed to talk to only Grace."

I saw Marisol's slight lift of eyebrows at the singular pronoun.

"Yes, well we come as a pair," Harry answered, "As I'm sure you'll soon understand."

Ric's ears pinked; his eyes skipped to Marisol, and back to Harry. "Cut the crap, Marsden. I, we, can talk to Grace here or at FBI headquarters."

Marisol's low, firm voice interrupted. "We can do this here and right now." She looked squarely at Harry. "Maybe you could make us some tea and get him," she nodded toward Will, "settled for the night. Don't kids have bedtimes in Pine Marsh?"

I saw Will's eyes flash anger. Nice to see I wasn't the only woman he disliked. "Daaaad!" His lips compressed to a straight line preventing another squeak from escaping.

"I'll put on the kettle," I volunteered. "How about coffee too?"

Ric nodded. Okay then, I thought. I handle refreshments, Harry handles Will, and Ric and Marisol handle perhaps their first jurisdictional conflict? I didn't care. I felt tired and a little nervous about having kept the little book. *Is this the reason for the visit? How would they even know the book existed? Maybe they found an inventory sheet in the box.*

Don't be paranoid. Who would inventory contents?

I would.

Yeah, you would. But I don't think Lieutenant Blackmore did.

"Grace? Grace, the kettle!" Marisol's voice intruded on my *mind speak*. I moved the kettle from under the stream of water and quickly turned off the spigot. The kettle had overflowed through the spout onto the counter and pooled around the ceramic canisters. Marisol tossed a towel over the water to contain it.

"Where did you go?" Ric touched the side of my head over my temple then, tucked a strand of hair behind my ear. "You're getting purple Gracie. Anything you want to tell me?"

My hands gripped the kettle and my mind raced from one explanation to another.

Rescue came from an unlikely source. Marisol must have had enough of Ric's use of my nickname. Touching my hair had to annoy a saint, let alone a woman with a gun.

"Grace, we won't take more of your time. Leave the coffee. We're not staying long." Her crisp tone brooked no argument. She nodded toward the nook. "Please, let's sit down."

I followed her lead and sat across from her. Ric, pretty much iced out of the arrangement, leaned against the counter. His face flickered with a tinge of anger followed by realization. I saw his eyes close, acknowledging his personal gaff, then, open quickly to settle back into character.

"Grace, we came back tonight to talk to you because the local police found a body in the haystack, yards from where you were standing."

"Oh my God!" My fingers pressed against my lips. I closed my eyes and took a deep breath, exhaling slowly against my fingers. The warmth of my breath calmed me. I did it again, then, had to do it two more times. My particular form of mania gains closure with the *evens* not the *odds*.

Apparently Marisol understood my need to settle down, or Ric had cautioned her to wait. I didn't hear movement from across the room so I guessed she got it or rather got me. I opened my eyes and swallowed hard.

"I thought I heard someone cry out or moan after the shot."

"Why didn't you tell someone?"

"It was the split second before they fired the volley and I heard the bullet hit the tree." My shoulders twitched with the memory.

Ric's voice pre-empted Marisol's next question. "Wait a minute. You heard one shot before the volley? Are you sure?"

"Yes. I thought he'd jumped the gun. You know like going offside in football, then everyone else fired."

Both of them looked at me with such intensity I knew I didn't want to ever get on their bad sides.

"Why are you staring? Does it matter?"

"Grace, if you heard the moan after the first shot and before the volley, it indicates someone other than those reenactors fired the fatal shot."

"I don't understand. They targeted the haystack, except for what's his name's last minute orders. Why would someone else be the shooter?"

"Because, darling, no one could be sure a body in the haystack would be killed." Harry slid in next to me. "Is that your thought Agent Nunez?"

Marisol leveled a cool look at Harry. I think she tried to determine if he purposely ignored Ric to annoy him or if he preferred to engage her because the FBI controlled the case. Her facial expression gave no clue to her decision. I made a mental note never to play poker with her.

"Exactly," she answered. "Whoever fired the fatal shot wasn't taking a chance on seven weekend reenactors who may or may not be marksmen. The quartermaster discovered a weapon and uniform are missing."

"Why go to the trouble of stealing equipment that might be missed? Why not wait in the field and shoot the guy with a more accurate gun, then blend into the crowd and leave?"

"Who blended better at that end of the field, you in civvies or a soldier?"

Ric's question made sense. Marisol nodded and made her own observation. "I'm trying to work out how you'd get a man to quietly sit in front of a haystack while you drew a bead on him."

"How was the body laid out?"

"She can't tell you that, Marsden."

Marisol shrugged. "Ric, I don't think we have the shooter in this kitchen. I'm okay with talking this out. Grace was there. Maybe with some more details she might remember more."

"Harry, when you ran across the field did you see anything or hear any comments?"

Harry rubbed his hand across his forehead. "Sorry, I was focused on getting to Grace. I saw her wobble a little and I didn't know if she had been hit. Not much use I'm afraid."

"Can't save the fair damsel and do black ops at the same time? Losing your touch, Marsden?"

Marisol pushed up from the table and whirled to face her soon-to-be (if he didn't screw it up) husband. "Ric, what's the matter with you. Geez, can't you two breathe the same air without all this damn drama!"

I giggled and clamped my hand over my mouth. *Oh crap, she's going to think I'm laughing at her.*

Marisol turned and looked directly into my eyes, which surely were purple. She narrowed her eyes and tilted her head so slightly, like someone looking at a painting on a wall. I waited for her to put up her thumb to sight over for a closer look.

"They really do turn purple. I've never seen that. How very cool." I had removed my hand from my mouth, hoping my eyes had distracted her from my outburst. Quickly she returned to the business at hand, but her tone had changed. "I might have been a touch dramatic myself. You two together," she waved her hand, pointer finger extended, back and forth between Ric and Harry, "always stir the pot." She sat down again. "Can we get on with the questions? I'd like to be in bed before sunrise."

Marisol ran her fingers through her long hair, pulling it away from her face and gathering the dark, straight hair at the nape of her neck. She slipped one hand in her pocket and withdrew a hair clip, which she used to capture and hold her heavy hair. In a moment the appearance of fatigue and familiarity morphed into crisp professionalism.

Oh, I like that. Even if I had one of those clips my hair would never do that. Sleek hairstyles didn't work on my thick wavy hair.

A scent of citrus wandered into my air space. Lost in my envious thoughts I'd missed the housekeeping tasks. A cup of steaming tea, Orange Blossom, the scent my clue, sat on the table directly beneath my chin propped up by my palms. I lowered my elbows from the table and mumbled, "Thanks," to the room, not sure who had served me.

"Grace, can you run through everything you saw and heard?" Marisol nodded toward the tea. "Take a sip, relax, and try to focus on the moments."

I looked into her dark eyes and rather than gathering my thoughts around her request, I thought about the beautiful babies these two gorgeous people would make–if they chose to become parents. I knew Ric wanted children; at least that's the leverage he tried to use on me when Harry's and my adoption bid ended up on hold so we could get to know Will.

"Grace? Can you do that?" Her crisp voice pulled me back through the rabbit hole.

"I spotted the cemetery in the distance and walked toward it. Jan and Dad stopped at a rope-making demonstration. Jan's become friends with one of the new reenactors, Mitch Trerra, who is also the event planner doing their wedding."

"That's convenient. How did they meet?"

"I don't know. One of those serendipitous encounters I guess. You'd be surprised at what these reenactors do for day jobs." I stopped and grinned. "Well, maybe *you* wouldn't be. Anyway, Dad said he'd be down the line spending time with the regiment's cook. I think they had recipes and samples. I lost track of Harry." I looked up at Harry. "Where did you go?"

Harry flushed and his shoulders lifted in a quick shrug. "I went over to the chap with the sabers; cavalry regiment. Because they rode horses they carried a curved sword. The infantry officers carried the straight swords."

I couldn't help the smile sneaking onto my face, tugging at one corner until I felt the curve complete. Harry noticed and flushed a deeper pink.

"Anyway, he let me swash it about out behind his tent. Nice fellow to do that." Harry picked up his cup from the counter and sipped the contents.

"You swashed it about?"

A glance at Marisol showed me her problem with the "swashing" visual as well. Her shoulders twitched and she looked down into her cup.

"Well, I didn't swish." Harry stood taller. "Perhaps brandished is a better word."

"Marisol, I know you think Marsden and I can't co-exist in the same space and time, and maybe you're right, but this is a typical Bait and Switch. You ask her questions, he redirects the attention. You ask him questions, she confuses the issue. They are masters at misdirection and obfuscation."

Ric folded his arms across his chest.

Marisol didn't respond. Instead, she closed her eyes, rolled her shoulders, and stretched her neck side to side. The movements looked inviting to imitate and I almost did, but stopped myself, worried she might think I mocked her. I lifted the length of yarn tied to my belt loop into my lap and began tying and untying bowlines to calm myself. I'd stretch my neck later.

She sat up straighter, exhaled, and opened her eyes. Marisol ignored the two men standing behind her in my kitchen. She looked directly at me.

"Grace, you and I are the only people in the room who matter at this moment in time. Please, continue."

She'd dismissed them out of hand. If they didn't feel the wall she'd thrown up around us I sure did. I'd have to reassess Ms. Nunez, but for now I would cooperate.

"I wanted to look at the grave markers. I've always

been fascinated by cemeteries. Marty photographs monuments for a hobby. I thought I'd check to see if this cemetery had zincers…"

Marisol lifted her hand palm forward. Her gesture brought me back on focus. The yarn felt scratchy on my fingers. I'd broken it in to a comforting texture.

"No one else was on the cemetery side of the field as far down as the big oak. I remember thinking maybe there might be some sort of agreement between the reenactors about not getting too close to the cemetery. The wire fence moves on an angle at that point and I ended up close to the oak. I planned to walk around the tree and continue walking the fence line, but I stopped at the tree."

"Why did you stop?"

"Two things happened. I saw the reenactors moving into position, and I thought I'd have a great view from there." I stopped and tried to see the events as they replayed in my head. "I caught a glimpse of a man in the cemetery. At least I think he was in it, hard to tell since the wire fence looks invisible and he stood further up the way. At first, I thought he might be visiting a grave, so I decided to stay put behind the tree."

I looked at Marisol. "Then I heard the shot and the volley and…" I shivered at the memory. I pulled my hands up onto the table and jostled my tea cup. Marisol's quick hands saved it from tipping over. She righted the cup, moved it away from my hands, and placed hers over mine. Her cool touch and light pressure felt comforting.

"You said 'at first' you thought he might be visiting a grave. Why did you say at first?"

Why did I? Figure of speech? I closed my eyes and tilted my head back. I watched me walking, detouring to the tree, turning to look across the field at the blue uniforms moving in place…

"Blue uniform. He wore a blue uniform. Oh my gosh, I can't believe I didn't remember that." My hands bounced under Marisol's and she lifted hers. "Could that be important?"

"Could be. We know a uniform and a musket are missing from the Quartermaster's tent. The dead man was a reenactor and he was wearing his uniform. It would seem you saw the killer disguised in the stolen uniform. Can you describe him?"

"Not a chance. I barely saw him and when I did I pulled back behind the tree. I don't think he saw me."

In my peripheral vision I saw Harry and Ric both step forward.

"She may be in danger."

"He knows someone was there now."

Harry and Ric spoke simultaneously.

My mouth gaped at the realization. "But I didn't see him clearly or for more than a second. I can't identify him. I saw the other soldier up close and…" I stopped talking.

"What other soldier?" All three spoke.

I looked from Marisol's cool dark eyes to my husband's worried blue ones and regretted my comment.

Harry crouched next to me and grabbed one of my hands. "What other soldier, Gracie?"

I felt tears pricking the backs of my eyes. I took a deep breath and looked at Marisol. I couldn't bear to see the concern in Harry's eyes. "I don't think he was real," I whispered. "He carried the box you took under his arm. I mean it couldn't have been the real box. I don't know." I looked down afraid of what I'd see in her eyes.

She leaned across the table and touched my hand. "You think you saw Lieutenant Blackmore?" Marisol had some psychic sensitivities of her own, but none as squirrelly as mine.

I nodded. "At first I thought he was a reenactor coming to tell us–me, Marty, and Will–that the cemetery was off limits." I paused and swallowed. "He walked through the fence towards us, but stopped and looked at the box under his arm, then at the grave under Marty's beeping metal detector."

"That's why you didn't stop them. You felt he gave you permission."

Harry's calm statement of fact lifted my mood. I marveled again at my good fortune to have met and married the only man who could support my peculiar type of normal.

I turned to stare at Harry's face and felt relief. I looked back at Marisol when she tapped the table with her manicured clear nails. "Grace, forget about the Lieutenant for now. I need you to focus on the man in uniform you saw first," she paused and I saw her face cloud with doubt, "unless you think it could have been Lieutenant Blackmore the first time."

"Wait a minute!" Ric sat down next to Marisol. He sat sideways on the chair so he could face all of us. "You think the victim was killed by a ghost wandering around his gravesite waiting for Miss Marple of the beyond to help him find justice, peace, and good pastrami!"

Ric's outburst proved one thing. We had exceeded exhaustion and ran now on fumes. He stroked his hand through his thick hair. Harry stood and stretched his back. Marisol propped her forehead against her steepled fingers. I rubbed my bit of yarn between my palms like rolling dough.

Marisol raised her head and spoke quietly. "Let's pick this up in the morning. Can you meet me at my office around 9:00? It's on Warrenville Road in Lisle."

"We'll be there," Harry said immediately, inserting himself in the equation. His tone said effectively, "You want her, you get me too."

I shook my head. "We can't, not both of us. We have Connor tomorrow."

Ric's face reddened. He'd not be in favor of Karen and Hannah adopting one child let alone two. He had some conservative mores and still struggled with Karen's lifestyle. He loved his sister, so he accepted what he didn't understand and couldn't approve.

Marisol asked, "How is your sister? I apologize for not asking sooner."

Harry nodded. "She's still quite fragile. The bullet did some nerve damage. The numbness in her arm and hand is still a problem. She's able to do a bit of physical rehab now, so we're hoping for improvement." He glanced at the clock. "In fact, if you'll excuse me, with the time change this is about the time we chat."

I touched his sleeve as he walked past. "Give her my love and tell her I'll send another video tape of Connor." I'd been videoing everything he did when he stayed with us, and sending the tapes to Hannah. I hoped seeing at least one of her babies would help her heal and bring them all together soon.

"Yes and I shall tell her about your latest escapade. It might lift her spirits." He winked and left the kitchen.

Marisol smiled at me. "You can bring Connor. We are quite civilized at the FBI. There is a daycare on site for the children of employees. I can arrange for Connor to have a 'drop in' pass. He can play with other kids."

"Thank you. That would be great. *Hmm*, on-site day care, very thoughtful. Didn't think the Federal government tried for a family friendly identity."

"They're not. It's good business. Parents are more focused in their jobs if they're not worried about their kids. The facility has 'sick baby' rooms so children aren't sent home. The tuition is subsidized and if longer hours are required, our daycare runs well beyond the standard six o'clock shutdown."

I'd been watching Marisol's face during her explanation. I couldn't decide if her enthusiasm peaked due to company pride or future use. Ric's expression showed boredom. He saw me looking at him and he tried to look interested.

Marisol added, "Let's make it nine-thirty. Goodnight, Grace."

She stood and walked out of kitchen. Ric stopped in the doorway and spoke in a quiet tone. "Gracie, I know you. If there is anything you're not telling us please come clean tomorrow. Tell them you forgot or were traumatized. These people are the Feds. Even Marisol, as sweet as she seems now with all the baby care talk, won't cut you any slack if you get in the way of her investigation." He brushed his fingers against my cheek. "I won't be able to help you. Please, Grace."

We both heard the front door close and none too gently. I leaned away from his touch. "You're the one who needs help. You know the way out."

Chapter Eighteen

I could hear Harry's voice rising, but couldn't make out the words. I moved closer to the doorway. I'd been cleaning up the kitchen, waiting for a pause in their conversation so I could say hello. He seemed agitated and I felt awkward. I was family, but this conversation seemed so private. I stayed in the kitchen and waited for a better break in the conversation. The room had turned cool and I pulled the thin fleece from the back of the chair.

"Hanns, you're confused. It's too soon to make decisions. We are all, every one of us, happy to continue caring for Connor. The little bugger has taken our hearts completely and irrevocably.

"What do you mean you and Karen counted on that?"

A suspicion, no more a gut feeling, crept into my mind.

Have I had an inkling of this from Karen's fears? Did I encourage those fears hoping for this outcome?

I recalled several late night conversations when Karen poured the wine and I'd spent the night at the brownstone. She had needed to talk out her fears with someone who wouldn't judge her, just love her.

Harry's voice shook with anger. "For God's sake, Hannah, they're not a pair of candlesticks to be divided amongst the family."

Had my comments helped develop the idea Hannah had planted with Karen? I pulled my fleece throw tighter around my shoulders, seeking warmth from a creeping cold.

Harry pleaded with her as he turned and paced around

the couch, no doubt trying to understand how his twin, whom he felt he knew better than his own heart, could abandon her son. My guilty conscience churned my stomach and made me nauseated; I turned on the tap for a glass of water.

With the water running I heard only blurred words and the pounding in my head. I sat at the table sipping from the glass, not able to swallow water easily past the lump in my throat.

Is this my fault? Karen always wanted only one and now Hannah wanted none.

Chapter Nineteen

We'd had little sleep after Harry's phone call with Hannah. She argued adamantly about her inability to care for Connor. She didn't want the responsibility.

Harry explained he understood the panic his sister still felt at being so close to death. She wasn't coming round. If anything she kept withdrawing from any involvement with people.

In the wee hours we had decided to agree with her wishes and adopt Connor, who already carried the Marsden name. Hannah told Harry she'd already started the paperwork with her attorney. We agreed to wait until after the wedding to spring the news. It would take at least a month to make it official.

We had settled into the car, with Connor strapped into his car seat, on our way to the FBI office before we caught our breaths. I drove my Jeep, more kid friendly than Harry's Jag. Gertrude and Walter had brought Connor over at eight o'clock. Gertrude planned to visit friends in Oak Park while. Walter offered to spend the morning at our house, showing Will how to cut down a dead tree near the barn. Harry had ordered a River Birch for the spot, so the tree had to come down. The nursery delivering the tree would remove the stump. Will had been trying to talk Harry into some sort of explosive solution to the stump problem.

"I can't fathom how one little tyke can cause so much disruption. He's a little bit of boy, aren't you, Connor."

I loved hearing Harry's "baby talk," and Connor loved it too. He grinned and prattled in his own language at the sound of his uncle's voice. I leaned back, correcting in my mind, his dad's voice.

"There's a good lad. Now when we're in the hoosegow, little man, and you're in amongst those other children, not a word about Auntie Grace and her antics. Mum's the word." He touched his finger against Connor's lips, who immediately tested it as a chew toy. "Ow, sharp little teeth." Harry sat forward and checked his finger. "He didn't draw blood, not like Claire did last week."

"Girls always have sharper teeth and nails. It's who we are." I grinned and made fast, biting motions. The clicking sound amused Connor; he *gaahed* in a high pitch tone that translated as happy.

We parked in the spacious lot, facing the main street, and entered the building. The security guard had our names, even Connor's, listed on his visitor's page. Harry signed in and showed the guard his identification. I handed Connor to Harry and showed my driver's license. As an afterthought, Harry pulled a bib from the side pocket of the small baby bag hanging from my shoulder, unfolded it, and showed the guard the name *Connor* on the front of the blue cloth. The guard wasn't amused; not even the hint of a smile moved across his craggy face. Instead he pointed toward the east end of the lobby and a bright yellow Big Bird type cutout on the wall.

Big Ben's Daycare expected Connor. I held his hand as we walked to the first small table set up with wooden blocks and plastic cups. Two children, both boys, who looked about the same age as Connor, stood on two sides of the table pushed up against the wall, leaving one open side. Connor reached the side and placed one hand on the table, but didn't let go of my hand. He started moving the blocks closest to him even closer, but still didn't let go of my hand.

"Okay, Sweetie Pie, Uncle Harry and I will be back in a little bit. You play with your new buddies." I started to wiggle my hand free. His eyes widened and his mouth opened in the same proportion. If he didn't look so pathetic, I would have burst into laughter. Harry did and his hearty laugh stalled Connor's onslaught of tears. The toddler looked up at Harry in confusion and began to smile in response to Harry's grin.

He was a natural with babies. Will's age frustrated him. Harry crouched next to his nephew and gently put the hand I released on one of the blocks. He held the hand and lifted the block to atop another. He slowly removed his hand. Connor squealed with delight and tapped the top block against the bottom. He used his other hand to pound the table. The tiny tower bounced on the table, bringing happy squeals from the other boys. When we said, "Bye bye," he absentmindedly responded, "Bye bye."

The elevator ride to the fourth floor gave us enough time to clean our fingers with the wet wipes I'd taken to carrying whenever we had Connor. Stickiness followed him. Although we never saw the source, we always ended up sticky. Harry scrubbed at a particularly resistant splotch on his fingertips. "Must have been when I crouched next to Connor. I set my fingers against the floor for balance."

"Must be what I felt on the bottom of my shoe when I stepped next to the table. Massive juice spill or something," I said.

A woman at the front of the car turned and chuckled. "First time parents, right?"

"No."

"Yes."

Harry and I looked at each other and laughed. The woman who'd spoken tilted her head in question.

"He's our nephew. We're filling in for his mom while she recovers from an illness." I spewed forth our "cover" story. Those family and friends who cared for Connor had agreed the same easy breezy explanation worked best in all situations.

She nodded. "Easier to spoil him and enjoy the gurgles and grins when you know he's going home." She smiled and faced forward. When she turned, her blazer flared open for a second and I noticed the gun in the holster at her waist. The door to floor four opened and she walked out, briskly moving down the hallway and turning right at the first corner.

"I wonder which office…"

"Good morning, Grace, Harry. Thanks for coming in today." Marisol had approached from the left and motioned us to follow her. She looked none the worse for her late night. Her dark hair was pulled off her face and held in check at the nape of her neck by a tortoise shell hair clip. Her high cheekbones showed the tiniest bit of blush, which served to accentuate the pastel eye shadow and hinted at color. Her dark lashes surrounded even darker eyes. The navy blue pantsuit would have looked severe if not for the lavender blouse Marisol had chosen. She wore low heeled navy pumps. Her entire ensemble said "professional, savvy, and feminine".

I inventoried my look. With my mind on Connor this morning my not quite shoulder length hair struggled against a wide headband. I, too, had brushed my cheekbones with blush, but I'd lacked time for shadow and mascara. I touched my purse slung over my shoulder remembering I'd put my eye makeup in there, assuring myself I'd have time to 'do' my eyes in the car or in the daycare or somewhere before this meeting. My lavender denim jeans and short sleeved white cotton crew neck sweater left me woefully underdressed for this meeting. I glanced at Harry who looked casually 'professional, savvy and masculine' in his navy blue dress pants, black tasseled loafers and Robin egg blue collarless tee shirt. The short sleeves displayed his lightly muscled arms and the material set snugly across his chest. I had noticed the approving glances from two women we passed on our route to Marisol's office.

"This is my office. Please sit down. Can I get you a beverage, coffee, tea, water?" She waited for a second then added, "I've already heated water so it's no bother," she said to Harry more than to me.

Because you're the coffee drinker. Don't get goofy here.

I know, I know. But why didn't I wear dress pants?

Sheesh, is that what's bothering you? What you're wearing?

No, of course not. That would be childish.

Good. By the way, smart choice wearing white. You got a little spot of spit up on it, but no one can tell.

I touched the crusty patch near my left shoulder blessing the choice of baby pears rather than carrots. "I'll have coffee, thank you."

"Tea would be lovely."

Marisol made light conversation. "I stopped at Joyful's Cafe after you served that wonderful coffee. This is Highland Grog." She handed me a mug and napkin.

She passed a cup and saucer with a tea bag tucked on the saucer to Harry. If she had offered crumpets I don't think I would have been surprised.

Once settled she wasted no time. "Our investigation has taken a twist. The victim, Keenen Putnam, recently joined as a member of the 10th Infantry. He supposedly transferred from another group in central Illinois, but his paperwork hadn't caught up to the membership person with the 10th."

"Paperwork, membership person?"

Marisol nodded at Harry. "Info for a particular soldier called a walk-on (not affiliated with a unit at a particular event) at least at every re-enactment I ever attended requires the re-enactor to fill out basic info and some kind of a release form. These soldiers are usually assigned to the OPs, other people unit. Many times registration is done by the unit, still requiring basic regimental records on the soldier, and still requiring him to sign a release for the current event. We interviewed Chris Lothrop after the Oswego police discovered the body. I know most organizations have some sort of regimental roster though no one does background checks. Might be my line of work, but it would make sense to do checks since reenactors do have access to firearms. You don't need a FOID card for weapons before 1898. Most of guys have them because different jurisdictions may interpret the law differently."

She stopped to refill my cup. I hadn't realized I'd emptied it.

"Thanks. So no one really knew him?"

"Right. He turned up at the living history event the regiment did at Cantigny in April and asked if he could join and participate in the Oswego living history event. Lothrop told him he could start sooner with the reenactment they had scheduled for May at the Naper Settlement. Putnam had mumbled something about not being ready and insisted June was soon enough. Lothrop had asked for a contact name and number and Putnam said the membership person had retired and he wasn't sure who the new person was, but he'd get the name and number to him soon."

"He never gave him a name?" Harry leaned forward.

"No, the strange part is he did give him a name of a lawyer in Ottawa, Illinois. I think Lothrop felt if a lawyer had taken over membership, our victim was probably okay. He admits he left a message on the lawyer's answering machine, but never followed up before yesterday's event."

"Has anyone contacted the solicitor?" Harry's English version always caught people off guard. Marisol paused for a moment until it clicked.

"This morning, in fact. Paul Garver returned my call and told me he'd never heard of a Keenan Putnam. He explained about the voice message he'd had and said he'd been out of town for awhile, then too busy to return the call until Friday. He'd left the message on Lothrop's answering machine."

Harry placed his tea cup on the edge of Marisol's desk and stood up. "Deadly phone tag it would seem. If Lothrop would have known about the bogus reference the victim may not have been on site to be murdered." He paced from the chair to the window. "The shooter wanted Putnam dead, but why? And why kill him in such a public fashion?"

"I've been asking myself the same questions. My team has started sifting and checking events and contacts for Putnam, leading up to his death. They started last night and have a few connections to investigate. One of my agents should be at the Ottawa Public Library about now checking out what Putnam checked out."

"You can do that?" I thought of my time as a librarian and the sense of "librarian-patron" privilege. Not that I'd protect a murderer, but totally wrong conclusions could be drawn about someone's library card entries. "I thought those records were private," I sensed I'd stepped on thin ice with

Marisol, "or something."

Marisol's eyebrow arched slightly. "When a murder is possibly connected to Federal interests, yes, I can and will."

All righty then, Grace. Way to set the tone for this interview.

"I've had your statement typed up. Please read it carefully. If it's correct, sign it and I'll get a copy for you." She snapped opened a manila file folder and slipped out the contents, handing them to me. I reached for the two typewritten sheets of paper staring at the double spaced typing, wondering how much truth or consequence I would read.

Marisol must have realized how brusque she sounded. She held the papers when my fingers closed over the edges. I looked up and she smiled slightly, an only lips, no teeth kind of smile. "Would you like more coffee?"

I nodded and held out my mug.

"This must be cold. I'll dump it." She left the room. Before the door closed Harry whipped around to her side of the desk looking at her neatly segmented papers.

"What are you doing?"

"Seeing what Agent Nunez isn't telling us." Harry lifted the corner of another file folder, skimmed the top page, carefully lowering the cover when he finished. He picked up a thicker bound file and fanned through those pages.

"Harry, don't. I'm in enough trouble." I hadn't meant to say that.

His head snapped up. "Anything more than the book from the box? Because that, I know about." He laid the file down in the exact position and moved easily around the corner of her desk, sliding smoothing into his chair as the door swung in and Marisol entered. She moved to the coffee pot and filled my cup.

I'd been holding my breath, fearful Harry would be caught snooping. Never mind how he knew I'd taken the book. Marisol glanced at me, and stared. I'm sure my eyes shone positively purple. She glanced down at her desk, then back at me.

"Here you go. Did you read your statement?"

I mumbled, "Thanks," as I took the mug. "Umm, you weren't gone long enough to read anything, I mean if anyone wanted to read, ah," *Geez Louise, Gracie, point a finger at Harry why don't you.* I inhaled, cleared my guilt, and exhaled. "Sorry, no. I didn't start." I took a sip of coffee. "Okay, I'm set now; won't take me long. I'm sure it's everything we talked about." *Okay, now shut up and read.*

The phone on her desk rang and saved me from myself. Harry sat ramrod straight in his chair with both feet flat on the floor. His arms rested lightly on the cherry wood arms of the chair, with his hands curled slightly around the wood. He hadn't looked at me while I babbled on, which had made recovering easier.

Marisol wrote quickly across the large notepad before she hung up the phone. "My agent in Ottawa found out Putnam considered himself the local Civil War enthusiast and historian. The reference librarian knew him well and had helped him with many of his searches for his book. His current research centered on a popular topic among Civil War buffs. According to," Marisol looked at her notes, "Lucy Stevens, the reference librarian, his book was titled *The Thin Gold Circle.* It's about an alleged missing gold shipment during the war."

"Is it true? I mean did gold go missing?"

Marisol's slight shrug at Harry belied the gleam in her eyes. "It's easy to catch gold fever. There are some legitimate possibilities of gold shipments meant for one side or the other disappearing, but most of those stories are based on hearsay and legend. If you want to read about what I think is an exciting story, but more fiction than fact, look up the legend of the lost gold of Keel Mountain. Will might enjoy reading it too, especially if he's been studying the Civil War."

"You don't think there's anything to lost gold somewhere around here? Why else would Putnam delay his start with the regiment to coincide with the encampment in Oswego? I think Lieutenant Blackmore's spirit chose this reenactment for a reason and not because he wanted to see if they got the details right."

As soon as the words left my mouth I felt a swirl of chilled air surround me and pin me to the chair. Marisol spoke, but I couldn't hear her over the din of the shouts and gunfire. I knew the sounds weren't real; more like a tape playing in my head.

Maybe he does want to make sure they get it right. Or maybe he is drawn to what he thinks might a group of his fellow soldiers. And if he can be drawn back through the divide between here and there, others might be able to come back. Lieutenant Blackmore seemed kind, but others pulled from their form of eternity might not be.

The air around me warmed and I felt a release through my body. The time my thoughts took must have slipped between real time.

"Grace, good thought about Putnam. I think more will come to light about him. Clements mentioned the librarian told him about a book Putman used extensively for his work, still checked out to him and apparently overdue. It's a book about the Knights of the Golden Circle. He's going to look for it at Putnam's apartment."

"Sounds like a secret society like Free Masons," I said wondering if they had noticed the tiny tear in time.

"You are spot on," Harry said.

Marisol and I both turned in surprise. He grinned and addressed me.

"I know you think I never did a whit of publishing during my employment by the British government, but I did publish several books a year. One of them, a fascinating story, almost a manifesto about this para-military bunch, the Knights of the Gold Circle."

Marisol moved a file from the center of her desk, the file Harry had looked at, and leaned forward on her forearms. She raised her eyebrows and tilted her chin up as if to say, "I'm all ears."

Harry got the not so subtle cue. "All right then. This secret society, established to promote the interests of the Southern United States, devised a grandiose plan to prepare the way for annexation of a circle of territories in Mexico, Central America, and the Caribbean to be included in the United States as slave states. During the Civil War some sympathizers in the North, from Indiana, Ohio, and Iowa, fought accusations of belonging to the Knights of the Golden Circle. Before the end of the war many citizens and politicians, especially in Ohio, joined as members of the organization."

"What's that got to do with gold? Have you ever heard reenactors talk about this Circle group?" I looked to Marisol for the answer.

"I've never heard about the Knights of the Golden Circle. Every now and then talk starts up at one of the encampments about someone with newly uncovered information. Mostly though it's rehashing *what if* and *here's how*, almost conspiracy talk with almost as many theories as surrounds the Kennedy assassination." She lifted her cup and sipped the coffee. "I've heard of one guy who studied topographical maps of a battlefield before and after the war and is convinced a rather high grassy knoll wasn't there before the war, so therefore must be where the gold is hidden. Fortunately, this grassy knoll is on government Parks land and will remain intact."

"There's no possibility it could be there?" I sounded like Will hoping for the big treasure find.

Marisol wagged her finger at me. "I told you it's easy to catch gold fever."

My face flushed and we had a chuckle at my expense. Her phone rang again. I finished reading the statement and signed at the bottom.

Marisol spoke quietly into the phone. Her shoulders loosened and the tiny tense lines around her eyes softened. She wasn't talking to her field agent. "Okay, five o'clock is good." Her other line rang and she clicked over to pick up the call. She straightened her shoulders and poised her pen over the notepad. This call was her agent. Marisol scribbled quickly. "Good work. Coordinate with the local police, then head back." She broke the connection and looked across the desk. Her face remained passive, but her eyes couldn't hide her excitement. They didn't change colors, though the color did deepen around the outside of the iris, almost like a darker circle. She had her own "tell" if you knew what to look for.

"Keenan Putnam must have uncovered new credible information about the missing gold. Agent Clements checked out Putnam's apartment and it's been tossed. Clements boxed up the papers and mail left behind. Maybe there's something in there to connect somebody to him. Whoever killed him might have done so after he found the information on the gold. Clements didn't find any manuscript or book."

"Seems logical he'd make sure he had the information before he killed the source," Harry said. He leaned forward resting his hands on his knees. "What if he went back to search because he didn't get the information?"

"Why would he kill Putnam before he had what he wanted?"

"What if someone else other than the shooter searched Putnam's apartment?"

"Why would you think there's another person involved?"

Harry and Marisol brainstormed with *what if–why* for a few more questions.

"Again, why do you think there's someone else?"

Harry stood up and paced between the chair and the desk, a scant four feet of back and forth, before he answered. "Because it's too convenient that Corvo happens to be told by a phantom Lieutenant–"

"You think Lieutenant Blackmore told Corvo to fire at the tree?" My voice squeaked.

"Sorry, darling, bad choice of words. I meant no one else spotted this random Lieutenant." He turned to Marisol. "Have you checked him out? Do you know this Corvo fellow? You yourself said you load your own weapon for safety reasons. You don't pick up a weapon you haven't checked and fire it."

I could tell by the dark circle in her eyes this was a new theory.

Harry continued. "He wasn't told to fire at the tree; he fired at the man in the uniform Grace saw moments before the volley. He fired at Putnam's killer."

Chapter Twenty

The expression on Marisol's face left no doubt this theory made absolute sense to her. "We'll talk to Mr. Corvo again." She stood up indicating she wanted to move on.

"Thank you for coming in this morning. I know you're probably looking forward to spending time with Connor." Her comments dismissed us. I thought of asking for another cup of coffee to buy more time, but I had the distinct feeling Marisol's hospitality ended with her acceptance of Harry's theory.

Harry remained seated. I stood behind his chair. "Agent Nunez, do you believe Lieutenant Blackmore stole the gold from the Ohio Reserve Bank?"

Marisol's eyebrows lifted and she glanced down at the file on her desk. Her stony gaze focused on Harry. "I didn't think I had to lock up files around you, Mr. Marsden. I won't commit that breach again. But you won't ever be in my office again." She opened the door and waited for us to make our way through it.

Her cool dismissal followed us to the elevators, daring us to look back. We didn't. We weren't alone in the car until the next floor. As quickly as the doors touched I turned to Harry.

"What was in the folder?"

Harry held up his finger to his lips and nodded toward the small round camera apparatus at the top of the control panel.

I'd seen those circular discs on many elevators and

never gave them a second thought. Then again, I wasn't asking my husband to reveal what he'd snooped from an FBI agent's desk in any of those other elevators.

The doors opened and within minutes we retrieved Connor from his two new best friends and headed to the car. We'd promised Connor Dippin' Dots, so our usual route home took a detour to Jo's Dippin' Dots ice cream emporium on Ogden Avenue. The store served great ice cream and it was family. My niece, Jolene had opened the ice cream shop three months ago.

We entered, setting off the bells over the door. Jolene looked up from the counter and grinned. She hurried around the glass cases and hugged me and Harry, saving a lift, hug, and twirl for Connor. He shrieked in delight.

I glanced around worried her customers might not enjoy baby shrieks with their Dippin' Dots. The only person in the shop sat opposite the counter against the wall. She seemed engrossed in her reading.

"Jo, honey, it's been ages." I hugged her again after Connor took Harry's hand to drag him to the ice cream case. Jo was my oldest brother's daughter. Joseph and his high school sweetheart, Darlene broke up when Joe decided to enter the seminary. He never knew Darlene was pregnant when she moved to Ohio after graduation. Jolene turned ten years old two weeks after her mom died and the Morelli family discovered her existence. She is the oldest of the grandchildren and though she came late to the position she is no less cherished.

"I know. This store has consumed my life. Sorry I missed Uncle Harry's party."

"You were sort of there. Your Dippin' Dots scored a big hit."

"Yes, I'm the best sort of guest." Jolene grinned.

"Have you stayed on at the zoo?" Jolene volunteered as a docent at Brookfield Zoo.

"The zoo's been great. Regi switched me to Tuesday since I work every weekend now."

I watched Connor's fingers touch the glass case repeatedly pointing at one container. "Looks like he has made his selection." We walked toward the counter; I stopped on the customer side; Jolene continued to the business side. She prepared Connor's little bowl of the colorful concoction and handed it to me, including the spoon and lots of napkins. Connor dropped Harry's hand like a hot potato and latched on to mine.

"So much for loyalty, little mate. Ah, well, the call of those dots is difficult to resist."

Jolene handed Harry his "usual"–a yogurt. Even his ice cream had to be healthy.

"Aunt Grace, nothing for you?"

I glanced quickly at Moose Tracks and Rocky Road, justifying a tiny bowl as my reward for the morning's ordeal with Marisol. Thinking of her reminded me of her slim, sleek look, which caused me to pause.

"Serve up one tiny scoop of each of those ice cream impersonators in a bowl for your aunt. She's had an unusual morning." Harry's face beamed with accomplishment as Jolene followed his instructions.

Connor had decided the person with one bowl of ice cream was good, but the person with all the ice cream would be better. He let go of my hand and wandered back behind the counter. Jolene hoisted him up onto the tall chair behind the register. She held her arm around him steadying him while he *gaaghed* at all the ice cream.

"Aunt Grace, hand me his bowl. I'll help him." Jolene looked around the shop. "It's not like I'm swamped."

I handed her the bowl. "Enjoy."

Harry had taken a table by the window opposite Jolene's other customer, whom I now recognized.

"Arlene, isn't it?"

The woman looked up from her book and smiled with recognition.

"We met at the encampment the other day; at Josephine's tent."

"Of course I remember you. I recognized your husband's voice as soon as he spoke, but I didn't want to intrude." She looked back at the counter. "Your little boy is adorable."

"Thank you," I said and smiled.

"He's not ours," Harry said, "but adorable he is."

Arlene looked confused. Harry filled in quickly. "He's our nephew, my sister's boy."

It would have been okay with letting her think he was ours.

No it wouldn't. Not yet until it's for sure.

Oh, stop. Just for once can't you ever agree with me?

Not when you're wrong.

Arlene cleared her throat. I'd missed a question.

"Sorry, I hooked a thought and couldn't shake it. What did you say?"

"I wondered if anymore had been discovered about the crime?"

Harry straightened in his chair, preparing to ward off bothersome questions for me; he donned his protective demeanor. I answered quickly. "We wouldn't be in that particular loop–not when it's murder."

Arlene's eye widened. "I wouldn't think so, but I meant the stolen gold?"

Now we sputtered in surprise. If we hadn't spent the

hour before talking about the Knights of the Golden Circle and diverted gold shipments we would have asked the expected, *what stolen gold?*

"Did Pete Corvo mention a gold shipment?"

Arlene tilted her head and assessed Harry's face with cool, hazel colored eyes. She answered slowly. "He did, on more than one occasion." She shifted in her chair to face him squarely. "I guess he got it right this time."

"This time? Did he have many lost gold theories?"

Arlene hesitated. "Not so much theories as a fascination for the entire subject. His new friend, Keenan Putnam was the historian."

"New friend?"

"They'd only known each other a short time, but they seemed thick as thieves. You'd think they'd known each other ages the way they understood each other, practically finishing each other's sentences." Arlene looked from me to Harry. "I didn't see it then, but looking back I think they knew each other a lot longer than two months."

"Yet Corvo didn't vouch for Putnam with the membership people. He must not have admitted knowing him. Curious, unless they had a reason to keep their friendship hidden," Harry said.

"You mean like they're gay?" I sat there confused.

"No, maybe friendship isn't the word; maybe partnership is a better description." Harry stood and faced the counter. "Jolene, have you a public phone in here?"

Jolene shook her head. "Sorry, no, but you can use the one on the wall behind the register."

"I'll let Agent Nunez know about their connection. She may want to look into that."

Arlene looked thoughtful, then, spoke quickly. "I hope I haven't put my foot in it. *Son of a Beethoven's First*

Symphony, sometimes I get on a roll." Her hands accidentally knocked pages out of her folder.

She blushed at her excited outburst and smoothed the pages. "I mean maybe they just clicked." She shook her head. "No, I'd swear, they knew each other."

"Another *son of a Beethoven's,*" I teased.

She laughed and nodded. "Yep. That's as strong as it gets." She took a spoonful of her ice cream and stopped before it reached her mouth. "Now Mitch Trerra, I'd swear they'd just met."

"He hung around with Corvo and Putnam?"

"Not really hung around, more met on occasion with Corvo. I never saw the three of them together, but I wasn't watching them."

I got the sense even if Arlene wasn't watching someone in particular she took in everything going on. Harry returned and sat down. "Agent Nunez is in a meeting. I left a message I'd call back."

"Arlene, back to your interesting comment about stolen gold. Why did you mention it as a real time crime, not some half baked theory? We were told not more than an hour ago how easy it is to catch 'gold fever'."

Arlene's cheeks reddened. She grinned. "There is that danger when you stay at encampments. There are always several low campfires on the grounds throughout the camp. People gather and talk, play cards by lantern light.

"We do try to keep it true to the time. Even though we bring our modern conveniences, most of us keep them undercover even when the visitors aren't present–helps you stay in character. We make sure store tags are removed from items we display; use worn looking rugs at our tent doors, keep lanterns handy, and some reenactors play music on instruments from the period. You always hear the sounds of a soft harmonica sending mournful notes up to the darkened sky." She shivered and straightened her shoulders.

"What's wrong?" Harry leaned toward her.

I had a sense of what why she shivered. I kept perfectly still, avoiding eye contact.

Her smile flashed small and tentative. "You'll think I'm over-reacting."

Harry looked at me, then at her. "No I shan't. Truly."

I looked up to add my unspoken support. Arlene got the look and must have remembered the comments Josephine made about me. She visibly lightened; her smile less tentative. "This last encampment felt different. I always get a sense of nostalgia at these overnights. I wonder if the period we re-enact had been a better time, simpler more honest. I think most of us fantasize about the bygone era."

"You felt more than nostalgia this time?"

She nodded at Harry before turning her eyes on me.

"I felt unsettled all night. I mentioned it to Josephine, but she pooh-poohed me and told me to lay off the coffee. At about one in the morning, still tossing and turning, I got dressed and slipped outside, hoping the night air would calm me." She took a deep breath. "You have to see for yourself what the encampment looks like at night with the fires banked, still glowing on the ground like a lighted path. Only a crescent moon lit the night sky, no clouds. Sometimes reenactors swear they see apparitions in the glow and tendrils of smoke from the low fires, like the Indian summer drawing they used to run on the front page of the Tribune–haystacks by day, ghostly Indians by night.

"I've seen fog turn spectral if you squint at it long enough. Not this night. I didn't see anyone, but for a few moments I felt and heard soldiers around me. It was as if an occult hand had opened a door to the past and for a brief time the dead mingled with the living. The sounds stopped abruptly like the door closed and reestablished the line which mustn't be crossed."

I shivered and rolled my shoulders to dislodge the heaviness weighing on them

"I know it sounds crazy, but somehow I think we pulled them back from their peace to our world."

Even my two-feet-on-the-ground husband paled at Arlene's words.

"Maybe they weren't at peace." I'd been thinking about Lieutenant Blackmore and his pleading look at his gravesite, and didn't realize I'd spoken.

Arlene straightened her shoulders and changed the subject. "Leave it to me to tell stories that put you off ice cream." She pointed at my nearly full bowl.

I had lost my appetite–unusual for me.

"Let's focus on those lost gold stories," Harry said. "Had you heard the current theory proffered by Corvo and Putnam?"

"They seemed convinced a Lieutenant from the 124th Regiment had taken a small band of soldiers with him and diverted a gold shipment from Ohio headed for the Confederate Army bivouacked near Huntsville, Alabama. The gold supposedly had been gathered by Northerners sympathetic to the South's cause."

The chimes on the door interrupted her for a moment. Five children, shepherded by two young moms, piled through the door.

I stood up quickly. "Go ahead, but I'd better get Connor." I hurried behind the counter to swoop him off the chair.

"Thanks, Aunt."

"Thank you, honey." I leaned toward Jolene. "Hope

they all buy triples." She grinned and gave me thumbs up. Connor belly laughed at the gesture and she did it again eliciting another round of baby laughter.

The children saw the exchange and five pairs of thumbs-up aimed at Connor. He shrieked with delight, which set off laughter from everyone. I didn't want to spoil their fun, but I wanted to get back to the gold conversation.

As I carried him to the table, Connor turned and twisted his neck to watch the children. "Soon enough, baby boy you'll have your own little band of mischief makers." The two moms laughed and nodded.

Harry motioned for Connor. He sat him down on his lap facing the table and my untouched bowl of mostly melted ice cream. Jolene had tucked a small towel around Connor's neck to act as a bib. I'd taken a few paper towels from behind the counter. We covered what we could and hoped for the best. Harry handed Connor the purple plastic spoon and guided his chubby hand around the spoon and into the bowl. Connor knew the drill.

Arlene backtracked for my benefit, explaining that the Northern businessmen who collected the gold had other motives beyond helping the South.

"Arlene, did Corvo or Putnam mention the Knights of the Golden Circle?"

"*Son of a Beethoven's First Symphony*, I was just about to say that." Arlene grinned. "That's the second time in less than fifteen minutes you've asked a question like you already knew the answer. Am I missing something?"

I looked at Harry and he nodded. He kissed the top of Connor's head and seemed content to let me take the lead. I filled her in on the metal detector debacle and disclosed the contents of the box, but withheld the fact I'd lifted the Lieutenant's book. Arlene made no comment throughout my "down and dirty" synopsis. I shrugged my shoulders. "If Blackmore had taken the gold he didn't put the map in the ordinance box."

"The gold could be buried deeper in the grave than the metal detector could find. I'd hate to think that's why Corvo and Putnam were so keen on this particular encampment." Arlene thought for a moment. "I have a friend who is a genealogist. If it's okay with you I'll give her a call and see what she can find out about your Lieutenant. What's his full name and do you know his regiment?"

"James Blackmore. I don't know his regiment, but I'll see if it's on–"

"Oops," Harry said and grabbed at the almost empty bowl. Connor looked surprised his yummy treat had tipped. I knew why he didn't have a clue. Harry had saved me from spilling the beans.

He mopped at a bit of gooey Moose Tracks and guided Connor's spoon hand back to the mother lode. "We're good. Sorry."

"See if it's on what?" Arlene hadn't missed a beat or my slip.

"On?"

"You said, 'I'll see if it's on'," she repeated verbatim. I felt my fingers twitch searching for comfort to calm my jitters.

"On his grave marker," Harry supplied smoothly.

"Good idea. I'm sure it's noted. Cemeteries kept good records. My friend tells me churches and cemeteries and census reports, of all things, are some of her best sources.

"I'm supposed to meet her here. She lives in Bolingbrook and this area is easy for both of us to get to."

My brain did a quick re-wind to the dinner party. I've learned there is no such thing as coincidence.

"Is your friend Barb Pardol?"

Arlene stared at me. "Now that's weird."

"Not really. We met her at a friend's house and I remembered she talked about genealogy. She said she lived locally so…"

"Nice deducing." Arlene smiled. "Barb is rather good so I'll put her on this Lieutenant's trail. All she needs is his regiment."

Connor, finished with his ice cream overload, clambered off Harry's lap, and made a beeline for Jolene, who worked at wiping down one of the table tops. She moved her dishpan of soapy water one tick before Connor reached for it.

"No you don't, buddy. Come back when you're older and I'll pay you to do this."

Harry stood, careful to grab the paper towels from his lap. He lifted the bowl and spoon and swiped at the table with his handful of toweling. "Right as rain," he pronounced and stepped to the trash container.

Arlene stood and gathered her book and papers. "It was wonderful to run into you." She put out her hand. Harry looked at his palms and smiled. "Best not, I'm a bit sticky."

Jolene had wiped off Connor's hands and jokingly said, "Over here, Uncle Harry, I'm great at 'sticky' removal." She held up the wet dishcloth.

I took Connor's hand and walked back to the table. "Arlene, I hope we didn't stop you from whatever you were doing. You looked busy."

She waved a hand at her pile of papers. "A welcomed break in the boredom. I'm writing a white paper on the history of the three gold standards which pre-dated the commodities market."

"I'd love to read it when it's ready," Harry said. "I

enjoy reading the history of what we take for granted now. In fact, if it's good and you've more on the subject consider expanding it to a book, maybe sixty-five thousand words."

Arlene stared at Harry and broke into laughter. *"Son of a Beethoven's First Symphony."* She wagged a finger at Harry. "I might hold you to it."

"It would be my pleasure," he paused and winked, "if it's good."

We said goodbye to Jolene and started walking out. Arlene called out to us. "There's a memorial gathering for Keenan Putnam tonight back at the field. Nothing big, just a quiet observation. Most of us didn't know him well, but he was one of the 10th Illinois Volunteer Infantry, if only for a few months. Maybe you want to come out." She opened her notebook. "You could check the grave marker."

I nodded and followed Harry and Connor outside.

I opened the back door and Harry lifted Connor into his car seat. I got in the passenger side and watched Harry tighten down and click everything in place around our precious cargo. "You know, I don't think she believed you when you said I'd look on his grave marker."

Harry closed the back door and got behind the wheel. "She would have believed what I said, old girl, if your eyes hadn't turned us out."

"She doesn't even know me; she couldn't know about my eyes. I mean I just met her with Jan and Josephine, and oh," I lifted my shoulders and let them drop, "I see." Anyone who met me through a friend usually commented on my lavender colored eyes, which always led to the great story about my personal "truth" barometer. "Are we going tonight?" Harry glanced sideways at me as we pulled out into traffic. "And, should we tell the Feds about it?"

Chapter Twenty-one

We decided to go to the memorial. The question of whether to tell Marisol stalled in the debate stage–until we heard the phone messages.

We'd carried a sleeping Connor into the house and placed him in his playpen. I unlaced his Buster Browns and removed his shoes and socks.

"We're popular, four messages." Harry pressed play.

"Honey, this is Dad. There's a story in Jan's Naperville Sun how the police have an eyewitness to the shooting at the re-enactment. What's going on? Is that you? Call me right away."

"Grace, this is Barb. Devin showed me an article about the shooting at the reenactment. Are you the local woman who witnessed the murder? You didn't tell me any of that. Are we walking tomorrow? I'll expect the whole story. Bye."

"Grace, this is Marisol. Did you talk to anyone at the newspaper? This didn't come from us. Call me at my office 630-555-0978. That's my direct line."

"Grace, call me. I'm worried about you."

Ric's terse voice ended our messages.

"Bloody hell!" Harry's hand slammed down on the counter. Connor awoke with a start and began howling. I rushed to lift him out of his Winnie the Pooh playpen. Harry came to my side. "Sorry, little chap. Lost my head there a bit." Harry held out his arms to Connor. He lifted him high against his shoulder and patted his back, murmuring the silly sounds and words we use on babies. Within moments

Connor hiccupped and calmed. Harry continued gently patting his back, swaying side to side. "Someone's put a target on you, Grace. We need Marisol and Kramer." Harry's words, spoken softly but so incongruous with his actions, chilled me.

Harry turned Connor toward me. His closed eyes and even breathing indicated he slept soundly. "Would that it were that easy for me," I thought as Harry laid him on his back and drew the thin blanket across his legs and bare feet. Watching Harry minister to Connor tugged at my heart. We had wanted our own babies.

He straightened and caught me watching him. He knew my expressions and put his arm around me and guided me to the living room. Harry squeezed my shoulders. I wondered if he mourned the children we'd never have together.

"I'm calling Marisol." Harry looked at his watch. "Almost three o'clock. Walter and Gertrude are picking up Connor at four o'clock. What time does Will get home today?"

I thought for a moment. "He has band practice until four and he'll take the late bus at four-thirty unless we pick him up."

"Too small of a window between Connor's pick up and Will's pick up. We could be driving to collect him and he'd be getting on the bus."

"I'll stay here with Connor and wait for Walter. You pick up Will."

Harry shook his head. "No, I'm staying close to you." He put up his hand to stop my comments. "That's not negotiable. I'll call Lily and see if she's in tonight. When Will gets home I'll send him over. In the meantime, you call your dad or he'll be on our doorstep."

I grinned at Harry's assessment of my father. "I'll call him from the bedroom." We had two lines on our bedroom phone.

I'd hung up with my dad after assuring him I couldn't identify the shooter and I hadn't said anything to the press. I told him Harry had a call in to Marisol. He calmed down, but exacted a promise to call him in the morning.

My head felt achy and my stomach churned. I searched the medicine cabinet for aspirin and shook out two into my palm before I realized I shouldn't take them on an empty stomach. I returned them to the bottle and the bottle to the shelf.

Half way down the stairs I heard the doorbell ring. By the time I reached the living room Ric Kramer and Harry stood huddled in a hurried conversation. They stopped talking when they saw me.

"Hi, Grace," Ric greeted.

I made a point of looking behind them toward the hallway to the front door. "Is this one half of a social call or one half of police business?"

The door bell rang again and I assumed it would be Marisol meeting Ric. Walter and Gertrude breezed through the doorway coming to pick up Connor for his overnight with them. Neither of them had children, therefore no prospects for grand children, or in the case of their ages, great grandchildren. Connor obviously brought them joy.

"We come early. Hope is no problem. If we are in the seats before four o'clock the matinee is less dollars," Gertrude explained while she hugged then kissed me on each cheek.

"He's in the kitchen. Let me change his diaper and slip on his p.j.s."

Gertrude and I returned to the living room with *kinder*

and his bag in tow. A sleepy Connor smiled when he heard Walter's rumbling voice as he explained to Harry, "*Ja*, the film is *Aladdin*. I *tink* he will like it, yes?"

"Spot on, Walter. I think you'll enjoy the cinema too. Princess Jasmine is quite the looker."

"Ariel is no slouch either," Ric added. He rumpled Connor's hair. "Maybe I'll take you to see that one," he said. Connor graced him with a grin.

Harry leaned in to kiss Connor's plump cheek. "See you come the weekend little chap." I smooched him once on each cheek. He giggled and unexpectedly wrapped his arms around my neck as I handed him to Walter.

Walter had him around the waist, his chubby circumference engulfed by large worn hands. I gently disengaged his arms and brought his hands to my mouth. His lip trembled and I felt my eyes filling with tears. I pretended to eat up his little sausage fingers making chomping sounds I hoped would make him laugh and hide my imminent tears.

He shrieked with delight and returned the favor by chomping on my nose.

"Oww!" My turn to shriek. Now at least I'd have a reason for tears. My outburst surprised him and he hovered on the edge of giggles and tears. Everyone's laughter at my expense settled him on giggles.

The door swung closed behind them and I could feel the mood in the room shifting from sweetness and light to something dark and scary.

Chapter Twenty-two

"Grace, did you by any stretch of the imagination indicate to anyone that you saw the shooter clearly enough to identify him?" Ric's question raised the little hairs on the back of my neck. I guess he had to ask it.

"Kramer, she's not stupid. Someone at the FBI must have said something."

I stepped between them before more words flew around the room.

"Stop. This doesn't help anything. I didn't say anything to anyone. Of course I wouldn't say I saw him. Why would I?"

Ric ran his hand through his hair. I'd seen him perform this nervous habit many times. This couldn't be good. He looked at Harry. "It didn't come from Marisol; she kept Grace's statement about seeing the shooter in her investigation notes, but not in the incident report. The file is on her desk. No one else has access to it."

Well we knew first hand that wasn't always the case. I looked at Harry before I could stop myself. He continued staring at Ric and spoke. "If it didn't come from Marisol, who is the leak? And more importantly, why? This person would have to know releasing the story would endanger Grace even if she isn't named. There's enough information in the article to figure out who the 'local Pine Marsh resident' is without any trouble."

"The information had to be passed yesterday because this," Ric held up the Naperville Sun, "came out today." He opened it to the page and read the byline, "George Romano. Do you know this guy?"

Harry looked at me. "Romano? Our insurance man?"

"Your insurance man is a stringer at the Sun?" Ric sounded incredulous.

I waved my hands for them to stop. "George Romita is our insurance man. I don't know a George Romano, but his name sounds familiar."

"Apparently he knows you because as he says, 'a source near the eye witness says she could see him clearly through the wire fence'. Who is this source?"

My stomach lurched and it had nothing to do with hunger. "Oh, no."

I looked at Harry to try and gauge how he'd take this.

"What is it Grace?"

Harry didn't take his eyes off me and I began to see a dawning in his eyes.

"Why are you staring at each other? You figured it out."

I nodded slowly. "Only a few people knew about the wire fence because they were there at the fence line. Danny Romano is a boy in Will's troop and in his class."

Harry looked at his watch. "I've enough time to collect him if I hurry. Kramer stay here with Grace."

The look on Harry's face made a storm cloud seem pale and fluffy.

"Harry, he didn't mean to cause trouble. It would be a big deal to be able to tell his friends about it. He embellished it to make it sound better; maybe even put himself in the picture." I froze. "Oh my God. Does it say anything about him in the story?"

I saw the flood of concern replace the anger on Harry's face.

"Don't panic," Ric cautioned. "There's nothing about Will. I'll stay with Grace. Go."

"He's a kid with a chance for fifteen minutes of fame," I said as Harry gave me a quick hug.

"He puts you in danger and you champion him." Harry kissed the top of my head. "He doesn't deserve you." He left through the garage.

"And *he* doesn't deserve you."

I turned to face Ric. In a split second before my eyes pinned his with confrontation I caught the tiny lift at the corner of his mouth.

"And I don't either."

I felt my posture shift from accusatory to confused. Ric's smile broadened. He stepped toward me and took both my hands in his. "We've meant a lot to each other over the years. We planned a life together at one time, loved each other, and then walked away from it all. Well, you walked. What I'm trying to say is I think I'm good with Marisol. I'll never love her the way I loved you, but I love her the best way I can with what you left me. I hope that's enough for her. She deserves better, but she's okay with it."

"Why are you telling me this?"

"Because as much as you don't belong with me, you belong less with him." Ric squeezed my hands to stop my outburst. Without them to wave about I pretty much remained speechless. "Listen to me. You've not had a normal life from the moment you said 'I do' to him. You honeymooned in London so he could meet with British Intel and accept an assignment that landed him in a South American prison. The nutcase jailed with him comes here to blow up your house with you in it." Ric hesitated and I knew he couldn't help remembering the injuries he sustained in the blast. "He discovers he's a dad and when you need him to protect you he's off in Europe catching up with his new found son. He played the big hero when he flew off to South America to rescue Hannah and Lily. He eluded the twisted son of the more twisted father he killed ten years ago to do it. It was heroic; I don't take anything away from him. But he is never here for you. Marrying you pulled him, I think, prematurely from a life he loved, thrived on. He is a danger junkie and that craving doesn't stop at the picket fence."

I couldn't believe Ric's diatribe. Where did this come from and why now? I yanked my hands out from his hold.

"You don't know what you're talking about. Maybe you're the danger junkie. First you're attracted to Nancy Royal the Lisle Police Officer, then, you find a bigger fish in Marisol, FBI. Maybe she's your connection to more excitement and danger than the River Forest P.D. can give you. Maybe you want the life Harry gave up willingly. Why didn't you go to South America to search for Lily and Hannah?"

I knew I'd hit a nerve. He ran his hand through his hair, creating a ridge where his fingers repeatedly sliced at the thick dark strands. I didn't want to fight with him or Will or anyone. I turned away and rushed toward the kitchen, but stopped when I realized Harry and Will would be coming home soon. I retraced my steps to stand in front of Ric.

"Leave it be Ric. Can we try for a semi-normal relationship for the sake of Karen and the kids and what we felt about each other–"

"Still feel."

"Make a life with Marisol or not, but let me go here." I touched the left side of my chest.

"I'll make a life, Gracie, but I won't ever let go." He closed the distance between us and in one quick movement gathered me into his arms and kissed me with a fierce tenderness so urgent it risked developing further. In my mind I glimpsed fractured frames of our relationship from our first kiss, to our lovemaking, to our painful separation, to this moment in time. I clung to him accepting his kiss, his heart, knowing this was his good bye.

Chapter Twenty-three

Ric left as soon as Harry returned with Will. He'd told us Marisol had talked to the paper and no further mention of me, erroneous or otherwise, would appear.

Lily walked over, planning to spend some time with Will and to bring him back to her house for supper. She tapped at the back door like family. I couldn't let her get under my skin, but I surely didn't want her present for our family discussion. As it turned out her presence made the discussion better.

She'd gone off on Will more than I would have ever dreamed of doing. Of course, she as his mother had all the parental rights to use his full name and play the 'I'm disappointed in you' card.

He apologized I'm sure from the sheer weight of two parents glaring at him rather than the thought he had really done anything too bad. He justified himself by saying the story got away from him. He blamed Danny for telling his dad, and Will claimed, adding 'some stuff' to make it sound better.

Harry called the publisher. He knew the blame landed squarely on Romano's shoulders for not checking his source. The publisher hemmed and hawed about part-time, local stringers.

It was nearly six o'clock before the tears dried and Will left with Lily.

Harry put his arms around me. "I've brought quite a bit to our lives, haven't I love?" He tightened his hold. "Hope you never wish you'd toss me out with the funnies after our first Sunday together."

I snuggled into his chest and lifted my head. Harry tensed and slowly released me. He stepped back and looked at me, his face awash with expressions of confusion, incredibility, and finally clarity.

"Grey Flannel." He turned and walked into the kitchen.

"Harry, wait. It wasn't like that." I didn't catch the scent of Ric's cologne on me, but apparently Harry had.

Dammit Grace! Why didn't you splash water on your face or brush your teeth or floss or something? Are you trying to end up alone?

The bizarre thought caused me to stutter-step after Harry, stopping to wonder why my subconscious would spew such a comment. I ran to catch him before he left.

He'd reached the door to garage when I lunged for his arm. I stepped off balance and he turned to keep me from tumbling into him. His blank expression gave no clue to his feelings, but his eyes spoke volumes. I saw the hurt and my heart ached. I swallowed hard to push the lump in my throat out of the way. I needed to explain.

Harry made sure I had my feet under me before he firmly disengaged my hand from his arm.

"It wasn't what you think!" I managed to squeak air around the golf ball-size lump in my throat. "He was saying good-bye."

"With an armful and apparently a mouthful of you. No simple, 'Have a nice life, good-bye Grace' for the two of you." Harry's slow, clipped speech frightened me more than if he'd exploded.

Tears streamed down my cheeks. I couldn't speak. I hoped he recognized the abject sorrow plastered across my face.

"I'll be at Lily's...perhaps saying *hello*." His face flushed. Perhaps he realized how hurtful he sounded, but he didn't back down. Maybe he meant it.

I watched my husband walk out of the kitchen and heard him close the door behind him in the mudroom. A quiet, more than just silence, descended over me like a too heavy jacket on a warm day, stifling, wicking away my energy. The sobs came and I let them overtake me, offering no resistance, instead cradling my head in my arms on the island counter top.

I became aware of furry friends rubbing against and circling my legs. As devastated as I felt, it's tough to keep sobbing when un-conditional love and comfort arrive. Hiccups from the aftermath of intense sobbing peppered my remaining sigh-like sobs. I sat down on the floor with my back against the island and accepted purrs and head butts from Elmo, Trey, and Patches. They'd all traveled through the small pet door in the mudroom, knowing dinner time loomed and tidbits could be bountiful. Elmo's tiny orange paw touched a tear on my cheek. He licked at the captured moisture on his paw. *Meow, meow.*

I didn't understand his comment, but I did understand his need to 'fix' me. I let him absorb a few more tears before I felt healed enough to change the direction of my mood.

I scooted backwards across the floor carrying them with me in my lap. Patches backed off the ride, anticipating our final destination and walked to the cabinet with the goodies. I fooled him and side-slid to the cabinet with the canned goods. I opened one side and pulled a jumbo size can of tuna fish from the shelf. "Okay, guys, tuna for everyone," I announced. I shifted to my knees and bounced to my feet, careful to miss any tiny toes. I gripped the counter, waiting for the lightheadedness to pass.

Whoa, girl. You're not sixteen anymore.

Heck, I'm not even thirty anymore.

I didn't think the sensation had to do with age as much as low blood pressure or maybe low blood sugar. Either way, I waited until my vision sharpened to run the can opener around the edge of the can.

The three tenors lost no time in bursting into *song* and weaving in and out of my legs. I pulled three small bowls and one larger bowl from the upper cabinet. With the crescendo of their musical demands I lowered the three bowls to the floor. I waited for the comical 'what did you get' stretch and sniff as each cat sniffed at each bowl. No matter how many times I put a bowl down in front of each cat, they never ate from their designated bowl, instead shifted positions until they stood in front of another bowl.

I laughed at their antics and wished them, "Bon Appetit," before spooning the other half of the contents into my bowl. I doctored mine with a dash of sea salt, pepper, a smidge of garlic powder, and a couple of shakes of hot sauce. I added a few oysters crackers smashed up in the tuna and joined my buddies on the floor. I used a fork.

Chapter Twenty-four

I scrubbed out the empty bowls and left them upturned in the drainer. No surprise my area of the floor showed bits of tuna smeared on the tile. I moistened a paper towel, applied a half dab of dishwashing liquid, and scrubbed the spot clean.

Oh no. The spot I'd wiped look so much cleaner than the surrounding tiles. *Gee, when was the last time I mopped?* The addition of Will and Connor to the household had significantly increased the spills and tracked-in debris. I wanted to walk away, go upstairs, and think. Instead I stepped into the dark garage to grab the mop; I could think while I swiped at the floor. I filled the wash bucket with hot water and Pine Sol and swished the long strands into the water rolling the handle back and forth between my palms, pulling the soaking fibers through the wringer.

I approached the floor like my mom had taught me, doing half, dumping the dirty water and rinsing with cold water, filling up the bucket for the second half, dumping the cooling, dirty water, and finishing with a cold rinse, ending at the door to the garage and the utility sink. I'd washed myself into a few corners as a kid; not so anymore.

The phone rang as I congratulated myself on a stellar finish. Hubris. When would I learn? The instrument sounded again like a taunt, *You can't get me.*

You didn't walk on the wet floor; you'd leave footprints. You didn't let the phone ring; it could be bad news. I walked on my tiptoes across the room to the phone.

"Hello?"

"Hi Grace, its Jan. Did I interrupt anything? I thought I'd get the machine you took so long to answer."

Jan's cheery voice lifted my spirits. No one could sound that happy and be delivering bad news.

"I was in the garage." Seemed simpler to not explain.

"Oh, on your way out?"

"No, in actually."

"I wanted to see how your day went with Connor. Jolene called her grandpa to tell him you'd all stopped by."

I marveled at how everyone in my family still kept tabs on me. More likely, I suspected Jan's motive was to find out about our trip to the FBI. I didn't blame her. She had a bit of *Nancy Drew* DNA. I realized I wanted to be out of the house, not waiting up for Harry to return, if he did.

"Meet me for a coffee? Unless you and Dad have plans. Are you at my dad's house?"

I heard a series of beeps. "Is that you or me?"

"Hang on, Grace. It's me."

The call-waiting feature on our phone still threw me. I twisted the cord between my fingers, but shifted to the yarn tied to it instead before a pattern could command my fingers to hopelessly entangle the curly cord.

"Grace, I'm back."

"Was that Dad?"

"No, Mitch. He had an idea for the champagne toast. I'm in Naperville. How about *Fanny's Place* in an hour?"

"Good call. See you then."

Jan lived in south Naperville and *Fanny's,* was west of Rt. 59 in Aurora. The restaurant had wonderful food, great big comfy chairs, and really good prices.

I thought about leaving a note for Harry and pulled the notepad from between the cookbooks lined up on the counter. The paperback size notepad displayed seashells across the top border with the heading, *A Special Note*...My note would be sour. I tucked the pad away between *An Invitation to Dine* and *St. Joan of Arc Parrish Cookbook.* I'll be back long before he is, I justified. The thought brought no comfort.

Chapter Twenty-five

Jan waved from a small table mid-way through the restaurant with only a few occupied tables. I slipped into the chair and leaned back against the oversized comfort.

"I won't feel guilty having a coffee and taking up a table, looks like the dinner rush is over."

Jan nodded. "They do a brisk business until about now, and pick up again when the movie theatres let out."

Jan already had coffee. I turned my cup up when the waitress approached. "Coffee only, thanks." She poured quickly and moved down the line to "coffee" the few remaining patrons. I took a cautionary sip. It wasn't Highland Grog. On the other hand, it wasn't tepid or burned.

"Okay, Honey. What's bothering you?"

Jan always direct, surprised me with this opening gambit a quick get-to-the-point-question even for her. I noticed from the corner of my eye when the waitress, *Meg*, her tag had read, poured, Jan had glanced at her watch. Had I sounded so pathetic on the phone she felt she had to meet me–an obligatory demand from her new *family?*

I couldn't sit there like a box of rocks. Meeting Jan was a bad idea. I couldn't spill my guts to a woman I'd know for a year. Could I?

"Grace?"

I sipped again thinking of an excuse, knowing she'd know if I lied. I met her gaze and hoped my eyes would not betray me. "Harry and Will are spending the night with Lily." My face flared with heat. Is that what I think? "I mean having dinner and spending the evening at her place. Probably playing Scrabble or watching a movie." I rushed to sketch a family scene.

"You took the higher path to enjoyment and asked me out for a coffee. Should I have brought my Scrabble board?" Jan's eyes twinkled. She didn't crush me with pity or questions.

My smile barely lifted a corner of my mouth. I envisioned a flat line between two lips pressed together to keep the tears from taking hold.

Flat line; my marriage's prognosis? I couldn't bum out Jan two weeks before her wedding. Do I want resuscitation or dissolution? I could move in with Karen, help her with the kids, get my old job back in the library, start writing again, this time with the perfect inspiration–Claire and Connor. Since Connor was a Marsden would Harry and Lily raise him and Will? Now that would be a proper family.

"Grace." Jan's tone snapped me out of my planning funk.

"I'm sorry, Jan. This was a bad idea. Thanks for coming out, but I'm going home."

"No you're not. You're coming with me." Jan openly checked her watch. "There is a memorial service for Keenan Putnam tonight at the field and several of us planned on attending. It's why I chose *Fanny's.* The memorial starts in thirty minutes and we can be there in twenty-five." She stood, put money on the table, and caught Meg's attention. "Can we please get two to go?"

"I don't know, Jan. I mean, I didn't think I'd be out long. I didn't leave a note."

"C'mon Grace. Scrabble can run long especially if you get into it."

I searched her face for a hint of malice. Her comment

struck a nerve. I knew Harry and Will would be enjoying themselves, especially Will, which would make Harry prolong their time together.

Like he wouldn't want to on his own?

Jan place the covered cup in my hand and nudged me toward the door. "Leave your car, I'll drive."

I mumbled, "Thanks," and climbed into her Explorer. I had no idea how to find the field. I had no idea what I'd find at home.

Candlelight vigil. Sounds right; for Putnam and my marriage.

Chapter Twenty-six

Jan offered the use of her car phone to call home and leave a message for Harry. "Hi, it's me. I'm with Jan and we're going to the reenactment field for the memorial. Bye."

"I'm sure that message will warm the cockles of his heart. What is going on with you two?"

"I never know what to say on a machine; never know who is going to hear it. Nothing is going on."

She shrugged and concentrated on the road. We'd driven only a few miles from the restaurant before the area had given way to empty fields and a two lane road. The nice thing about Jan was she wouldn't keep asking. I relaxed and leaned back against the seat, enjoying the childhood sensation of watching the scenery fly by. I watched the new cornfields march past the window. I felt myself dozing. I wished I could wish myself home, climbing the stairs to bed, not preparing to participate in a depressing memorial for someone I didn't know.

Why are you going to this? You really don't want to, do you?

No I don't. Jan's driving and I'd make her late if I asked her to take me back to the restaurant.

You should have driven your own car.

I should have stayed home.

My head nodded forward and the movement snapped me awake.

"Perfect timing, we're almost there. I have a bag of mints in the glove box. Would you get them? I have severe coffee mouth." I pulled out the bag of multi-colored starlight mints and strained to find one with purple stripes.

"What color?"

"No matter, anything to kill the taste."

She obviously didn't savor coffee mouth the way I did. I felt anxious about being here and something to keep my dry mouth from becoming parched sounded good. I handed her the usual red while I unwrapped the grape-flavored quarter size-candy.

"Thanks." Jan unwrapped the mint and popped it in her mouth, working her mouth to increase saliva around the candy. "Darn, it's starting to mist. Hope the serious rain holds off. I have an umbrella and a poncho, maybe two, somewhere in the back."

A line of taillights, with left turn signals blinking, appeared around the curve of the road. Jan slowed and flipped on her signal. The field looked eerie in the misty darkness. The area recently festooned with rows of tents with regimental flags planted at their forefront, with animated people costumed in period garb demonstrating skills almost lost, if not for their passion, with the aroma of Burgoo Stew simmering in a cook pot blending with the pungent smell of cordite lingering in the summer air after a staged skirmish, now stood empty and forlorn.

Only the ghostly imprint of what had been remained in the pressed-down hillocks of grass and the jagged holes, circled with dirt disturbed by the removal of countless poles jerked from the ground.

Jan handed me a poncho and pulled another over her head. She shoved her purse under the seat and I did the same. I grabbed the umbrella from the back seat. "You never know."

"Okay, but you carry it. I prefer hands free." Jan

reached under her poncho to put her car keys in her pocket, and brought out both hand palms out.

I didn't mind carrying the small telescoping umbrella. Coming from a family of four eagle scouts I'd learned all kinds of ways to transport stuff. I tucked the seven inch bundle in the back of my waistband. I waved my empty hands at Jan. "Me too."

She grinned. "Can't wait to see how you handle sitting."

We pulled up our hoods and walked toward the growing group of people gathering around a low campfire. Several people holding lanterns low at their sides created a lighted corridor to the campfire.

I'd traveled campgrounds at night by the light of lanterns, but those sojourns had been for fun. This lighted pathway added solemnity to the sadness I could see on people's faces.

I whispered to Jan. "I don't feel right being here. I didn't know him."

Jan nodded agreement. "I didn't think it would be so, so haunting. I thought it would be more like the encampment."

I slowed my steps. "Maybe we should leave. No one has–"

A lantern swung higher and cast light over us. "Grace is that you?" Josephine's ample voice cut through the darkness. "Over here," she directed, swinging her lantern, creating alternating light and dark across the ground like pulsating checker board.

"You were saying," Jan said. I heard the sigh in her voice. No chance to leave now.

"Let's get over there before she gathers a crowd." Jan and I walked toward her. In one of Josephine's backward arcs with the lantern, the light cast against the gated entrance to *Eternal Rest Gardens*.

Against reason I knew who I would see. He stood silently illuminated in the arc of light indistinguishable for the time it took Josephine to swing the lantern forward, then visible again in the backswing of the arc. The illusionist's taunt ran through my head. *Now you see him, now you don't.* The arc lifted toward the cemetery. He was gone.

I tripped over a sturdy tuft of grass and caught myself against Jan.

"Sorry."

"Josephine hold the light down and steady. That lantern's not a disco ball."

I recognized Arlene's husky voice and saw her outlined behind Josephine.

"Give me that." Arlene spoke softly now, with a smile in her tone. She took the lantern from Josephine's hand. "Go hug. It's what you do."

We stood before Josephine and received anticipated hugs. "Ladies, I am so happy to see you. Under different circumstances this would be a delightful encounter. Stand with us until the memorial service begins."

Jan cleared her throat. "Josephine, I didn't know Keenan well and Grace didn't know him at all. I sort of brought her with me on a whim. Maybe we shouldn't be here. I don't want the 10th to think we're here like 'tourists'."

Arlene and Josephine both resisted the idea we didn't belong, and offered to keep us with them the entire service.

When a man with a crate of cold lanterns approached them they turned to speak with him.

I leaned close to Jan. "That went well, didn't it?"

Jan rolled her eyes. "Yeah, I spoke so eloquently they'll probably keep us front and center. No chance to melt into the background now."

Melt into the background. The rain would come and we would melt into the ground; the quick and the dead, all the same.

I searched the darkness at the cemetery gate and spotted his outline. I wouldn't go to him, he couldn't come to me. We stared at each other through the deepening darkness. *What do you want me to do? I don't understand.*

Clear my name.

Chapter Twenty-seven

"Clear my name. That's all I want."

I jumped at hearing the words outside my head. Pete Corvo spoke. "Everyone thinks I messed up. They don't say anything, but I know that's what they're thinking," he complained while he lifted a lantern from the box and handed it off to Arlene.

He noticed me and Jan, especially me, and changed his tone. "Thanks for coming, Mrs. Marsden. I'm really sorry."

I stood feet away from the guy Harry and Marisol suspected of trying to kill someone. I couldn't see it. I held up my hand to stop further apology. "Please, it's over. I know it was an accident."

"Thanks," he mumbled and thrust a lantern in my uplifted hand. "I'd appreciate if you'd stand next to me during the circle service. Let people know you don't hold a grudge." Without waiting for my agreement he turned and practically sprinted off to the next group of lantern recipients.

Jan clapped me on the shoulder. "Way to keep a low profile, Gracie."

Arlene lifted the glass and motioned for me to hold it while she struck a match and touched the flame to the wick. I guided the chimney back on its seat and shifted the lantern to my left hand, holding it low next to my leg.

"Why don't the two of you take up the next position about ten feet away or until you're out of our light?" Arlene pointed back the way we'd come.

More people streamed in from the parking area. The mist evolved to definite rain drops. Jan and I positioned ourselves outside the end of Arlene's light, creating another half arc of light across the ground.

"You're my witness I didn't go looking for this. Right? I mean if something bizarre happens I didn't come out here trying to get involved."

"Hey, you're scaring me. What do you mean bizarre? What's going to happen?" Jan's head snapped from side to side looking for danger. I instantly regretted alarming her.

"I'm sorry. I'm jumpy. I don't want to be here and now I'm involved."

"Grace, it's my fault. C'mon lets go. Hand the lantern to the next person who comes in or put it on the ground. Let's get out of here. I'm getting nervous."

What had I done to the happy-go-lucky woman I'd met a year ago. I'd turned her into a bundle of nerves, searching the night for shadows.

I lowered my lantern to the ground, looking for a flat spot. Pete Corvo materialized at the edge of the light. "There you are. We're going to begin now because the weather report is predicting a storm front in an hour." He picked up the lantern and handed it to Jan. "Would you mind waiting out here for a few more minutes?"

I intercepted the lantern and returned it to the ground. "Put all the lanterns on the ground, and no one has to wait for latecomers." I hoped Pete would agree because I wasn't leaving Jan.

"Great idea. I'll pass the word."

So much for escaping unnoticed. I glanced at the cemetery gate. His outline grew clearer in the light of a moving lantern. He shook his head.

Warning, disapproval, what?

Chapter Twenty-eight

What I thought had been one campfire in the distance turned out to be several small campfires in a circle around an area about eight feet in circumference. I couldn't determine any hierarchy to the structure of the circle. People gathered and formed circles from the campfires out. It seemed rather a grouping of individual clumps of friends. I saw Jan scanning the people nearby.

"Are you looking for someone?"

She nodded. "Mitch said he'd be here. I thought I could kill two birds with one stone; still trying to figure out the flower scheme."

Leave it to Jan to find the only wedding planner who also engaged in Civil War reenacting. Actually, he'd found her at a living history and handed her his "day job" card when he'd heard of her impending nuptials.

"He probably checked the weather and made the smart choice."

The rain drops shifted from fat plops to beady, pelting drops driven by an increasing wind. As the campfires smoldered and appeared to succumb to the rain, people holding the remaining lanterns walked around the fires and placed the lanterns in a tight circle. Movement from the opposite side drew my attention. I nudged Jan. Ten reenactors in uniform walked in two rows toward the outer edge of the circle. They split ranks and continued around the campfires at a slow, solemn pace. They stood at attention with their muskets at their right side, stock down. I expected them to raise the muskets and fire a salute over our heads. Instead they dropped to the ground to end up with one knee touching the ground, the other bent 90 degrees, with their heads down and their muskets under their right arms, with the point of the bayonet and musket mussel pointing to the ground and the trigger guard up. The lack of gunfire made the tribute more eerie.

Pete Corvo began to speak words of friendship for a friend. His voice carried clear, with only a word or two slurred with emotion. He stood bare-headed taking the rain on his face as he spoke, holding his lantern chest high to provide a focal point to the voice coming out of the darkness.

Arlene stood to his right and Josephine stood on my left next to Jan. Josephine motioned Arlene to her side to share her umbrella. I remembered the one tucked in my waistband and moved back from Pete's side to rummage under my poncho.

Pop. Pop. Pop.

A weight slammed against my chest and I heard someone scream. I staggered back, fell to the ground; the air knocked out of me.

Pop. Pop.

I waited for the third *pop. Where's the third pop?*

Who cares! Get up; someone's shooting at you!

My brain registered the weight as Pete Corvo's body, pinning me to ground. Beyond that realization I heard screams, shouts, and the thudding of footsteps running from the danger. I heard Jan shouting for me, her voice fading. Either she moved away from me or I had melted into the ground.

I heard a different set of screams and shouts. The smell

of cordite filled my nose and gun smoke clouded my vision. The screams of men in pain, falling to the ground, dying alone in battle surrounded me. I heard the shouts of *Medic* and the grunts of soldiers, carrying their fallen brothers, trying to reach cover before they were cut down. Suddenly the weight lifted, without any one there to grapple Pete Corvo from my body. It was if an occult hand had lifted him. Only there was no Pete Corvo, only me standing off to the side near an Oak tree barely as big around as me. The sparsely populated cemetery lay behind me. A sprinkling of tombstones glowed grey-purple in the waning light.

How can it be dusk? I touched my poncho and looked at the ground. It hadn't rained on this ground in days. I scrutinized the field and began to see the differences. More haystacks, smaller stands of trees, fewer graves all pointed to the answer. I stood on the same field. I existed in a different time. I remembered their term for the wrong time. I was *farby*.

My heart filled with terror. Am I dead? How could this be happening if I wasn't? If I am dead where's the light I'm supposed to go into where my mom and Nonna Santa are supposed to be waiting for me?

Oh geez, what if there wasn't a light for me? Oh man, I didn't want to go to hell. Fighting, pain, dying all around me; is this hell?

The screams and terror I'd heard earlier disappeared. He walked toward me from the direction of the field. He didn't see me, but looked beyond. He looked exactly as I'd seen him 130 years in the future except the stain on his uniform gleamed fresh and still wet with his life's blood.

I followed his gaze and watched his shoulders slump in pain as he watched a family, his family I thought, gathered in anguish, crying over his grave. The wind shifted, blowing directly into my face. With the shift I heard words carried on the air. A woman in widow's weeds lifted a tear-stained face to a man standing close to her. "I will never believe he took the money. James was a patriot, a hero and the Department of the Army can say what they choose and deny him a military funeral. I know my husband." Her voice held love and anger, pride and stubbornness for the man she lost. The gentleman next to her placed his hand on her arm in a conciliatory gesture. She pulled her arm away and motioned for two children to come to her. Mrs. Blackmore gathered them under her arms and they walked slowly up the slight incline and curved path to the carriage waiting on the road. She turned at the carriage for another look.

My eyes locked on hers although she saw through me to the grave beyond. Her eyes squinted, then widened. I whirled to see if he stood behind me. Did she catch a glimpse of her dead husband? Was their love so strong they snatched one last look? Or was his search for justice so intense it kept him earthbound?

Earthbound? Melted into the ground? Am I here forever? I don't want to walk with them. I want to go home. Will Harry cry at my grave site; will Lily place her hand on his arm? My dad will cry–a parent should never have to bury a child. My heart is pounding. I can't breathe. I'm dying. Someone is coming for me. They know my name; they sound nice. I see a light, bright shining like the sun.

Something's wrong. I can't hear the sweet voice calling me; it's drowned out by a harsh gurgle, a guttural noise in my ears. And the light, it's wrong too. It's too bright, painful. Patterns explode behind my eyelids and in my head. I don't want to melt into the ground. Please, God.

Chapter Twenty-nine

The weight lifted from my body. Nonetheless, I couldn't move a muscle. I realized I lay on the wet ground, raindrops pelting my face.

This is good. Where I was, make that when I was before, the earth was dry. I'm back in my time.

Sharp pinches shot throughout my left side. I heard my heartbeat resonating in my ears, slowing, slowing.

This is not good. I'm not breathing.

Someone pushed down on my chest; compressions, one, two, three, four, five. A different someone leaned close to my face and air rushed into my mouth down my throat and stopped.

"No good, something must be blocking her airway. Get her up, now!"

Rough hands pulled me up to a sitting position, then standing. The pain in my side escalated from manageable pinches to sharp stabbing make-you-nauseous-pain. Hot breath coming in panicked gasps wet the back of my neck. I felt lighter. Despite knowing my chin rested on my chest, I saw a bright light, not the glaring kind, but a gentle welcoming light with hope and love shimmering at its edges. I could float there if this person would let go of me. His arms encircled my chest holding me upright for a moment.

Thanks for standing me up. Now let go so I can walk into the light.

His arms tightened then jerked hard against my chest. The pain returned with a vengeance and the light disappeared. Again, he pulled his fists into my chest. I felt a scraping and burning in my throat. My mouth opened in protest and expelled a lump of starlight mint.

Harghhh, harghhhh, hurghhh. I grabbed enough air to fill my flat lungs. *Hurghhh, hurghhh.* The pain in my side lessened until I took another deep breath. If I took shallow breaths my side hurt less.

"Lay her down," someone directed.

"No, keep her upright," someone else countered.

That's right, don't jostle me.

I shifted in my rescuer's arms and felt fairly certain I could stand on my own power.

"She's coming round," he said, his voice so close to my ear I realized the speaker must not be much taller than me.

I raised my head and let it tip back against his shoulder. The rain had slowed to a gentle sprinkle that felt fresh on my skin.

"Gracie, oh my God, Gracie. Can you hear me?"

"Jan." I wanted to say more, but I hadn't the strength to push the words past my lips or hold up my head to look at her.

She took one of my hands in hers. "Her hands are like ice. We need to do something. At least get her under some cover."

Snap. Swoosh.

"Hold it over them."

The rain, blocked from my head and shoulders, tapped lightly above me asking for permission to enter. The lack of rain felt better.

How odd I didn't think so before.

Everything about you is odd.

That's not fair.

We're not talking about fair, just fact.

The muscles in my legs quivered and lost strength. The arms tightened around me. "She's losing consciousness; I think she stopped breathing."

"I've got her. They don't have another gurney."

Stronger arms, one under my shoulders the other under my knees, lifted me off my feet and up against a warm, dry chest.

We moved quickly over the uneven ground.

"Thank God you're here." Jan's voice puffed behind me. I imagined her short legs pumping like pistons to keep up with the long stride carrying me toward the flashing lights.

The saturated ground, turned to muddy potholes, sucked at every step we took. The umbrella carrier, shorter strides by the sound of the more frequent but lighter squelch sounds lost ground. The rain found me. The drops pinched my skin. They felt angry.

I turned my head toward the comfort of the familiar spot between his shoulder blade and chest.

Chapter Thirty

I couldn't convince the attending at Silver Cross Hospital I didn't need an overnight observation but rather dry clothes and hot coffee. They gave me a warm robe in exchange for my soaked clothes, but they wouldn't let me have a coffee until someone determined I had no injury beyond shock, a sore throat, and bruised ribs.

At the field the EMTs had got me breathing again. The Heimlich had worked, but the trauma had caused my windpipe to swell and block my airway. A quick injection of a drug reduced the swelling and now my vitals looked good and the preliminary work-up came up good. Jan had given them most of my info except for personal things she wouldn't know like the date of my last period, boxers or briefs, and my mother's hat size.

My mind skipped across the events of the evening like a flat rock over smooth lake water. Jan had stayed by my side in, during triage, and had left a few minutes ago after squeezing my hand and assuring me she'd be at the house in the morning…with my dad.

Marisol Nunez had poked her head around my curtain. "I'm glad Jan finally went home. She looks done in."

My personal FBI agent (so it seemed) sat in the chair recently vacated by Jan. "Why were you out there?"

"No 'hello, Grace? Fancy meeting you here'. By the way…"

"Grace, I don't have time to play nice with you. Three people are dead and you–"

"What!" I lurched to sitting position, my arm flailing against the pole holding the 'get-over-shock-solution' bag. The thin tubing leading to the needle in my arm straightened and tugged but held. I pulled up my feet and dug in my heels to squooch up in bed.

"Cripes, Grace, hold still." Marisol fingered the remote and the head of my bed rose toward my back.

A nurse came around the curtain, checking on the commotion. Her name tag read Cherry Ames. Did nurses use pseudonyms?

"Everything okay?" She expertly eyed the IV apparatus. She looked at her watch. "You're due for another bag in ten minutes. I'm here now, might as well replace it now."

Marisol held up her badge for the nurse's inspection. "Could you give us the ten minutes?"

Cherry Ames nodded, her wide eyes making me think she had more than the Hippocratic Oath in mind. She whipped around the curtain, resolved to keep patient-doctor confidentially I hoped.

Do nurses take the Hippocratic Oath? I'll have to ask Tracy.

My head hurt from the abrupt movement, but my stomach needed immediate attention. I gagged and reached for the kidney shaped bowl they'd left for me.

Marisol shoved it into my hand in the nick of time. She scooped up the sides of my hair, transferred all the hair into her left hand, stretched her right arm to a container on the wall, and pulled out a handful of paper towels.

I lifted my head and she released my hair.

"Thanks," I mumbled.

She took the bowl from my hand and replaced it with paper towels.

I scrubbed at my mouth, pushing the saliva onto the

paper, and wadding it over and over.

Marisol pushed the table to the back of the examining room. I heard cabinets opening and closing. She appeared at my side and handed me one of those pink spongy balls on a stick.

I ran the spongy ball over my gums and teeth, cleansing the aftermath of being sick, and freshening my mouth. Marisol handed me a fresh pink ball and I repeated the process. "Where were you during my college years?" I think I smiled, but my lips felt fat and tight like after Novocain.

"From what I hear you and Karen had each other's back." Marisol smiled, and then turned serious. "Grace, I need to ask you some questions."

I remembered my outburst and the consequences, so I stayed calm, asked quietly, "Who is dead? I heard shots but I may have been hallucinating. I hit my head; it still hurts like the dickens."

Marisol stared into my eyes. I didn't like what I saw. "Ric and I were coming up the path when the shots started. It's standard operation procedure for law enforcement to attend funerals, memorials of a victim on an open investigation. The perpetrator sometimes returns to be present in the crowd of mourners.

"When we heard shots fired we circled around the crowd trying to pinpoint the shooter's location. He got away. I radioed for back up and EMTs. We lost the shooter in the crowd. He probably holstered his gun and ran for cover like the other eighty people trampling each other in the panic."

"Who is dead?" My voice didn't reach much above whisper, not for lack of trying. My throat felt raw and each swallow hurt.

Marisol's lips stretched tight across her mouth before

she spoke. "Pete Corvo, Terry Stock," she paused and licked her lips, then continued in a rush, "and Josephine." She grabbed my hand. "Grace, I'm so sorry."

I swallowed quickly several times ignoring the pain. "Why? Who would do this? Why Josephine?" My throat tightened around more words.

Marisol retreated to her FBI mode. "We think the shooter came for the witness who could identify him."

The room turned cold. Every surface seemed to shimmer with an icy sheen. The *whoosh plick, whoosh plick* of the monitor in the next room sounded as clear as if I carried it on my shoulder like a medical boom box.

I shook my head hard and recoiled from the flash of pain behind my eyes. The sheen dulled and my ears heard only the heavy pounding of my heart against my ribs. I wrinkled my nose at the sour smell from the metal bowl and feared for a moment I'd be sick again.

Marisol moved past me, headed for the offensive bowl, but I grabbed her hand. "Me? He came to shoot me?"

She stopped dead in her tracks and swung round to face me squarely. "No, not you. Pete Corvo. We don't believe a ghost told him to shoot toward the tree. We think he knew the shooter. My team has uncovered more connections to Keenan Putnam and a diverted gold shipment."

A part of me sighed with relief since my presence hadn't caused Josephine's death. I lay back against the upright mattress.

How could this be? Why Josephine?

"Grace, I need you to think about last night and answer some questions. You were standing between Josephine and Corvo would have had the best chance to notice anyone across the circle who might have been acting suspiciously."

My head turned slowly toward her until my eyes locked on hers. "Suspicious? It was pouring down rain and pitch dark except for a few lanterns. People huddled under umbrellas, tucking their heads deep inside their poncho hoods." I felt the tears of frustration filling my eyes slip down my cheeks. "I didn't even look across the circle." Anguish and fear burst from my throat in short wrenching sobs. I wouldn't have recognized the hoarse choking sounds as mine except I was the only one in the room crying.

"Marisol. What the hell? I said I'd question her." Ric's recrimination filled the small room. He whipped the curtain closed behind him and stood on one side of the cubicle, glaring across the bed at her.

She rocketed around the end of the bed and stood in front of Ric. "You don't tell me how to run my investigation. Back off." She lifted her hand to punctuate her comment. Ric caught her fist and held it.

Marisol lifted her chin in defiance. "You are close to assaulting a Federal Officer."

"Holy cripes, stop it both of you." My dad left the curtain open behind him. Maybe he thought an audience would diffuse the situation. He'd left it open for Harry who lagged a half step behind him.

"Grace." Harry skimmed around Dad and filled the spot Marisol had left open. "Grace, oh my God. I sat at home for an hour before I noticed the call light on the phone." Harry nodded his chin at Ric. "He called to tell me they were headed to the field to watch for the shooter. I told him you had gone there, and then I left to find you."

That explained his wet clothes, matted hair and, I imagined if I looked, muddy boots.

"It was a madhouse in the field. I kept asking about you. No one knew anything Finally, someone told me a woman had been shot. I found Arlene and she told me you'd been taken here. Grace, the woman shot didn't make it. It was…" Harry's voice tightened. I saw him swallow hard.

I touched his hand. "I know, Josephine."

"I could only think, 'Thank God it's not Grace.'" He tilted his head back and breathed out through his mouth.

My dad clapped a hand on Harry's shoulder. "She's fine, son. You look like hell. Sit down." He pulled the chair closer to Harry and pushed down on his shoulder. "Sit."

Cherry Ames began talking before she turned the corner into my cubicle. "Okay, you've had your ten…minutes…" She slowed to a stop at the end of my bed. She assessed the body count and transformed into a lean, mean nursing machine. "Everybody out!" Her firm voice wasn't louder than before, but her resolve *pinged* like metal.

"Nurse Ames, I'm her father and this is her husband. We only arrived a minute ago. He's been searching for her." Dad stepped aside and pointed to Harry's lower half.

Her eyebrows rose. Before she could speak Harry cleared his throat and turned in the chair to face her. "Please don't ask me to leave. I've only just found her. I thought she'd been the one who'd been…" He left off, not needing to finish.

There aren't many women who could have said no. She wasn't one of them. She turned to Marisol "You had your ten minutes. You need to leave. And you?" She raised an eyebrow at Ric.

"Inspector Kramer, homicide."

The word landed heavy in our midst. Harry's hand sought mine. My dad stepped closer to the bed. Marisol looked up into Ric's face. Ric stared straight into Nurse Ames' eyes. "I'd like a minute with Gra–the family."

Marisol whipped her head around and looked at me.

"I'll talk to you tomorrow." She stepped boldly past Nurse Ames. Of course she did, she carried a badge and a gun.

Cherry Ames looked at the three remaining occupants. Dad spoke up. "Nurse, I'll step out. I've seen her with my own eyes. Life is good." He touched his chest over his heart. "Thank you for helping her. Can you point me toward the closest coffee machine?"

"That stuff is awful. Come with me and I'll get you a cup from the nurses' break room."

He smiled and motioned for her to lead on.

"Five minutes. We'll be back in five minutes."

My dad discreetly pulled the curtain closed when he followed her out.

"Kramer, can it wait until tomorrow. At least Nunez had the decency to leave."

"Harry, wait." I squeezed his hand.

"I wanted to make sure she was okay."

Ric and I spoke at the same time.

"Dammit, Kramer. She is not your concern. Don't you get that?"

Ric stood quietly looking into my eyes, ignoring Harry.

I didn't break eye contact. "Thank you. It was you."

Ric's lips pursed with emotion. He nodded and swallowed several times. "How did you…did someone tell…"

"Grey Flannel."

Chapter Thirty-one

I turned to Harry and saw the confusion in his eyes.

"Pete Corvo's body slammed against me and knocked me down. I was pinned under his weight. The mint in my mouth lodged in my windpipe. I choked on it. Someone…" I looked at Ric. "Do you know who helped me?"

Ric shook his head. "Not yet, it's crazy out there, but we'll find out."

I turned back to Harry. "A man did the Heimlich on me and the mint popped out of my mouth. For a minute I felt strong, but I started drifting and having trouble breathing. Not like before where I couldn't get any air, but different like I could breathe in but not out." I took a deep breath and released it slowly. I would never take that simple pleasure for granted again. "The EMTs wouldn't have found me in time. Ric carried me across the field to them."

Harry's voice choked with emotion. "I owe you everything." He nodded at Ric. "Thank you."

Ric ducked his head and looked away. He fingered the tubing lying on my bed and raised his face to meet Harry's gaze. "You don't owe me anything. *You* never entered the picture. It's about being there when it counts." The last part he said looking at me.

My dad and Nurse Ames walked around the curtain. She held another bag for my IV. Dad held a tray with three coffee cups.

"We still don't have a room available. I'm afraid you'll have to spend the rest of the night here. Your vitals are excellent, but we want to monitor your breathing and we want to get some fluids back in you." She stepped past Ric and deftly switched out the flattened bag for the plump new one.

"Can one of those fluids be coffee?" I eyed the tray in my dad's hands.

She checked the chart on the table. "Yes, it can. Enjoy. I'll bring you some ice water and…" she wrinkled her nose when she replaced the chart and looked at the back counter. "Why didn't you tell me you vomited?" She placed a hand on Dad's arm. "No coffee for her. Not until I know her stomach is settled." Nurse Ames looked at me. "I'll bring you something for the nausea." She lifted the bowl and covered it with a paper towel.

"I'm fine, really. Please?" I pleaded at her ramrod straight back as she ducked around the curtain.

Each of the men in my life, in unspoken agreement, lifted a cup from the tray and took a step back from the bed.

How the human mind finds humor during tragedy is beyond me, but in that moment I began to laugh and point at each of them in turn.

"Oh, yeah, keep the coffee away from Grace 'cause she might jump out of bed and kick your butts to get a cup."

The tension broke. They didn't actually guffaw but they did smile.

My dad made a show of placing his cup on the table well out of my reach. He leaned in for a kiss. "I'm spending the night at Jan's. Call me if you need anything. We'll meet you at home tomorrow."

"Thanks, Dad."

"Okay, fellas, carry on." He nodded at Ric and Harry in turn, lifted his cup from the table and left.

Nurse Ames popped in with a glass of water and pink

tablet in a tiny plastic cup. She waited for me to swallow the pill. "I'll bring a pitcher of water if everything stays down." She tucked a clean kidney-shaped bowl on the bed next to my hand.

"Gentlemen, it's past her bedtime. Get some rest," she paused, looked them over head to toe, "get cleaned up, and come back in the morning."

"I'm staying with her."

"I'm not leaving her."

Harry and Ric spoke simultaneously.

Cherry Ames stiffened her shoulders and took a deep breath. Her facial expression set a no-nonsense demeanor.

Code Blue triage A. Code Blue Triage A.

Nurse Ames expelled her breath. Her expression changed to brisk efficiency. She turned to leave and measured her words, "Figure it out, but only one of you can stay." She stopped and turned back. "And keep your voices down, we have sick people here." The curtain snapped behind her.

"Kramer, I'm her husband."

"I'm her bodyguard."

"I don't need a bodyguard."

"She doesn't need a bodyguard," Harry echoed.

"You're never around. She needs someone she can count on."

"You're a bloody fool!"

"Really. Where were you tonight?"

Harry's face conveyed his feelings of guilt.

"Harry, it's not your fault you left me for Lily's."

"He left you for Lily?" Ric turned on Harry. "What are you, stupid in addition to arrogant and, and English."

"Don't think I've the market on arrogance. I'm grateful for what you did tonight. Can't ever repay you, but dammit, she's my wife." He turned to speak to me, "And I did not leave you for Lily." His voice softened. "I love you, Grace."

My eyes pinched and I swallowed hard. "I said 'Lily's', he said 'Lily'."

I looked at Ric. "He went to Lily's because Will was there and because, um, he smelled Grey Flannel on me."

Ric's face reddened. Even through his mud-streaked cheeks his embarrassment showed. He opened and closed his mouth, like a guppy in shallow water, over apparently the wrong words as he groped for the right ones. "We, I mean, I, hugged her. Hugged her goodbye. I mean, really goodbye." He raked his fingers through his hair, pushing matted strands off his forehead.

"Big goodbye hug, eh? She reeked with your cologne; I could taste it on her skin. I've had enough of you. You want to say goodbye to my wife, shake hands like any other casual acquaintance, because that's what you're going to become around our house."

The vein in Harry's temple throbbed with anger, all the more frustrated because their 'shouting' match flared in low, harsh whispers. If I weren't exhausted, saddened, and generally depressed I would laugh at the two of them sparing like roosters. My imagination withered their arms and plumped out their chests. Sturdy cock's combs sprouted atop their heads and hard, gritty beaks stretched out from their lips.

Fine specimens, the both of them. Either one would make an excellent breeder.

Oh, great, now I'm hallucinating about roosters vying for me. Get out of my head!

I'm going but remember the goal is to keep their bloodline intact; it's a fight to the death.

The fowl accoutrement retreated from their faces. I

could have smiled if not for the bitter words spewing from their lips, hurled across my personal space, bits of tone and language spattering me like hot oil.

"Stop."

"Stop!"

My shabby whisper and her firm command spoke at once.

Marisol stood at the curtain.

"Are you two cretins finished? So much for decorum and confidentiality." She turned to Ric. "Do I have to hear from two cubicles down facts about this case?" Marisol whipped around to face Harry. "And how nice for Grace to have her relationship bandied down the hallway. Do you really love her or is this a tug-of-war?"

The rhetorical questions went unanswered, but her comments added additional grist for the hospital gossip mill. You couldn't help but hear.

"Please leave."

Ric and Harry looked at me, waiting for clarification. Each still held the hand they had grabbed during their face off. I wiggled my fingers and slid my hand out from their grips.

"Both of you leave."

"Gracie, I'm not leaving you. Don't send me away."

"You need protection. Don't get pig-headed."

Marisol stepped up to the foot of the bed. "She needs rest, not two roosters pecking and pushing at each other."

How did she know about the roosters?

She held up her hand to ward off protests. "You love your wife; go home, clean up, get some rest, and come back," she looked at her watch, "in seven hours with clean clothes for her."

She turned to Ric. "You love me, get out of my face

and let me do my job. I'm on this watch. Frank is spelling me in three hours. Go home or go to my place, but leave, now."

Yikes, I thought, she's hard as nails. I looked at the petite woman at the foot of my bed. She stared at each man in turn, waiting for them to back off. Ric "blinked" first. He looked down at me. I saw his eyes shift to the lock of hair matted to my cheek from rain or mud or tears. I knew he wanted to lift it free and tuck it behind my ear. I locked on his eyes. *Don't do it.*

Either mental telepathy worked or he came to his senses. He tapped the top of my hand and smiled. "Behave, Gracie." He spoke to Marisol when he left, words meant for her ears only. Her face gave no clue. *For sure, I wouldn't play poker with her.*

Harry leaned close to me. "I want to stay." He felt me stiffen. "Please, Grace, don't shut me out." I closed my eyes to gather strength. He freed the lock of hair from my cheek, guided it behind my ear, and kissed the spot he'd cleared. I opened my eyes. "I need my clothes and the animals need care. It's too late to call and ask Devin to do it. Will might be home early and you won't be there."

"Right, all right. As soon as things are sorted out at home, I'll be back." He leaned in and brushed his lips against mine.

I knew a thirteen year old, undisturbed, would sleep till noon, but Harry, new at parenting, let the Will comment convince him.

He was turning out to be a great dad; the husband part gave me pause.

He stopped to talk to Marisol, with clear words for anyone listening. "She is precious to me. You'd better be as good as they say or at least as good as Kramer."

Chapter Thirty-two

"Whew, those two act like they came straight out of a Barbara Michaels romance."

"You read romance novels?" I couldn't keep the incredulity out of my voice. "I guess I thought you'd read grittier stuff, you know like stuff you do."

"First, what I 'do' isn't usually gritty. It's a lot of paperwork, tracking, following process, and not much actual 'shoot'em ups' or stalking serial killers; for which I'm grateful." She pulled the chair closer and sat down. "Second, I don't want to read in fiction what I read about in FBI bulletins and alerts and case files. I live and work 'true crime', 'police procedurals', 'thrillers' and even, I'm sorry to say, 'horror'." She leaned back and grinned. "I'll take a romance or a cozy any day."

I sat up a little straighter. "The shooter wasn't after Pete Corvo." My calm statement surprised her.

Marisol's eyes narrowed. "Who has been telling you stories?"

"Okay, maybe Corvo started out the intended victim but the shooter had more than one target–"

"Grace you don't want to start speculating on what you don't know."

"I'm not stupid and I'm not speculating." I held up one hand ticking off points on my fingers. "One, Ric says I need protection. Two, you come back to sit with me. Three, you've arranged for your department to be involved, so it's not just a 'feeling'. You know something. Four, the two people standing on either side of me are dead and I'll bet the other person, Terry, was standing on the other side of Corvo." For emphasis I pushed down digits starting with my pinkie, so now I had a loose version of 'thumbs up'.

"I never thought of you as stupid. I didn't know how well you felt and didn't want to upset you further."

I'm glad she spoke up; I didn't have a fifth point to make. Her comment annoyed me. I pinned her eyes with I hoped a contemptuous glare.

"Not feeling well enough to hear about a homicidal maniac who tried to kill me? Not well enough to handle how he missed me, but killed a friend who had, moments before, moved next to me when Jan left my side to talk to Arlene."

Oh, God. It could have been Jan dead because of me. I hadn't remembered her moving until that moment when I replayed the minutes prior to the shooting.

I continued to stare at Marisol. I felt no contempt only icy fear.

Marisol must have seen the expression of horror on my face. Her eyes widened and she reached toward me half rising from her chair. "Grace you're as white as this sheet. I'll get a nurse."

I grabbed at her hand. "No. I don't need a nurse."

She sat down, but stretched forward to not break contact with me.

"If I don't see some color coming back and more focus in your eyes, I'm getting the nurse." She placed her hand over mine. "You heard what your husband said. Nothing's going to happen to you on my watch."

She smiled and squeezed my hand. I knew I had to respond appropriately or she'd call Cherry Ames, and who knew what she would do. I pushed thoughts of Josephine's death and Jan's near miss to the back of my mind, trusting the part of my brain that never turns off would sort through those feelings.

I inhaled deeply. Nothing brings color to your cheeks and clarity to your eyes like a dose of side-splitting pain. I set my face, held the breath for a delicious moment, releasing it slowly, hoping the pain would diminish in the same increments.

"Much better," Marisol pronounced. She relinquished my hand and sat back squarely in her chair completing the shift from concern to cop. "I told you earlier you weren't the target. I wasn't entirely sure, but felt I shouldn't panic you."

"What's changed?"

"Two things. We received more information about Putnam and Corvo." Marisol seemed to make a decision. "One of the ambulance drivers reported being questioned by someone at the field."

"That's cause for alarm."

"It is when the person asking the questions insists on knowing if you'd been brought in to Silver Cross or Edwards."

Goosebumps erupted on my arms and I shivered. I pulled the thin hospital sheet closer around my shoulders as though the fabric could keep out the cold.

Marisol pursed her lips in response to my actions. "Yeah, exactly. Creepy." She rolled her shoulders to shake off her thoughts. "By the time he finished with his patients and reported the conversation to an officer, it was too late to search the field. He couldn't describe the guy any better than a dark-skinned man, average height and build, wearing a poncho with a hood obscuring his face. The guy reached out and grabbed his arm to get his attention and the EMT noticed his hand, otherwise we wouldn't have skin color.

"The EMT told him he didn't know who went where and he would have to check with each hospital. The guy pressed him again to ask if they had picked up a woman with your description. The EMT, who thankfully wasn't the one Ric had carried you to, told him he couldn't release patient information anyway. He wouldn't have reported it, but when he didn't have an answer for him, the guy called him the 'n' word and flipped him off."

"Wait, Marisol. The EMT is black?"

She nodded. "Why?"

"Keenan Putnam was black. Pete Corvo was Hispanic. Josephine was black. Maybe it's not about me but a racial thing."

"Why would he be asking about you?"

My shoulders slumped. I'd wanted to believe Josephine had died not because she stood near me, but because someone with a twisted soul had targeted her.

Marisol flipped through her notebook. She lifted her head quickly. "The other deceased, Terry Stock, was black. Maybe there is something here."

"It doesn't make sense. Why is he asking about me, unless he thinks Italians are a minority?"

"Maybe that's not it at all. Maybe it shows his concern; making sure a bullet hadn't hit you. You went down when Pete Corvo collapsed."

"This is even creepier. Why would he care?"

"I'm not saying he does. Honestly, it's more likely he had targeted you, too, and he wanted to know if he'd succeeded."

"You don't think it could be racially motivated?"

Marisol washed her face with both hands. The fine lines around her eyes looked more pronounced, deepened by fatigue or the unflattering light in the cubicle.

She rolled her neck and seemed to come to a decision. "I've already thrown out the rule book with you and Harry. I probably shouldn't be heading this investigation because of our," she rolled her wrist around in a circle, "all of our connections, but my gut tells me I need to stay on this one. I think the shooter is after you because of what he thinks you saw."

"Yeah, well Will didn't mean–"

"This creep would have thought you saw him even without the newspaper item. Once the story about the 'near miss' spread throughout the encampment it would have been easy for him to find out who you were. My instincts tell me he already knew of you, maybe even that you would be attending the memorial."

"That's impossible. I didn't know until the last minute."

"Right. So Pete would have been his primary target tonight. He knew Pete would attend and probably deliver a eulogy since he knew Putnam. I imagine he counted his lucky stars to find you in attendance."

"One thing, Marisol. In the rain and the dark people had hoods up and umbrellas out. I don't know how he could have recognized me."

I yawned and rolled my shoulders from side to side. "*Hmm.* I think nurse Ames slipped me a sleeping pill with the nausea pill."

Marisol smiled. "I think your adrenaline level flat-lined hours ago, but you've been pushing to stay keyed up. Let it go and get some sleep. I've got some ideas about how to proceed–totally outside the rule book."

Chapter Thirty-three

The exchange from hospital to home went smoothly. I hadn't noticed when Marisol left and Frank, her partner, took her post. I slept soundly through the IV needle being removed from my hand, through the clatter of morning rounds. I instantly opened my eyes when I felt the brush of lips against my cheek.

Harry stood over me, staring at me the way a woman wants a man to look at her. He picked up my hand in one of his, turned it palm up, and bent to gently kiss the spot under my thumb.

"Good morning." He waited for me to take the next step–pardon or snub. His eyes searched my face. "Didn't mean to wake you, well perhaps I did. Gracie, I'm miserable without you. I don't ever want us to–"

"Me too," I interrupted.

"I love you, Gracie girl. God I do." He leaned down and kissed my forehead. "It's early. Sleep a bit more if you can. I'm afraid the house will be bedlam."

"Now for sure I won't get back to sleep. Bedlam?" Harry had a tendency to exaggerate, or maybe his word choice painted more interesting pictures. "Do you mean confusion like 'sixes and sevens' (one of Harry's English terms) or do you mean craziness like my family is circling?"

Harry grinned. In that moment of boyish abandon, all the years and pain we'd share fell away from his demeanor. "All right then, old girl, no rest for you. Don't say I didn't warn you." Harry lifted a small duffle bag from the chair to the bed. "I think I've brought it all except for those clippie things you like for your hair–couldn't find those buggers anywhere."

He referred to banana clips which I hadn't worn since I cut my hair. I'd given them to Jolene, but I gave him credit for trying.

"I brought your soiled clothing home last night and popped them in the wash this morning." He beamed like a schoolboy waiting for a gold star.

Nurse Ames cleared her throat before she entered. She glanced sideways at Harry, then turned her full attention on him. "Good morning, Mr. Marsden. You surely look different from last night."

She apparently approved of my freshly scrubbed husband. His soft blue polo shirt pulled snug across his chest and the color accentuated his cornflower blue eyes. I had to admit he was an eyeful, but I knew the best had yet to unfold.

Harry smiled at her, making her feel like the only person in the room, heck in the hospital, with him. "You look as lovely as you did when you attempted to throw me out of here last night."

She blushed and sputtered, "I, ah."

Harry captured the hand not holding the clipboard and held it in both of his. "You had every right to do so. I've only gratitude for the excellent care you've given Grace. Seems a simple 'thank you' isn't worthy of your efforts."

Sheesh! What do you with him?

I dunno; love him.

I cleared my throat. Nurse Ames reluctantly removed her hand from my husband's gentle grip. She gave him one long look. I swear she gave herself a shake as if to wake up from a fantasy.

She cleared her throat again and looked directly at me. "Mrs. Marsden your vitals are excellent. You can get dressed. Doctor will be in shortly to release you." She turned to Harry and handed him the clipboard, although I'm pretty sure she would have rather dipped into his arms. She looked back at me. "When you're ready, sign at the bottom. Keep the second page for contact information. Your primary physician will get the results of the tests. I'm going off shift now." She looked at Harry and back at me. "Good bye, good luck."

Harry remained at the curtain. "I'll stand guard whilst you get dressed," he crossed his arms over his chest, "unless you require assistance."

"Stay," I ordered, "or we'll never get out of here."

Chapter Thirty-four

We had three hours before the Morelli's descended. The bedlam Harry referred to was the scheduled wedding rehearsal. With the wedding less than two weeks away we had to have at least one run-through.

I had resisted Harry's offer of assistance with my shower, certain his plan to dally in places we didn't have time to visit trumped his offer to help. I rethought his motives, however, when pain shot through my side as I attempted to shampoo my hair. Lather and rinse would be enough today. I'd give myself the deluxe package when lifting my arms didn't hurt so much it made me nauseated.

I chose a button up shirt, rather than a pullover top, and settled on adding a light-weight summer vest to hide the fact I went braless. No way could I blow dry my hair. It wasn't the length, but rather the thickness that took so much work to dry and tame. My best shot was to brush it straight off my face and wear a head band. Not stylish, but neither was the purplish bruise on the side of my cheek or the abrasion along my jaw line. I sat down at my dressing table ready to do battle with my hair. Harry stepped up behind me. He lifted the hair dryer and my brush from the vanity top. "Lean back and relax."

Harry learned to tame ladies locks at a young age. Having a twin with deliciously long hair, he would help his sister untangle and manage her hair after her day of adventure. He'd resorted to scissors once when Hannah had ended up with tar in her hair.

Harry's strong hands began pulling the brush through my hair and applying the powerful stream of air first to the base of the strand then the middle, and finally directing the air over the curled tips. The drone of the motor filled my head with a pleasant, calming noise. I found myself drifting with no particular thought in mind. How pleasant not to talk, not to think. The warm air soothed me and led me to a drowsy place. A light coating of mist covered the mirror. My features faded into the fog.

Wagon wheels creaked protest against the rutted road. The mule driver cussed another round against the 'dade blamed' officer who'd ordered him to take this route.

Gattlin' guns for the troops. Crates so heavy mules pulled the army buckboard across prairie miles on a route hopefully hidden from Confederate scouts.

Mule driver, Private Osborn Wilson, grumbled to his 'shotgun', Private Jerimiah Putnam, "Can't make no time on this Godforsaken Indian path. Ain't even a real road. I seen the map; I know where we're headed. I know a better road, a shorter way, and the ruts won't jam our backbones into our skulls."

The soft noise in my head stopped. Harry switched gears from hairdresser to masseuse and gently gripped the top of my shoulders on either side of my neck. He kneaded the muscles slowly, working out knots as large as walnuts. "*Hmmm*. You're hired." I looked in the mirror and saw Harry's reflection above me. I glanced away and thought I caught another reflection from the corner of my eye: a young man in uniform, holding a small book. My head snapped forward; no fog, no soldier, only my face and Harry's.

"Did I hurt you," Harry asked lifting his hands from my shoulders.

"No. It feels great. I thought of something I have to do before everyone gets here."

Harry leaned down and slipped his arms around me so they crossed over my chest. "I thought of that, hours ago." He uncrossed his arms and let his hands slide up over my breasts. "Ah, the 'girls' are relaxing today."

I'm sure he could tell the 'girls' were anything but relaxed. He led, I followed. After all, how does one tip the best husband-hairdresser-masseuse?

On the dot, the entourage arrived, my dad first through the door. He and Jan immediately checked me out, pronouncing I looked better than last night.

"I'm feeling much better. The bruises look worse than they are."

"Hey, Sis, nice shiner."

My father tapped the back of Marty's head. Will giggled, then stopped, not sure if it was appropriate to laugh. Dad smiled at Will. "Just so you know I have permission from your folks to administer 'love taps' to you when necessary." Will's face split in a grin.

My cousin, Nick, gave me a quick hug and peck on the cheek. "Mom and Dad say hello."

Mitch had hung back watching me, studying my face.

I must look worse than I thought. Best get some make-up on those bruises.

After minutes of pleasantries, and beverage orders, the real work began. I left Jan, Dad and Mitch on the patio. Jan had suggested setting two vintage baskets filled with colorful pashminas for the guests. When Dad said, "What kind of flower is that," and Mitch rolled his eyes, I thought I'd leave them alone. I heard Jan's, "Mike, you remember, they're shawls in case a guest gets cold." I didn't hear his response. I could imagine it and grinned.

I returned to the kitchen and found Harry and Will lifting lids from the containers to check out the food my Dad had brought.

"I don't know if we've enough room in the fridge for all this," Harry said. "Exactly how many people are eating here? He's brought enough for a small town. Please tell me we're not having a small town to lunch?"

Will and I laughed at Harry's exaggerated concern. "Look here, Will and I can sort this out." In a stage whisper he added, "And sneak a few tasty morsels, whilst you go have a lie down. At the slow rate they're moving out there it will be lunch time before we have to take our places. Besides, Jan's daughter, Judi, called to say she's running late. Can't rehearse without one of the maids of honor."

Stretching out on a comfy bed in a quiet room sounded lovely. Will and Harry confirmed their capability of handling the kitchen. Mitch would convince my dad that garlands of green orchids and crystals were a 'must have' and Nick and Marty moved well on their way to weaving strands of tiny lights through the lattice pattern on the white arbor delivered earlier today.

I climbed the stairs to our room, intending to snooze until summoned. Instead I detoured to the lingerie drawer in my dresser. From childhood I'd always tucked special papers or treasures under my underwear. As undershirts and girl type boxer underwear gave way to high school bras and briefs I still hid important stuff from prying eyes. I'd discovered my brothers believed, above all other drawers, my underwear drawer to be sacrosanct. I'm not sure if my Nonna Santa or my dad established that boundary.

I rummaged under my half slip for the thin book I'd hidden there. I hadn't had the time to look at it until now. If

I could find any way to follow the plea I heard on the field last night, *clear my name*, it could be in this book. My fingers found it easily under the black lacy slip–the texture of the leather so foreign in a landscape of silky *frou frou.*

I had a small one-cup coffee maker I kept plugged in and loaded at the corner of the window seat. I lifted the lid to be certain I had filled it with coffee and checked the carafe for water. Good to go, I pressed the on button. An orange light blinked on. Soon, I would have a steaming cup of Highland Grog. I pulled a lightweight throw off the back of the rocker and curled up on the window seat, shifting against the plump pillows. I turned over my coffee mug anticipating the series of *gasps* the coffeemaker emits when it has finished its brewing trip.

Never possessing the virtue of patience, I opened the book to page one, page two, and page three, and four, and so forth, until about page twelve. I skimmed pages filled with large, loopy writing, reminiscent of third grade penmanship papers. Each page held a few 'housekeeping' notes; the salt pork container cracked–needed a new one. Cook got drunk again and "mess" turned out the best they'd had since his last bout with the "Snake Oil Potion" one of the sutlers had sold him. Another entry notated they needed more wheel grease.

Fascinating as the daily drudge of running a regiment read, I searched for references to gold. On page twelve, and for six more pages, each page depicted some kind of terrain–a drawing of an area with circles and squares and X's interspersed over the terrain. I had seen topographical maps. I could be looking at the layout of Blackmore's farm back home, a travel route for his regiment, or the plot in Eternal Rest Gardens. I needed someone who worked with maps, actually found places using them; I needed Harry.

I filled my mug and went downstairs to find him. Harry had made himself a cup of tea and sat at the nook watching my brother and cousin, on ladders, hanging lights on shepherd crooks placed along the perimeter of the yard; solar powered lights ready to blink on at dusk.

He looked up when I entered. He nodded at the book in my hand. "Probably not the best of times or places, but I've been dying for you to haul it out of your panties drawer and give me a look see."

"You knew where it was?"

"It's where you put everything important." He grinned. "One of the things I love about you."

"Shove over so we can look at it together."

He obediently slid further along the bench.

"I thought this might be a diary he kept, but after the first twelve pages there are only maps of some kind. At least I think so."

Harry flipped through the pages once quickly, then again more slowly. He pointed to initials and dates at the bottom of a few of the pages. "This is curious; seems like a bit of code with the letters, but the dates seem straightforward enough. Wish I knew more about your Civil War. The dates are definitely near the end."

"There is someone who will be here later who is pretty much an expert. He's the reason Jan got interested in re-enactments. She met him through the Elmhurst Chamber when she had her business."

Harry's eyes widened with comprehension. "The minister is a reenactor." I nodded grinning at his expression.

"Yep. Reverend Jerry is a man of the Union cloth."

Jerry Kowalski, a long time friend of Jan and her family, a rabid Civil War reenactor, and also an ordained minister.

"Wait, I know your brother has been assigned to Rome, but I thought your father's priest would be officiating? Perhaps he's a Civil War buff also."

"Napoleonic Wars. He's short and a control freak, but a good priest and nice guy. We've know Father Moffat since grammar school at St. Domitilla."

"Why didn't he marry us?"

"He was laid up in the hospital from a spill he took off his motorcycle."

"I think I shall like meeting the good Father. And why isn't he officiating this time around, another accident?"

"He retired two years ago. Doesn't do the entire Mass anymore, does only blessings. Reverend Jerry does the ceremony, Father Moffat does the blessing, and Joseph wrangles a visit for them with the Pope when they honeymoon in Italy."

"They do know how to compromise, those two."

I grinned. "Not about baskets of pashminas."

"Not so," Marty said from the doorway. "I heard Dad say okay to the shawls, but Jan had to include Chinese lanterns for the inside of the tent." Marty smiled at me. "Remember your Sweet Sixteen birthday party?"

I feared he would reminisce, but I saw his eyes find the booklet partially covered by Harry's hand. He looked at me his eyes gleaming.

"Is it from the box, Gracie?" He stared at my eyes daring me to lie, knowing he'd know.

"Why would you think that, Marty?" Harry tried to distract him. My youngest brother, the closest to me in spirit and temperament, knew if he stared at me I'd give it up in three shades of purple.

"What does it say? Does he tell where the gold is buried?" Marty approached us. "Shove over so I can see it."

I stood up and effectively blocked his path.

"See what?" Nick stood in the doorway recently abandoned by Marty.

Harry groaned. "Did anyone ever have privacy in your home?"

"Not in our home," my dad's voice answered from behind Nick. "Too many kids, one bathroom, one phone with one extension." Dad slipped around Nick and stepped into the kitchen. "Wanted to let you know Reverend Kowalski is here and we're ready for 'take one'."

"What about Judi?"

My dad shrugged. "We've gotta' get the show on the road. Karen is going to stand in for Judi. She got here a few minutes ago. Claire is a little princess," my dad smiled. "Present company excluded."

One half of the twin set had arrived. Gertrude and Walter were bringing Connor. With the kitchen full of prying eyes I felt stupid for bringing out the book. I had to figure out how to get it back to safety under my bras and panties.

"Dad, why don't we serve lunch first? We planned to do one run-through, break for lunch then do another one. Let's eat first and run through it twice. This way for those who have to leave early they still will have eaten."

I knew making sure people ate ranks high as part of my father's mission statement. I felt a twinge of guilt for deceiving him with his good intention. He gave me a bear hug and beamed at no one in particular. "The apple doesn't fall far from the tree."

His hug caused more than a twinge.

"Oww."

"Gracie, honey, I'm sorry." He held me at arm's length. "You okay?"

I nodded and took short shallow breaths.

Harry seized the moment, and the book, and stood next to me. "Mike, I'm going to take her upstairs, make sure she rests before lunch." He looked around the room at the guys who were all looking at me. "Can you fellows get things going? Perhaps call a few of the ladies to help out. I'll be back in a Tinker's tic."

We left the room amidst assurances they could handle it. Harry and I raced up the stairs and rushed into our room giddy with our successful ruse. I marched over to my dresser and opened my lingerie drawer. Harry dutifully tucked the book under a pair of black panties which he fondled a nanosecond too long. I slapped his hand and snugged the drawer closed. "Safe for another time," I pronounced.

Harry stood at attention and mimicked a salute. "I shall protect milady's knickers with my life."

We dissolved into laughter. He gently grabbed me up in his arms. "You mean the world to me, Gracie."

His serious tone, like a "but" coming, froze my heart. "You're scaring me, Harry."

"No, no my darling. I shan't ever cause you fright again or allow anyone to hurt you." He lowered his lips over mine and masterfully drained the tension and fear from my body. "Trust me."

Those two words touched a chord in my soul. He had spoken those words to me the night before he'd left for South American over ten years ago.

Chapter Thirty-five

The rehearsal went well with the minimal amount of glitches. They were still undecided on Jan's entrance.

Jan and I toyed with the idea of having her driven in a carriage from Lily's house to our yard; Dad would help her alight from the carriage, and then walk her down the aisle and through the arbor. I thought it would be romantic and give April a shot at attending the wedding. I had requested extra crystal cording for her mane.

I found Nick and Mitch, the last two to leave, in the mudroom. Nick wanted to show Mitch the final lighting arrangements.

"Oh, I thought everyone left."

"I wanted to show Mitch the electrical connections in case he needed to know."

"You have a beautiful home Grace. Interesting architecture. Nick says you and your husband designed it. I particularly love the back stairs." He pointed to the wrought iron staircase. "Leads up to the family space. Very clever."

"I don't know about clever, but it's handy."

"About finished in here?" Harry stood in the doorway.

"Yep. We're done in here. C'mon," Nick motioned to Mitch, "I'll show you the set up outside."

Nick opened the back door and let Mitch go first. "I have two bottles of Mike's Hard Lemonade if you're interested," he said.

I closed the door and leaned against it. "Whew, I thought they'd never leave. They sure got buddy-buddy."

I stepped toward Harry and looped my arm in his. "I think we rehearsed well. I am satisfied we will be the best husband-wife team of rice bundle distributors the wedding scene has ever–"

Harry interrupted, "Or will ever,"

"Have the pleasure of watching in action," I finished.

"I must admit Gracie, you caught on to the 'lift lightly from your basket and offer with a flourish' directions faster than I did."

We walked into the living room. I patted Harry's hand. "It's all in the wrist."

Harry groaned. "I knew you were going to say that. My wrist hasn't had as much action as Mitch's apparently."

"You and my dad are so wrong about him. He is not gay."

"Who's not gay?" Will had come in from the mudroom.

"No one." I looked beyond Will. "I locked the door, how did you get in?"

"Nick used the key in the corner of that cement coffin."

"Sarcophagus," Harry and I corrected.

"Yeah, that thing. The wedding guy thought he forgot his planner book in the house." Will shrugged and spoke to Harry. "Anyway, the minister is back. He said you wanted to talk to him about a Civil War book or something. The wedding guy and Nick are talking to him outside."

"Thanks, son. Why don't you go upstairs? We've some plans to go over with Reverend Kowalski. Wedding plans."

"That's probably what the wedding guy is doing." Will started up the stairs and stopped. "So who is the gay guy?"

"William," Harry started.

"Okay, okay." Will clumped up the stairs.

Harry turned to me. "I don't like Nick showing a stranger where we keep our key."

"He's not a stranger. He's Jan's wedding planner. He'd probably be lost without his book. Nick was just being helpful."

"I'm moving the key. Only you, I, and Will shall know where I've hidden it."

"Fine. You go find the Rev and I'll put your kettle on to heat."

"Not for me, too hot. I'll take iced tea."

Harry left to find the minister and returned shortly with Reverend Kowalski, Mitch Trerra, and Barb Podol.

"What an unlikely grouping," I thought when Harry herded them into the kitchen.

Barb spoke as soon as she saw me. "Hi Grace. I didn't mean to interrupt your afternoon. I saw you had company so I was going to leave some papers for you with Barbara. She insisted it was okay to come over. By the time we finished our beverages most of your guests had left. I spoke with Arlene and she asked if I could gather this information for you."

Barb handed me a brown envelope the size of a magazine. It wasn't heavy. In fact, felt empty. Of course, two or three pages of paper didn't weigh much.

"Thank you. Ah, sit down, please. I'm making coffee."

"We haven't met. I'm Mitch Trerra. I know Arlene from the 10th Regiment reenactors." He did a quick mock bow and said, "Quartermaster at your service."

Quartermaster. Perfect job for a wedding planner. Organize, inventory, set up.

"Oh, too bad the Lieutenant wasn't from the 10th," Barb said and smiled.

How were we going to separate these people? I couldn't bring up the book with Barb and Mitch here. I wanted to read the file she'd brought with her present in case I had questions.

Mitch turned his attention to Reverend Jerry. "You're the National Chaplain for the Sons of Union Veterans of the Civil War." Mitch stretched out his hand to Jerry. "I didn't make the connection earlier. I used to get the newsletter."

"Actually, past National Chaplain, but you know once a Rev always a Rev." Jerry's laugh boomed through the kitchen. He looked at his watch. "In fact I'm giving the blessing at a dinner this evening. You said something about a book?"

"From the Civil War?" Barb's eyes gleamed. "About people?"

"That would be a real find," Mitch added while his gaze scraped the counter and table top. "Could be valuable."

I didn't like the way everyone keyed on the book like a juicy bone. I had a bad feeling about where this was going.

"Civil War? No, not hardly. Don't know where that intel came from. We've found an old book of hymns at a church jumble. Might date back to the 1860's, but don't think so. We thought if the Reverend had some time he could help us choose some pieces for the wedding, maybe a collage or medley if that's a proper term for hymns."

Harry is a brilliant liar; a worrisome thought at times but not this time. You could see Mitch's body language shift from in-the-hunt to boredom. Barb lost interest as well–nothing noteworthy about people in an old hymnal. Good thing Harry didn't say Bible or Barb would have been asking to check the family page.

Mitch stood. "I guess I'll be going. Don't want to hold you up." He turned to me and Harry. "Thanks for your help today. I think we are on target for a wonderful wedding. I have a couple of decorations to bring over this week and get in place. Will you be home tomorrow night?"

"I will." I looked at Harry. "You're at the scout meeting."

"No problem, I can leave them on the patio." Mitch shook hands with Harry and nodded toward Jerry and Barb. "Nice to meet both of you." He extended his hand to me. I felt a stream of cold air between us. Our hands clasped in an icy current that, apparently, only I felt. A second later the temperature returned to normal.

Nothing is ever normal with you.

Shush, we have company.

Barb stood up. "I'd better be going too. If you have any questions, call me. My card is in there."

"I'll walk out with you," Mitch said. "In fact, I find genealogy fascinating. May I have a card? I might be able to send some business your way. Brides and grooms may want to do a search to complete their family trees. It's a connection kind of time for couples."

It sounded innocent enough, but I had the feeling Mitch would find out the contents of my envelope before I did.

Harry had sprinted up to our room as soon as the door closed behind Mitch and Barb. I poured Jerry a cup of Highland Grog. Before I could lay out the napkin and spoon, Harry laid out our thoughts about the pages in the book.

Reverend Kowalski sipped at his coffee while Harry explained the circumstances, the sanitized version, of how we came to be the keepers of the book.

Jerry put down his cup and reached for the book. He paged slowly through the first few pages, faster through more pages. He stopped "Can I use your phone? I gotta call a man about a blessing."

Chapter Thirty-six

He called a friend who would be at the dinner, and asked him to fill in on the invocation. He hung up and turned to us with a grin. "They don't need a man of the cloth, just a nice touch. The mayor will be at the dinner, he'll do it. Tom loves to talk."

He returned to his chair and accepted a refill.

"So tell me again what you think you have here?"

"We hope," I said as I pulled the sheets of paper from the envelope, "we have an idea of what happened to the gold shipment Lieutenant Blackmore was accused of diverting. We don't believe it's buried with him. I don't think he did it. The reenactor killed at encampment last week had information some people apparently thought had merit. He was writing about the Knights of the Gold Circle."

Jerry Kowalski's dark eyebrows rose. "Those Knights surface most seasons. Someone always has a new theory or an old theory with an addendum." He looked down at the book he'd closed. "This is different. You've examined the topographical maps. You're sure they're not of this area?"

Harry nodded. "Afraid so. I did a bit of checking and from my limited skill I'm certain we don't have this topography in this area. Maybe Southern Illinois or Southern Indiana. Only a convergence of rivers causes these types of rolling hills." Harry opened the book and pointed to different pages.

"Could your geography include Southern Ohio?"

Harry thought for a moment. "I suppose. Why?"

Jerry loosened the string tie he'd worn. He was a big man, but the vest and tie looked good on him. He rubbed his big boned hands briskly and settled into the chair.

"In 1863, the National Bank of Athens, Ohio, released gold bullion in the form of bars to a group of investors whose sympathies lay with the South. The gold, on its way to Huntsville, would support the Confederacy. Before it reached Huntsville, Union soldiers captured the wagon and made their own arrangements. They needed to get the gold out of the South quickly before they were relieved of it.

"Historians tracked the shipment, which had been hidden in bales of cotton, onto a steamer on the Ohio River, surreptitiously headed to the Midwest market.

"The shipment made it to the Illinois River for its final destination further north. At this point, the shipment was offloaded by a Union officer charged with getting the gold to safety in an Illinois bank with no connections or compassions for the South.

"This is where it gets dicey." Jerry stopped to take a sip a coffee. He leaned forward and we moved closer like kids sharing a secret.

"The young lieutenant, according to his orders, was to send out two buckboards on two different routes. One was, of course, a dummy shipment, the crates, marked 'munitions' filled with rocks instead of gold bars.

"His letter back to command indicated he would not send a small patrol to lag behind the buckboard because the area couldn't conceal the soldiers easily and they would draw attention and suspicion. Instead, he'd send out patrols forward of the trail and the wagon. They would travel back towards camp providing protection in the sense that they stayed visible, but not seemingly connected to the wagon. Once the patrol passed the wagon they would wait a few hours, then head back to their forward point, eventually passing them again as men on horseback made better time than a wagon."

"Brilliant strategy." Harry said. "Did it work?"

"Half of the plan did. The dummy shipment was hijacked. Bet those rebels were purely put off when they pried up those lids and found rocks." Jerry grinned and sipped at his coffee. "The other half, the real gold shipment and the two soldiers, went missing without a trace. The Lieutenant had split the patrol with one contingency leaving their forward coordinate and traveling back to camp on the same day the wagon left camp and with the other members of the patrol leaving a day later. The Lieutenant's report indicated the first patrol passed them coming and going and the second patrol passed them coming in to camp, but when they turned back to pass them from behind, the wagon had disappeared."

"How?"

"They never found the wagon?"

Harry and I asked at the same time.

Jerry swung his head from me to Harry. "The muleskinner must have left the trail. One theory proffers him as a Confederate spy who struck pay dirt when his team was tapped to carry the real McCoy. Another theory is the Lieutenant had men waiting on the trail, who forced them deeper into the hills. They'd know the timing of the patrols. Another theory says the muleskinner and his 'shotgun' figured out what the crates they hauled carried and decided to steal the gold." He held up his hands palm open. "There are as many theories as people who have an opinion."

"What's your opinion?" Harry asked.

"It might change if there is something I don't know about Lieutenant Blackmore in those papers." He inclined his head toward the envelope.

I undid the string on the flap and slid the contents onto the table. The first sheet's banner read, HISTORY of the 124TH REGIMENT in big bold letters. I read further. Illinois Infantry Volunteers, otherwise known as the 'HUNDRED AND TWO DOZEN'. The history ranged from August 1862 to August 1865.

"This is compiled by Richard L. Howard, Chaplain." I slid the papers toward Jerry. "One of your people." I smiled.

He fanned them out so we could each read pieces.

"Says here he hailed from the Montgomery area and mustered out of Camp Butler, Illinois. They moved out to Jackson, Tennessee in the fall of 1862."

"How about a refill, Reverend Kowalski?"

"Thanks, Grace," he held out his cup, "and call me Jerry."

I poured a fresh cup at the counter and brought that to him, accepting his empty. I topped off my angel mug and slid in next to Harry to read some other sheets.

"Wow, the 124th covered a lot of ground and fought in so many campaigns. They saw action in Mississippi and Alabama after Tennessee. The Lieutenant mustered out at Vicksburg, Mississippi and received formal discharge at Chicago August 16, 1865."

Harry pointed to a long run-on sentence indicating the regiment, in total, lost 190 men: 1 Officer and 40 enlisted men killed in combat; 2 Officers and 147 enlisted men killed by disease.

The sobering statistics cast a pall on what had started to be a stimulating paper chase. It became real in a heartbeat.

Jerry shook his head. "I don't know if this is our guy. The story connected with this lost gold claims the lieutenant in charge was drummed out of the army. You know, dishonorable discharge." He tapped the sheet he'd been reading. "There is no indication of such a discharge with Lieutenant Blackmore."

"That can't be. I heard 'clear my–"

Harry slipped his hand over mine. I caught my slip; I hoped in time.

"You heard what?"

I looked into my cup. "I heard it was more innuendo that plagued the lieutenant rather than a dishonorable discharge."

Harry interjected some ideas and drew Jerry's attention. "This sheet says he died in 1893 in Aurora, Illinois. He's buried in the cemetery next to the encampment field. Perhaps he spent those years after the war trying to find the shipment and clear the smear on his good record. Do you know the destination of the gold in your story?"

"Castle Bank, National Association, DeKalb County," Jerry answered. "Practically in his backyard."

"Jerry, do these initials at the bottom of the pages mean anything to you?"

"I've been looking at those. If we accept this lieutenant as the guy with the gold, then these two initials and date could be the soldiers assigned to drive and the date they left. It loosely correlates to when the gold may have made it to Illinois. Each page with a different topography has different initials. Could be the patrol leader and the day they would have been passing the wagon."

Harry turned a sheet around to face Jerry. "Would it help to have the roster?"

Jerry rubbed his hands together briskly and nodded. "Now we're cranking." He flipped back to the first page of the journal. "Look for names with initials OW and JP."

I leaned closer to Harry to read the names. The pages

marked at the top 'Best Copy Possible' hardly deserved that notation. The small, cramped writing filled the ledger with a listing of un-alphabetized names. The former librarian in me bristled at the disorder or maybe the current OCD in me caused the reaction.

"Here's one," Harry said, "Osborn Wilson."

I'd been scrolling the list with my finger. I stopped near the bottom and tapped the name. Harry's eyes found the name.

"That's not a coincidence," he said quietly.

Jerry craned his neck to see. "Jeremiah Putnam?"

Harry nodded and stood. "I'd best call Agent Nunez." He slowly walked to the phone. I knew why he hesitated. He'd have to turn me in, in a sense, when he told Marisol about the journal.

"The man killed at the encampment was Keenan Putnam," I quickly explained to Jerry. "He's probably related to this man."

"I would wager he also had an excellent idea of where the gold ended up. That idea could be what got him killed." Harry surmised.

Chapter Thirty-seven

Jerry's eyes gleamed. "Whoa, I've never been this close to finding out if any of these gold legends are true. Maybe we should do a little investigating on our own before the police take over and close us out."

Harry lifted the receiver. "No. Four people have been killed over this legend. I'm not contributing to a higher body count."

He dialed her private number. "Agent Nunez, this is Harry Marsden. I'm afraid I haven't been quite forthcoming with you."

I jumped up from my seat. "Harry, no."

I don't know if he thought I didn't want him to reveal the existence of the journal or I didn't want him to take the fall for me. He thrust out his hand in an indisputable *stop* command and continued with Marisol.

"Something was removed from the box and it seems there is a connection between Keenan Putnam and the original owner of the box."

He listened and hung up without saying goodbye.

"Jerry, you'd best skedaddle. The FBI is on her way and you don't want to tangle with her."

Jerry didn't seem dissuaded. "Maybe I could decipher more of the journal, more initials. You know kind of consult with the FBI."

"Sorry, old chap. Jan would have my *guts for garters* if I caused her minister to be incarcerated. I'd have to deal with my father-in-law as well. I'll take my chances with the

FBI, but you are not involved after this point."

Jerry shrugged. "You'll have all the fun." His mischievous grin belied his pastoral background.

Harry clapped him on the shoulder and guided him out the back. "Be a good padre and put in a word or two for us."

"Will do, but I still think I could help. Call if you need me?"

"Absolutely."

Harry waited outside for Jerry to leave and Marisol to arrive. It wasn't long before I heard the back door open and the ensuing conversation.

I could hear Harry's voice rising, but I couldn't make out the words. I moved closer to the doorway.

"When were you going to tell me about this? Posthumously?" Harry's voice shook with emotion.

"When were *you* going to tell me about this?" Marisol sounded just as angry. I could only assume she meant the journal. I had no idea what Harry meant.

Ric's voice chimed in. "Listen, they are connected and both credible. We need to sit down and work through this, not tear each other apart."

Ric, the voice of reason? I began to get a queasy sense of pending disaster.

They burst into the kitchen, still squabbling over protocol, stopping suddenly when they noticed me. *Talk about feeling like the eight hundred pound gorilla in the room.*

"What's wrong? You each look dreadful. Not bad; I mean, full of dread. You know like something bad has happened or is going to…"

Harry closed the distance between us and took me in his arms. "Sssh, we'll figure it out."

I babble when I panic. I couldn't stop myself. "Figure

out what? Don't lie to me or for me. Are you being arrested for keeping the journal?"

Harry held my shoulders and pulled me away from his chest. He looked at me with an expression of abject sorrow and edges of fear. "Grace, sit down."

My stomach lurched. The coffee I recently relished seemed capable of turning on me. Harry guided me to the table and gently pushed me into a chair.

Marisol sat down across from me, holding the journal in her hand. "Grace, I won't mince words with you. You and Harry are in danger. We know the threat is somehow connected to the reenactment, but we don't know who is targeting you."

My head whirled with her words. Harry sat down next to me. Ric leaned against the wall behind Marisol.

"Someone really was trying to kill me at the reenactment? Why?"

"No not then. We believe the shooter thinks you can identify him. That's the danger to you from him.

"The connection you discovered is one we confirmed a few hours ago. My field agent interviewed people who knew Putnam, and found his former girlfriend, Molly Jamison. Apparently they'd been together for years but Putnam would never commit to marriage until he found the gold. She finally dumped him six months ago. The break-up pushed Putnam into high gear. He contacted her and told her he knew the location of the gold and had enlisted the help of a friend, Pete Corvo. According to Molly, Keenan wanted to recover the gold and return it to the Army and record the search and recovery in his next book."

"Does the killer know where the gold is now?"

"We don't think so. It gets complicated." Marisol pulled her heavy hair and snapped a clip around it. I began to realize her hair clipping was her "tell" under stress.

"Molly still loved Keenan and she wanted him to succeed. The last conversation she had with him unsettled her and she came north looking for him. He had told her he suspected his friend, Pete, was going to double-cross him with a third guy and keep the gold."

"Is the third guy a reenactor too?" I was trying to follow the storyline.

"The third guy is the shooter. We don't think he's a reenactor, because of the stolen uniform and musket we found. Molly told us Keenan showed her a box he'd found in his great uncle's belongings. She identified the box Marty dug up as the same box."

My eyes popped. "This isn't complicated, it's crazy. How can that be?"

"Remember we commented on how well preserved the box appeared to be, and Marty mentioned how close to the surface he found it?"

"It would have been helpful to have been part of that conversation Harry." Though Marisol used his first name, her voice held no friendliness.

Harry's ears pinked. "We erred badly. I am sorry I didn't give you the book immediately."

Marisol suddenly flipped through the pages and ran her finger along the inside seam. "His girlfriend said he had waved two small pages, with ripped edges, at her, saying these would take him to the gold."

Harry cleared his throat. "How did Putnam get Blackmore's effects?"

"We thought everything in the box belonged to Blackmore because it was in his grave, obviously a bit of unintentional misdirection on Putnam's part. The journal belonged to Blackmore but everything else in the box belonged to Putnam's great grandfather."

"Maybe that's why I felt drawn–"

"Grace."

"Gracie."

Harry and Ric's voice sounded together.

"It's okay boys. I knew Grace was the one with the sticky fingers." Marisol arched an eyebrow and looked straight into my eyes. "Must be comforting to have two guardian angels."

My face flushed fast and hot. I didn't speak, didn't break eye contact. What could I say?

Marisol looked at Harry. "We're not sure how Putnam got his hands on the journal. The only way it could have been in his great grandfather's belongings would have been if the elder Putnam stole it from Blackmore before they left, or got it from him after he returned from the mission. I wondered about that. Looking at this," she thumbed through more pages, "I can see these map pages are some of the last entries in the book, so I would say Putnam stole the journal before he left on the mission."

"Sounds like Wilson and Putnam planned a diversion of their own." Harry said. "Blackmore lived around the Aurora area, so he'd know the terrain and different routes."

"Is there anything in the journal written in another hand? Maybe Putnam kept notes on where they hid the gold."

"Keenan Putnam wouldn't have left those notes in the journal."

Marisol flipped through from the back of the book and shook her head. "Nothing. Would be nice but way too easy."

"Wilson and Putnam probably couldn't read or write. Education wasn't mandatory to be in the Army; you only needed your four front teeth according to Jan." I tried for a smile, but my lips felt stuck in a straight line.

Marisol's lips curved a little, then settled back with a determined slash across her beautiful mouth. "We think these two, Wilson and Putnam, decided to take a different route. Because they couldn't read or write, they recorded their new route, and possibly where they hid the gold, using the same topographical method. Or they were ambushed and killed and this journal ended up in Putnam's box and the gold ended up who knows where."

"Does Molly know if Jeremiah Putnam made it through the war?"

"No, she doesn't. She said Keenan had family stories, but nothing concrete until he found the box."

"So he comes to the area where he thinks the gold has been hidden for some hundred and twenty-five years and enlists the assistance of a friend who knows the area." Harry said. "After all, if his friend knows the area well he might be able to identify the topographical location from the pages Putnam shows him. It could be open field, an office complex, or a cemetery by this time."

"What pages would Putnam have?" I stared at the book in Marisol's hands.

Marisol looked at Harry with growing suspicion in her eyes. "Did you take–"

Harry waved off her question and nodded at the book under her fingers. "There is a page, or possibly two, missing toward the back. I think only one page, because there is only the slightest break in continuity when you fan the pages. It looks like it has been carefully sliced out. I'd say more the mark of an historian being respectful than a common soldier ripping out directions. Putnam brought that page with him to show Corvo."

Marisol fanned the pages, this time catching the break. She looked up at Harry with a different expression. "You're good."

"Who has the page now and does it mean anything to him?" I looked around the table.

"We think at this point the killer is cutting his losses and killing anyone who can identify him. The gold is probably lost to him, but he's desperate to keep his identity and place in the community safe. Which is why we are going to work with the local police, and assign some surveillance and protection for you and for Harry."

"Harry? Why Harry, he didn't see anything. I didn't either, but apparently this guy thinks I did."

Their faces turned *dread-filled* again.

"What? You're all scaring me."

Harry lifted my hand and held it between his. "When I went in to the jungle to find Hannah, I'm afraid I stirred up old wrongs and set something nasty in motion." He squeezed my hand. "Before my mission went haywire, ten years ago, Derek and I killed Antonio Salizar. His son, Luis, was a teenager. Salizar's older sister raised him, took him in with her own family.

"When he learned I had entered the country he set those men on me; the men who almost killed Hannah." His voice crusted with emotion.

"You and Hannah made it. You're safe."

Harry's eyes filled with pain. He slowly shook his head, but remained silent.

Ric spoke from the wall he'd been holding up. "This Salizar is ten times worse than his father ever was. He's clearly a sociopath. He has taken his father's local cartel and boosted it to international. His drugs are showing up in Miami and working their way throughout the country."

Marisol cleared her throat and took over. "We know they've made it to this area, because a few of the small busts have turned out to be his blend of cocaine. Some of these drug lords are so vain they hire experts to create a line specific to them–like a signature perfume."

I wiggled my fingers under Harry's hands. "I still don't get the danger to you."

He swallowed hard. "Luis Salizar has put a contract out on me. And because Hannah is my sister, on her as well." His eyes brimmed with tears. He pulled his hands away and scrubbed his face, taking a deep breath.

My stomach churned with fear. "There's more isn't there?" I looked at Marisol, not Ric. I couldn't stand it if his face crumbled under my scrutiny.

"We can't be sure, but this bastard is so twisted he most likely has included you and Harry's son."

I had to mouth breathe to get enough oxygen to keep my mind clear. No good, thoughts and impressions careened down neuro-pathways and bounced off each other in a desperate flight to escape this awful reality.

I continued to stare into her serious dark eyes, centering my concentration on her, fearing if I looked away I'd shattered into pieces or crumbled into bits of rubble. Either way I'd never stay whole.

Those seconds of calm from her concerned, but not involved, eyes gave me the strength I needed.

"One person wants to kill me, maybe two. One person wants to kill you." I pointed to Harry. The tiny part of my mind that uses humor to survive registered I was "winning" in the kill count.

"What do we do?"

No one spoke. I expected action plans, strategies; the silence continued.

Finally, her soft voice laid out their plan. "We've learned two facts about the contract. It's what they call, *con el permiso.* It means an individual has requested permission to carry out the contract, like calling 'dibs' on it. From what we've been able to determine from sources, Salizar has given his *permiso* to one person with a defined period of time. He is perhaps repaying a favor or giving a favor by keeping everyone else on hold until this person gets a shot." Marisol stopped abruptly. "A chance at fulfilling the contract," she finished.

Ric leaned away from the wall and sat down next to Marisol. He seemed to be moving closer to me to provide support. Dear God, there couldn't be more.

Marisol spoke more slowly. "The second fact we've learned is the contract is *última venganza.*"

Harry's hand jerked away. "Oh, God." He moved closer and put his arm around my shoulders.

Marisol continued stopping and starting, trying to get the explanation out. "*Última venganza* is an insidious form of revenge or vendetta. The contract is laid out to kill in a certain order. The main target is left for last. Left to be tortured by watching his family removed one by one. We don't know if they would start with the youngest or with the target's parents or spouse. It is most likely impossible to protect everyone."

My head filled with noise and motion. I knew only Harry's strong arm kept me from pitching forward. Tears filled my eyes and rolled down my face. I turned my head into Harry's chest and choked back the lump in my throat. I had to get control over my emotions or I'd curl up in a ball and be useless. My stomach twisted and I felt another kind of lump moving up my throat.

I wiggled free from Harry's arm, shot out of my chair

and rushed to the bathroom. I heard another chair scrape against the tile.

"Wait. Let her calm down. We need to talk," I heard Marisol say.

I lunged into the bathroom in the nick of time. In a perverse way I felt better after vomiting, almost like expelling an ugly fear. I took my time rinsing my mouth and washing my face. I ran a comb through my hair and adjusted my head band. About the time I caught myself applying lip gloss and pinching my cheeks I realized I was performing routine grooming tasks to avoid facing the awful reality of my life.

I picked up the length of yarn looped on the towel holder, lowered the lid on the toilet, and sat down. My brain clamored for order. I began to easily loop and back loop and pull through until the blue cord folded neatly into knots. A number popped into my head. *Twenty-five.*

I could do that, would do that–I had no choice. The repetition and sense of doing helped me regain control in some small sense. As long as I could create a point of calm in me, I felt I could go there if things got worse.

Twenty-five knots completed, I laid out what had been a three foot cord on the vanity. I left the bathroom and quietly returned to the space outside the kitchen.

"We have two different shooters," Marisol said. "We have to eliminate the immediate threat to Grace. We can only do so if we can draw him out."

"Are you two crazy?" Harry slammed his fist against the table. "You want to use her as bait?"

"Marsden, I'm not sure there's any other way. Think about it. If this contract killer has permission for a short time, the danger to Grace and all of you is increasing by the hour. We have to get one of them corralled to concentrate on the other. Their styles of attack will be different."

"What do you want me to do?"

"Grace, no."

"Harry, we can't live looking over our shoulders. Wouldn't it be better to take this risk?"

"There is another way." Harry's voice, soft and low, further calmed me. He motioned me back to my chair. He reached for my hand. "I have friends from before, who could help us disappear."

I stared at my husband, trying to add meaning to the words I heard. "What do you mean disappear? Hide for awhile? Take a vacation?"

"He means the equivalent of our Witness Protection Program," Marisol answered. "Our government would like Salizar ousted, but can't take that stand publicly. Unless you had information in an ongoing investigation on Salizar, not saying there is one, we can't relocate you."

"No. I'm not leaving my family, my friends, our home. No. This is where we belong."

"Grace, these same friends might be able to pluck this jackal off his throne. I'll have to make some calls. I know they'll do all they can."

Harry turned to Marisol. "How does this *con el permiso* twist work?"

"The contractor has a small window of exclusivity. If he can't complete the job the contract could be awarded to another exclusive hit man or it could be offered globally."

"So we're lucky this Salizar is granting this kind of favor?" I couldn't believe I felt grateful for a one-at-a-time contract. How we frail humans grasp at straws of any kind.

Marisol nodded. "You could look at it that way. We're checking to see who has recently come into the country. If we can pinpoint an associate, we have somewhere to start."

"Why would this Salizar give this 'honor' to a mere associate?"

"What do you mean, Harry?" Marisol asked.

"Harry's right," I chimed in quickly, grateful to have a thought toward the problem. "Wouldn't he be more likely to allow someone closer to him, a trusted friend, or a family member this opportunity?"

Marisol's mouth twitched. "Trusted and friend don't work in the same sentence for this guy, but the family member could be an angle to check out. Can I use your phone?"

"If the two of you and Will disappear would it be here or in England?"

"We're not going anywhere."

"England. I have more contacts."

Harry and I spoke at the same time.

"Darling, if we can't stop the contract by disposing of Luis Salizar, we won't be safe here. I won't stand by and let some mad bastard kill my family."

He turned toward Ric. "I have a concern for Connor. His last name is Marsden. If they are searching for my son he may be the target. Lily's intention, to legally apply to change Will's name to Marsden, didn't get done because of the accident."

"That paper snafu may keep Will safe."

"May keep him safe, but we can't be sure the killer doesn't know about him. Maybe we've been under surveillance. He might know about Will."

"Marsden, you'll go crazy with all the 'what ifs'. Right now we know the targets are your parents, your sister, and Grace, with maybe Connor."

"And I'm the bloody link." Harry's voice dripped with venom he directed at himself.

The phone rang and Marisol jumped up. "That will be for me." She lifted the receiver before the second ring and listened. "Okay, thanks I'm on my way."

She turned and addressed Harry. "They might have turned up a lead. We actually have someone in Salizar's camp on a lower level. Lucky for us thieves talk as much as country club matrons. I'm assigning some men to your house. They can't get here for thirty minutes. I know you have a weapon. Do you need more fire power?"

Harry shook his head. "I'm prepared."

"Good. I'm heading into the office, but I'll be back. Meantime, keep her away from the windows and definitely no going outside. Lock up after us. I'll call before we arrive. If you don't answer we're coming in, guns drawn."

We stood at the same time, energized with purpose and, hopefully, success. Ric pulled at Marisol's arm. "You have someone in place in Salizar's camp. You didn't tell me."

"A need to know basis, Ric." She looked up into his stern face. "You didn't need to know."

"We know now," Harry said. A look passed between him and Ric. Marisol caught it and immediately swung round to face them down.

"I see what you're thinking, both of you, and the answered is no. No black ops are going to happen. We have been building a case for two years and have lost one agent. No cowboys are going in on my watch."

Ric took Marisol's arm. "I'll stay onboard here, get a position outside." He turned to us. "I'll be right back. You won't see me, but I'll be out there." He looked at Harry again with an easily readable *talk to you later* expression in his eyes. He and Marisol left by the front door. I heard the click of the automatic locking mechanism.

Chapter Thirty-eight

"Harry, please promise me you're not going back to try and kill this Salizar."

"If I get the chance to go two for two, I'll take it. Would you have me stand by and watch everyone I loved slaughtered?" The vein at his temple twitched and his fingers curled into fists at his side.

"I'd rather hide with you for a lifetime than have no lifetime with you. Please, make the arrangements. We'll say goodbye and disappear."

Harry visible struggled with my words. He had campaigned for my agreement an hour earlier, but had changed course when he discovered there could be a way into the devil's lair.

I stepped closer to him and lifted his arms around me. He held me tightly, uncurling his fingers to rub and pat my back.

"Please promise me you won't go," I murmured into his chest. I felt him nod against my head, but he didn't speak.

After a moment he released me and leaned down to kiss my forehead. "I'd best get ready in case…"

I knew he'd bring out the small arsenal he kept under lock and key.

"Should we bring Will to Lily's for the night?"

"I've taken care of that, called Marty while you freshened up in the loo. He should be here any minute to collect Will, who is upstairs throwing some things in his backpack. He is absolutely thrilled about a day off school and a zincer trip. Walter is going with them. He thought he'd like to become a zincer explorer."

I smiled at the thought of Marty and Will on an adventure, with Walter as their protector.

"Grace, we also decided to flush out the reenactor chap with a bogus article in the paper, stating the trauma of your near death experience jogged your memory about the shooting. Marisol called that Romano fellow and his editor to make sure it got in the evening edition."

"All this happened while I was in the bathroom?"

Harry nodded. "You spent thirty minutes in there."

I wondered how many other plans had been discussed and decided on while I'd sat on the toilet, braiding my brain into some semblance of calm.

The doorbell rang and Harry hurried to open the door to Marty.

"Hi, Sis," he greeted me, and kissed my cheek. He looked at the coffeemaker. "Seems like I was just here," he joked, but his eyes looked edgy. He looked at the empty carafe. "What, no coffee?"

"I'll make some; I don't think Will is quite ready." While I busied myself with water and coffee grounds Marty sat quietly, making small talk about his afternoon.

A burst of coffee aroma rushed my face when I lifted the tight lid on the canister marked with a coffee mug sticker. I inhaled deeply and listened marginally to my brother's light chatter. He seemed more talkative than usual. Marty ‘chattered’ when he became excited or nervous.

I brought two mugs of coffee to the table and sat down. Marty stopped talking and looked at me for my full attention. He had it.

"Nick came home from the rehearsal apparently higher than a kite. Katie recognized his condition immediately and when she realized he was lethargic and unresponsive she called 911. They took him to St. Alexis where they pumped his stomach."

"Is he okay? Why didn't Dad call? Oh, my gosh, we should be there." I didn't know what to say first. My wonderful Nick, in the hospital.

"He had a bad reaction to whatever he took and started convulsing." Marty grabbed at my failing hands. "Gracie, he's going to be okay. They have him sedated to keep him calm and give him a chance to recover."

My eyes narrowed. "Dad doesn't know does he?"

Marty squirmed under my gaze. "We didn't tell him. Geez, Grace he's getting married in two weeks. We didn't want to mess up his and Jan's plans tonight. They're checking out the hotel where they're spending their wedding night."

"Checking out, like *trying out?*" I felt the rush of heat to my face.

"Yeah," Marty answered, a little pink in the face.

"I see your point, but Dad's going to be mad no one told him about Nick. He's his favorite nephew."

Marty shrugged. "I made a decision. I'll live with the consequences."

This was a mature side of Marty we seldom saw.

"How did Nick get whatever he took? He doesn't know drug dealers. Does he?" I hadn't been as close to my twenty-four year old cousin in the last few years as I had been when he was younger and spent time at the house.

"Katie says no. She says Nick wouldn't take drugs, but whatever got into his system could have killed him."

I shivered and rubbed my arms. "Can you take a drug and not know it. I mean, eat it or drink it."

"I don't know. Katie said they found a small plastic

packet, with a little bit of powder in it, in his jeans pocket. The police have it and I guess will test it. I don't know but Nick is always concocting those protein drinks. Maybe this was some kind of protein gone bad."

Marty rubbed his hands over his face. "Don't you worry what this world will be like when Connor is a teenager?"

I swallowed hard to stop the tears threatening to well up in my eyes. If only Marty knew my worry was Connor wouldn't get his chance.

"Uncle Marty," Will practically squeaked from the doorway. His twelve-year-old hormones played havoc with his voice. He rushed to Marty's side.

"Hey, kiddo. Ready to hunt the elusive zincer?" Marty ruffled Will's hair. "We gotta be up at the crack of dawn to get a jump on the day."

"Yeah, sure. I'm ready." He hoisted his backpack over one shoulder. "I brought my compass like Dad said."

"Excellent. We'll pick up Walter on our way."

Marty hugged me and whispered. "I don't know what's going on, but don't worry about Will."

I wondered what reason Harry had given my brother to get him to drop everything and take on Will's custody for a day or two.

Will hugged his dad and headed for the doorway.

"Whoa there, kiddo. Hugs all around. You wanna be part of the Morelli *famiglia* you gotta hug hello, goodbye and sometimes how ya doin'."

Will, so anxious to start his adventure, enthusiastically hugged me. I gripped him close and quickly kissed the top of his blonde head. "Have fun; keep your uncle in line."

He stepped back and laughed, but when he looked up at me I saw a shade of confusion clouding those blue eyes.

He turned to look at his dad who missed getting a grin plastered on his face by a nanosecond.

Marty saw the crisis forming. "Man, this kid takes to hugs. Are you sure we weren't separated at birth 'cause our hug pattern is very similar."

Will laughed. Even Harry and I smiled at my brother's sense of humor.

"See you in a few." Marty threw off a jaunty wave as he turned toward the hallway.

"Yeah, see you in a few." Will turned to look at his dad for reassurance for maybe what he thought he sensed.

Harry high-fived him. "You bet your Nelly."

Will rolled his eyes and groaned. "It's bippy, you bet your bippy."

We heard Marty asking in a stage whisper, "What's with your dad and the Nelly stuff. You'd think he grew up somewhere weird."

The door closed on Will's giggles.

Chapter Thirty-nine

I went up to our room to begin the painful process of writing good-bye letters to people I knew I wouldn't see before we fled into anonymity. I wrote to Tracy and my brother Joe. I asked Joe to keep us in his daily prayers. I wouldn't leave without seeing my dad. I wrote to Glenn, my other younger brother, who was camping in Canada with my friend Joan and her husband Dave. I wrote to Joan, too. We'd been friends since grade three at St. Domitilla grammar school.

I took a break from the words and the tears, and came down since I thought Harry might be on the phone with Hannah. I could say goodbye and promise her I'd guard Connor with my life.

They were discussing more than Connor's new parents. I knew he had broken the horrible news of *última venganza* because his comments were affirming whatever Hannah was saying.

"I've spoken to Dad and he's closing up the house. He and mum are taking a holiday in Scotland. I think it would be best if you work with Kingsley and choose something remote, but not isolated."

He had his back to me. He listened and paced. His agitation permeated the room like a force of unrest moving from his core to fill the room. "I don't know Hanns. I don't know if this madman is starting with the youngest or the oldest." His voice cracked. I knew his heart was breaking.

I needed to move away from the tension or the tears

would flow again. I turned toward the dining room to calm myself and waited for a better break in the conversation.

The knot in my throat churned my stomach and made me nauseated; I slipped into the kitchen for a glass of water and sat in the nook staring into the water, not sure if I could swallow.

I heard Harry slam down the receiver and waited for him to come into the kitchen. I realized he thought I had remained upstairs and I started to stand.

I heard two sounds at the same time; a loud *pop* and glass breaking.

I lunged for the floor, reacting even before I understood the cause of the broken glass. I heard the *thud* of the next bullet hit the wooden paneling. My palms scraped along the cool tile as I flattened against the floor.

The engine whine and spurting movement of a motorized vehicle sounded outside the window. I heard another shot, a lower pitched pop, yet another shot, again a different timbre. I heard the engine whine at a higher pitch, scraping along the pecan shell path then relative silence. Harry's footsteps pounded through the house and he burst into the kitchen, sliding to the ground on one knee beside me.

"Grace." His voice choked with concern.

I rolled and sat up, pushing into his arms. "I'm okay, I'm okay."

Harry's arms tightened around me. "I thought he might try. I meant to be outside waiting. Oh, God, Grace I thought you were upstairs."

He swallowed hard and held me tighter, kissing the top of my head.

I moved my head to feel those kisses on my face. Sweet as they felt my legs were not meant to bend in this fashion for long. I wiggled around to get my feet under me. Harry stood and lifted me to my feet. Standing in the kitchen, I felt vulnerable and couldn't help glancing at the shattered window.

"He can't hurt you. Trerra's dead." Harry's soft voice carried no regret.

"Mitch Trerra is the killer? He's a wedding planner for God's sake. Has the world gone crazy?"

Harry's arms tightened around me. "He wasn't who he appeared to be, Gracie. Marisol found out he befriended Corvo and Putnam to find the gold. He befriended Jan for a far worse reason. And for that he had to die."

I knew Harry had killed before, in his life with British Intelligence. This was different. Harry had been expecting him. He'd set a trap. Actually Marisol had set it, but couldn't be involved.

How would the police view what he'd done?

As though he read my mind, he kept his arm around me and moved to lift the receiver on the phone in the kitchen. "Suppose I'd best call it in through the proper channels, turn myself in and all." He saw the shock on my face.

"Don't worry, darling, it's obviously self-defense." Harry lifted the receiver and dialed 9-1-1. "Wish I could explain that other bloke out there," he muttered more than said.

"Someone else was out there?" I remembered the different gun sound.

Harry tersely reported the situation and hung up. "We're to stay inside and wait."

Like I'd be running outside anytime soon.

"Someone else stood in wait out there," Harry began. "I didn't see him but he pushed me out of the way. He may have saved my life." Harry's voice echoed in my ears. The floor tilted under my feet and Harry's arm held me upright. "Stupid of me. It wasn't nearly so dramatic. Sorry, darling."

His words told one story, but his eyes couldn't hide the tinge of shock he experienced; he'd almost been killed.

Harry guided me to the couch then retrieved my water glass. "Here, sip this." I reached for the glass. It was as if an occult hand knocked the glass from my grasp before I could tighten my grip. I shivered as I remembered Arlene used the same words to express when she felt the dead had joined the living. The glass landed on the cushion spilling its contents.

"Damn!" I started to rise.

"Sit, I'll get a towel."

The room turned cold the moment Harry left. Blackmore stood at the hallway to the mudroom. He carried his musket and nodded toward the kitchen and Harry.

Thank you. We know you didn't steal the gold, but we don't know where the gold is. Without it I don't know if that's enough to clear your name.

He looked resigned to carry the injustice through eternity. The room temperature rose as quickly as he faded.

Harry returned with two dish towels. He dropped to one knee and mopped at the water, scrunching the towel to absorb the fluid. "Ouch!" Harry pulled back his hand. He turned over the towel and saw the shard poking through the thin fabric.

"Nasty bugger that would have been." He lifted the glass.

"It's not broken." He swirled the glass in his hand. The tinkle of glass bouncing against the sides answered the question. "This glass is from the window. You could have swallowed glass." His face paled. "And I gave it to you."

I took the glass from his hand and stood it upright on

the rug next to my feet. "I'm fine; I didn't drink it. Blackmore wouldn't let me."

I took Harry's hand, turned it palm up, and kissed the tiny pinprick of blood.

The sound of sirens pulled us back to our immediate dilemma–a dead body in the backyard. "I'll clean up, you let them in." He left me carefully dabbing the couch for any more pieces of glass.

Chapter Forty

Double headlight beams bounced over the window. I wondered about the two cars until I heard Harry at the door.

Sergeant Peterson, from the private security company, and Agent Marisol Nunez and her partner, Frank Jeffers, pulled into our driveway.

"Peterson, good to see you. Marisol, Agent Jeffers, come in." Harry led them first to the kitchen. I stood next to the doorway feeling surreal welcoming them to my home. *How do you do? How do I do? Not so good you see, there's a body–*

Marisol touched my arm. "Grace, are you all right?"

I blinked several times to refocus my thoughts. "I'm good. I dropped to the floor as soon as I heard the shot, well no, the glass breaking, I think maybe the shot or–"

Marisol squeezed my arm and guided me to the island. She pulled out a stool. "Sit here and put your head down on your arms." She glanced around the kitchen and spotted my fleece throw draped on another stool. I didn't remember taking it off or putting it there. She moved to lift it.

"Don't," Harry cautioned her. "It's got bits of glass on it; she was wearing it when…" He stopped and looked at the fleece. "I've got better." Harry strode from the room and returned with his favorite hand-knitted blanket. Hannah had made it for him when she learned to knit in grade ten. He gently covered me with the maroon and gold striped blanket and leaned close to kiss me. The slight woodsy scent of his aftershave lingered on the strands of yarn.

"You heard 'the man'," he said, referring to Marisol's orders. "Head down, eyes closed. I'll be back in a tic."

I felt his fingers brush against my cheek as he guided a piece of hair behind my ear. He straightened and moved away from me.

"He's out back. You'll need some transport," I heard Harry say as he led them through the house. "And another thing," Harry lowered his voice, "I heard another shot; there was another shooter."

"Could it have been Trerra firing at you?"

"No muzzle flare. The shot came from my right."

"An entire crime scene unit will be here soon, including the ME and her bus." Jeffers spoke for the first time. "I'll secure the back."

"I'll wait out front for them," offered Petersen.

"Thank you, Sergeant."

Harry and Marisol moved out of the kitchen, but still within earshot. "It could have been Kramer but the timing is wrong. He said he'd start the sweep from the wooded path at Lily's end of the compound."

Harry's voice sounded terse. He questioned Marisol in a low tone, but I could make out the words.

"You found out Trerra was the third person in the gold search. Did you know before we set the trap? Couldn't you have arrested him and not placed Grace in danger? I only agreed to the trap because you said it would be the only way to draw out the killer."

"We had no proof of him as the shooter. We suspected when we connected him to the other two, and to the recreational drugs being sold to reenactors and some locals. The common denominator turned out to be Trerra. We've questioned several reenactors and his name came up. Apparently Josephine had been telling people to steer clear of him. That couldn't have endeared her to him."

I remembered how Josephine had reacted about Mitch. She may not have known exactly what he was up to, but she sensed it was no good. In his paranoid mind he must have thought she knew more than she did. Just like he thought I could identify him. Another thought pushed to the surface. Had Nick bought drugs from Trerra earlier today?

Marisol continued. "He acted clever enough to steal the uniform and musket to make us think we should look outside the group of reenactors. When I called the office this afternoon I had them run the names our agent in Salizar's camp sends back to us as he hears them. Most of them are dead-ends and don't lead to the States."

"Mitch Trerra is connected to Salizar?" Harry's voice shook with anger.

"We can't connect him, but Salizar's sister married a Trerra. It's a common name and we're checking to see if he is Salizar's nephew."

"I can't believe this connection. Jan trusted him. Mike never liked him, but what guy likes a wedding planner. Oh my God, he would have been at the wedding."

"Not if he could have killed Grace first." Marisol added, "I like him for the drug connection. I have a feeling Putnam and Corvo signed their death warrants as soon as they involved Trerra. We ran Corvo's name and found out Corvo's family and Trerra's family name in registries from the same small town in Venezuela. The common connection must have started their friendship."

"Do you think he planned to kill them; to keep the entire amount?"

"Absolutely. He knew from Corvo that Putnam wanted to turn in the money. I think he convinced Corvo to double-cross Putnam and split the gold two ways. I don't think

Corvo suspected Trerra's drug business. If I were Trerra, I would have played along, offered to fence the gold for cash then disappeared with all the gold. He could buy significant quantities of drugs from his connection."

"Why would he kill Putnam before he had the gold?"

"I'm stuck there. Either Putnam tumbled to Trerra's plan and threatened to cause trouble, or maybe it's Trerra who has the missing sheets from the journal. Maybe he thought he had all he needed and killed Putnam after he stole the pages. Putnam probably hid the box in the grave, figuring it safer there; not knowing the pages were missing."

Marisol's voice turned edgy. "There are some things we'll never know with the last player dead. I would have liked to be able to clear the lieutenant's name, since I believe him innocent of the gold heist. I hate that, but the best we can do is piece it together and live with the holes."

Harry's voice rose, "I don't give a tinker's damn about the gold or the lieutenant. We know why he was stalking Grace. If it turns out he was Salizar's nephew, could he be the *con el permiso* assassin?"

"If he turns out to be Salizar's nephew the contract will go global instantly. We have to keep his identity under wraps until we know for certain."

I had trouble focusing on their conversation, losing bits and pieces as my brain turned them away. They moved further into the living room and I could hear only murmurs.

Warmth, part blanket and part dream, enveloped me. I drifted, body whole, mind quiet to the safe haven in my universe. My thoughts floated through my life, lingering at pleasant places, and rushing past pain and sorrow, finally stopping to gaze in the window of guilt. I wanted to look away. Instead, I peered beyond my reflection and recognized the people in my life I had betrayed in ways small and large. My grade two teacher, Sister Mary Albert, from whom I'd taken an extra holy card, stood benevolently behind me and to my left. Mr. Switzer, the pharmacist, stood nearby. I'd swiped a nickel eraser from his drug store at age nine and returned it three years later with a tearful apology.

My mother stood directly behind my right shoulder. She raised her hand and placed it gently on my shoulder; I couldn't feel her touch, but it was nice to see. I'd been a horrible daughter, acting out after being admonished for making her nervous, for being too headstrong for my fragile mom. I should have been softer, gentler, and held her when her demons became too strong for her to fight back. She must know I'm hosting the wedding party for her husband and another woman. I like Jan, and I know my dad loves her. Does she feel betrayed? By him, by me?

Ric stood there as well Harry. I'd taken back my love from Ric once I learned Harry was alive. I'd given my heart to someone else within months of believing Harry was gone. I betrayed them both. They stood shoulder to shoulder. What did that mean? Was I about to betray one of them again?

I saw another figure reflected in the crowd behind me. James Blackmore moved closer to me, stretching out his hand, offering me what it held. I felt a slight pressure against my arm.

Something furry bumped my elbow. *Meow.* Elmo fluffed at my hair with his tiny paw. The thick strand he tousled moved to and fro under his control. I slowly returned from the introspective place in my mind and turned my eyes outward; actually, opened my left one slightly to squint at the orange creature sitting half on my arm half on the table. I thumped my arm up and down to unseat him. The fluffing stopped. *Meow*. He knew he woke me.

"Fine, I'm up." I lifted my head and slid my arms off the table.

"She'll have to move." I heard Marisol's low tone. "The techs are entering the compound; they'll be here in minutes." Her radio *squawked* confirmation before she dialed down the volume.

Harry touched my shoulder. "We've got to let the tech lab chaps sort out things in here."

I nodded and stood. Harry slipped his arm around my shoulders.

Meow. Elmo walked across the table to the very edge, his paws curling over the wood, tiny claws gripping the oak.

"You too." Harry presented his other arm for Elmo's use. The orange bundle leisurely stepped from the table to Harry's arm and climbed to his favorite perch atop Harry's shoulder.

Petersen had guided the techs into the house. They stood at the kitchen door waiting for us to vacate the room. We, including Marisol and Petersen, walked into the living room.

Marisol and Petersen remained standing. Sergeant Petersen spoke first. "I'm finished here; they've got it now."

"Thank you, Sergeant." Harry stood and shook hands with him. "Pity we keep seeing you under these circumstances."

Petersen nodded, trying to squelch an inappropriate grin. "You and Mrs. Marsden do keep our blotter full."

In an attempt to keep the charade going for the benefit of Sergeant Petersen, who we knew would tell the cops, Marisol cleared her throat. "I've read your file and in the last two and a half years you've had over–"

"Are we on your radar, *too*, Agent Nunez? It seems activity in Pine Marsh ends up on several blotters." Harry looked at her, a slight smile forming on his lips.

She picked up on the emphasized *too* and knew Harry referred to Ric's interest in Pine Marsh and me. Marisol reddened. "My concern is this investigation, which should wrap up nicely as soon as I get the ME's report."

Petersen seemed anxious to leave. He tipped his head to me, then Marisol. "Ma'am, agent." He knew his way out of the house.

With Petersen gone and the techs in the kitchen out of earshot Harry asked Marisol, "Didn't Petersen think it strange you got here as quickly as he did?"

"Yeah, could be a problem. Hope he doesn't dwell on it. I meant to be here earlier and settle in for the night. Trerra must have come in from the golf course; on his motorcycle. We missed him. We set up to monitor the entrance and the woods behind the properties."

"We?" My voice lingered on the pronoun.

Marisol hesitated. "My partner, Frank, had the next shift. He was involved in an accident on Route 53 and radioed me he'd be late." She looked down at her shoes and inhaled deeply. She lifted her gaze to my eyes.

"You know Ric insisted on being part of the surveillance team." She held up her hand to stop any comments. "I know it's out of the realm of FBI protocol, but he was going to be out there with or without the agency's blessing." Her expression turned hard to read. "So I figured I'd better work him into the schedule." She looked toward the back of the house then spoke softly. "Jeffers is out looking for him. I thought he'd come in once he saw us arrive."

"When you," she indicated Harry, "said you heard

another shot I figured it was Ric. Since he hasn't come forward, now I don't know."

"What do you mean? Is he out there now?" My voice rose with the question.

"He was supposed to back up Frank. We–I, thought it would make more sense for them to work together." She paused. I wondered if she second-guessed her decision to leave her fiancée's 'back' to someone else. "When Frank radioed me about the accident, I radioed Ric I had to leave the surveillance to certify Frank's involvement with a civilian."

"What? Why would you leave?"

Harry touched my shoulder. "Grace, someone other than the involved law enforcement entity has to certify or sign off on the accident before the officer can leave the scene. In this case, Marisol being the closest agent and also senior in the team, could sign off and get him here."

She nodded. "I was out of the compound for twenty minutes. My people patched in the 9-1-1 call to my car. I would have been on your doorstep before the cordite settled if it weren't for the accident."

"Could the accident have been staged?"

"No, a stupid lapse on the part of the civilian. He said he looked away to adjust the radio and when he looked up Frank's car was stopped at the light."

"Well, where's Ric? Why isn't he here?"

"She's right. Regardless of your impending nuptials, Ric Kramer would have been in here when he heard those shots, making sure Grace was safe."

"How well I know. I expected him to be here." Marisol shook her head slowly. "I don't know where he is. Jeffers took another agent with him; I have two men looking for him." Her voice no longer reflected the agent, only a woman worried about her lover. "We're finished here. I'm going out on the search." She strode toward the back of the house.

"I'll help you." He hesitated. "We'll help you."

The radio in her pocket crackled with a disjointed voice. "Nunez, something you should see at the ambulance."

That's it, something you should see at the ambulance? Not someone?

Chapter Forty-one

The two paramedics and the ME waited at the back end of the ambulance. The body of Mitch Trerra, harmless in death, lay on the gurney. Dr. Hepplegate climbed into the vehicle and motioned for Marisol to join her.

"Agent, we've got a circumstance here." Joyce Hepplegate pushed a lock of her curly, reddish brown hair off her forehead. The petite medical examiner pulled a thin metal clip from her pocket and hurriedly jammed it into her thick hair in time to keep the surly lock from tumbling onto her low brow. "Gotta' get a haircut. No damn time." She cleared her throat and pointed at Trerra's body. "He has been shot three times, here, here, and here; all kill shots," Hepplegate paused. "Dead before he hit the ground."

Marisol waited; we all did. The ME folded her arms across her chest and faced Marisol. She spoke slowly, "Three shooters, three guns."

"Three, that's crazy." Marisol swung round to look at Harry. "Marsden you said you shot once and heard one other shot."

Harry's face gave no hint to his thoughts. He looked beyond the ambulance, up the driveway, and toward the barn area. "He never returned my fire. I'd stayed on the phone too long with Hannah, explaining, arguing. I'd only moved into the shadows to wait when I heard the shot into the house."

Marisol's jaw clenched and she looked away. She turned to the ME. "Can you tell caliber from the wounds?"

Hepplegate shrugged. "Looks like something small like a 22 caliber, something a little larger like a Glock, but this third wound," she shook her head, "I can't say until I get the body in autopsy."

"It's a musket." Harry spoke so softly I couldn't tell if, with her back to him, she'd heard.

Hepplegate turned slowly. "*Hmm*. It could be the same wound pattern. Am I going to find a ball like I took out of Keenan Putnam?"

Harry nodded. "I believe so."

Marisol put her hands up in front of her, palms out, signaling a stop to the conversation. "Wait a minute. This makes no sense. The dead guy is Mitch who used a musket to kill Keenan Putnam. If Marsden's .22 and Kramer's Glock fired lethal shots who fired the musket? And where is Kramer?"

The hours dragged as more officers joined the search for Ric Kramer. Dr. Applegate and her "patient" had left. The techs had finished and left the kitchen. Only the bouncing lights from handheld flashlights marked the progress of police personnel crisscrossing the grounds, searching for a fellow officer.

Petersen and some of his men came back and joined in the search. The *whap, whap, whap* of the helicopter that Marisol convinced her superiors would help sounded alternately closer then farther as it followed its own grid search.

I wondered what my neighbors thought, wrenched from their sleep by the sounds and lights of the search.

Harry and I allowed the police to use the mudroom as a command center of sorts. Searchers checked in and out with completed search grids. One of Marisol's dispatch people showed up, straight from an evening out; the cocktail dress and stiletto heels gave her away. Andrea Morris had dropped her date off and turned up to help. She was on Marisol's team and her maid-of-honor. I'd met her twice, once socially at the engagement party and once over a year ago at the hospital when Marisol had been injured because of a nutcase after me.

I waited at the door for Andrea to finish checking off coordinates before I spoke. "I have three air pots of coffee and a tray of sandwiches." I looked at all the areas covered with papers and gear. "Where do you want it?"

"Grace, thanks so much. Everyone will appreciate this. Um, over here on the bench. I'll clear off our stuff, you bring it on." Several thick strands of her light brown hair, earlier done up in a glam do, dipped over one ear in a style her hair professional would disown. "Oh, Grace?" Andrea pointed to a black checked wool shirt hung on a peg. "Can I borrow that? It gets cold in here every time someone comes in. Who knew night time temps would drop into the forties."

I felt the cooler air when Harry walked into the room. He looked tired. His blonde hair stuck up over his left ear, a smudge of dirt streaked his cheek.

I flipped the shirt from the peg and tossed it to Andrea.

"Thanks." She dove into the warm fabric and immediately focused on her chart.

I moved closer to Harry and noticed a gouge filling with blood under the mud on his cheek. "What happened?" I grabbed a small towel from the shelf. "You should wash it out."

He took the towel and turned on the faucet in the sink, letting the warm water soak the terrycloth. "I dropped my torch and when I bent to retrieve it I immediately fell headlong into a tree." He gingerly patted the cloth against his face doing his best to remove the dirt from the wound.

"I'm going to get a heavier shirt. I'll be right back, and I would love a cup of tea if you could find one amongst the coffee." He grinned at me and winced as the effort tugged at his ripped skin. Harry held the terrycloth against his face and took the back stairs up to the second floor.

I'd already heated water, in case someone else wanted tea or hot chocolate. I went to the kitchen, poured the water into a thick mug, added some loose tea to the silver ball, and set it in the mug to steep. I moved a few sandwiches to the next layer and tucked Harry's mug on the tray to bring out to the mudroom.

Andrea lifted the last pack from the bench. She took the tray from my hands. "I bet the mug is for the big guy with the dreamy accent. I'll keep it safe."

I smiled at her description. Andrea was shorter than I and about fifteen pounds thinner. Harry would love being called "big guy", but I wasn't going to tell him.

"I'll be back with the pots and sugar and cream."

Andrea set the tray on the bench. She lifted the mug and one of the ham sandwiches and settled back in her chair.

Harry stood at the bottom of the stairs when I left Andrea. I peered at his face. The mud was gone and the scratch pimpled with fresh blood. At least the wound was clean.

He slipped his arm around my shoulders and walked with me to the kitchen. "How are you doing?"

I handed him two air pots. I picked up the creamer of milk and sugar bowl. "I'm okay. It should be over now with Trerra dead. But it's not. Where's Ric? Why can't they find him?"

My hands trembled and a bit of milk sloshed over the rim. Harry nodded toward the mudroom. "C'mon let's get this to the search people; they can use it."

We set up the air pots and Styrofoam cups next to the sandwiches in silence. Harry retrieved his mug from Andrea. He looked over her head and his eyes motioned for me to join him outside. He swung a lantern from the shelf next to the door. I pulled my jacket from another peg, and hurried out behind him. He'd lit the lantern and kept it low, casting light only a few feet ahead. No matter; we knew our way out here in the dark.

Harry walked to the barn and waited for me to pass in front of him. April and Cash's soft snorts greeted us when we entered. I automatically moved to rub April's silky outstretched muzzle. My hand stopped inches from her nose. I caught the scent of Gray Flannel. I turned knowing he'd be there.

He wasn't alone. Ric stood in the shadows next to Marisol. Harry stood forward of Marisol blocking the light from the sputtering lantern.

The somber mood made no sense to me. He was found. He was alive. He looked whole though I couldn't see him clearly.

Marisol said, "You knew he was here before you turned. How?"

If she hoped for a psychic phenomenon I disappointed her. "Gray Flannel. I have a good nose."

She said over her shoulder, "You'll have to change that."

Even in the low light, my confusion must have shown on my face. I understood Ric was fine, had never really been in danger. I looked at Marisol and asked the next question. "You really looked worried when we were inside. Did you know?"

Marisol answered slowly. "Yes and no."

I turned to Harry. "And you?"

Harry shook his head firmly. "Not until an hour ago."

"I don't understand. Why are you hiding in the barn? There's a bunch of people out there searching the woods, the golf course, everywhere for you. There's even a helicopter." I pointed at Marisol. "That she insisted on."

"We had to make it look good."

"Make what look good?"

Ric stepped around Marisol and walked to stand in front of me. He raised his hands to hold my arms below my shoulders. His face lowered to within inches of mine. His dark eyes pinned my eyes and I couldn't look away. "I'm going undercover for the FBI. You'll hear some stories, that I was wounded, that I'm a dirty cop, maybe worse, or maybe that I'm dead. I couldn't go without seeing you, letting you know I'm alive."

The pressure on my upper arms increased with the intensity of his words, low and just for me. "I would never put you through that, Gracie." He leaned closer and mouthed more than said, "I'll always love you." He straightened and said in a normal tone. "I need you to tell Karen. I know she'll believe it from you."

"Ric, you've got to go. The search is getting too wide to keep moving you." Marisol's brisk voice broke our eye contact. His eyes shifted away, but returned quickly as he removed one hand to cup my chin. Again in a tone only for me he said, "Don't forget me."

I grabbed at his hand when he removed it from my chin and squeezed it, holding on to it as though the contact would be enough. "I won't," squeezed past the lump in my throat. Ric backed away loosening my grip. He faded into the shadows beyond the light cast from Harry's lantern. Ric touched two fingers to his lips and turned them toward me.

Marisol walked ahead of him making for the small door at the back of barn. Harry glanced out the window to check for searchers. Tears streamed down my face. It was as if an occult hand had reached between us and pulled him slowly away to his destiny; one that would never include me.

Harry's arm around my shoulders guided me out of the barn. He pulled me closer and prevented me from looking over my shoulder. No matter, Ric wouldn't be there.

Chapter Forty-two

The reality of daylight streamed through the sparkling windows, casting aside the darkness of the deeds carried out last night. The ramifications of those deeds might take years to come to full light.

Marisol had called off the search in the early morning hours. Harry had insisted she spend the night with us. Her partner, Frank, had agreed to the idea since Marisol's apartment in Wrigleyville was at least a forty-five minute drive, even at three in the morning. I suspected the invitation had less to do with English sensibility and more with some kind of plan.

"That's the last of your crew." Harry closed the door and leaned his forehead against the frame. "How will this work?" He spoke so softly and toward the wall I barely heard his words. Marisol who had turned away when the taillight of the last car blinked out of view didn't hear him.

"How will what work?" He didn't move. Marisol, however, whirled around and walked to his side. Her jaw muscles clenched. She touched his shoulder. He turned.

"It's done. Your part, his." She stared at Harry until he nodded.

"What's going on? What's done?" I grabbed Harry's hand and held it between mine. My eyes searched his face. I saw the sadness in his eyes. "Please tell me."

Marisol put her hand over Harry's wrist and pulled his hand away from mine. She took my hands and motioned toward the living room. "Let's sit down. What I'm going to tell you doesn't leave this room."

Her tone scared me. Harry's easy acquiescence terrified me. I turned my head to make sure Harry followed. He stepped behind me and kissed the top of my head. "I've a few calls to make. Marisol will explain then we'll talk."

My heart thumped against my chest and no amount of slow breathing would calm me. I watched Harry walk upstairs to make the calls that would shape our future.

Chapter Forty-three

Marisol carried two mugs of coffee into the living room and motioned for me to sit. I accepted the coffee, more for something to do with my hands. I gripped the ceramic mug with both hands and took small comfort from the heat transfer to my cold fingers.

"We weren't sure of Trerra's connection if any to Salizar, but during the night we nailed down the relationship. Mitch Trerra was Salizar's nephew. Our agent inside confirmed the *con el permiso* had been granted to someone in the United States."

The catastrophic news swept over me like a wave hitting at the knees, knocking my legs out from under me. I heard Marisol's voice from the depths of icy water filling my ears and eyes. The room turned opaque, the table lamps shimmering in the distance.

Marisol pried my fingers from around the mug and placed it on the coffee table. "Grace." She shook my shoulder, rubbed her hands briskly over mine. "Grace."

I forced myself to focus on her voice and not the droning of water in my ears. Her tone sharpened in my ears and I felt the warmth from her fingers seeping into me.

I looked at her and saw concern in her dark eyes, as well as a touch of impatience. I knew I wasn't mentally tough like her.

Heck, Gracie, an eight year old is mentally tougher than you sometimes.

Go away, I don't need this now.

Sure, but I'm never far.

I squared my shoulders and took a deep breath. "Why has Ric disappeared and who is Harry calling?"

Marisol's eyes widened at my tone and question. I saw impatience replaced with approval. For a tiny moment I felt pleased with the "cool girl's" acceptance.

This wasn't high school and the pleasure I'd felt turned sour in the pit of my stomach.

"Ric applied to the Bureau seven months ago, and he's been approved. This isn't the usual way we transition police officers to the bureau, but most agents don't come to us with a black ops mission in hand. We've known we have a leak somewhere in our task force. We needed a fresh face. We have to find out who the mole is quickly. Events are escalating. This *venganza* wrinkle makes it more dangerous, but even more necessary."

The dread I felt at her words poured into me like concrete flowing into a wooden form hardening around my heart.

"Ric and a special ops volunteer are literally flying in under the radar to try and find Salizar. The United States supports the popular party in his country and it would be in everyone's best interest if Salizar were removed. The plan would never work with a group of agents swarming the presidential palace, but two 'specialists' have a good chance of pulling it off and getting back alive."

In a gut-wrenching moment I realized if Harry went back a third time he'd never make it out alive.

Chapter Forty-four

I looked at Marisol. I knew my eyes must be a crazy purple. She'd chalk that up to nerves, fear…and she'd be right.

"They won't make it back. You know that, don't you?" I didn't expect her to answer.

She looked tired, the fine lines around her eyes etched deeper, and lack of sleep smudged under her eyes. Marisol shook her head and spoke calmly, with a finality of sadness. "I don't see them with us for the wedding, but they will stop Salizar."

Not with us for the wedding. I hadn't thought they'd leave before the wedding.

She doesn't mean that.

Okay they're leaving now and they won't be back in time for the wedding.

She doesn't mean that.

I know…

I reached out and touched the top of her hand. *Tough FBI chick* my brother had called her when she first came on the Morelli radar.

Not so tough now. She ached as much as I did for a man she loved and would lose.

"Isn't there any other way; other people who could go?"

"Salizar's removal is on our government's wish list, but not on paper or tape or anywhere official. This is the only way, and only those two have the motivation to get it done."

I swallowed hard to force the lump out of my throat. "When?"

"Two days."

"How long will it take?"

Marisol shrugged and rolled her neck side to side. "In and out they call it; no more than 48 hours on the ground."

"Is there any other way?"

Harry answered from the bottom of the stairs. "Only for all the Marsdens to disappear. My parents and Hannah are in the process. Once the people secure them I won't know where they are until this is over."

I'd already made my peace with this. Why couldn't he? We could be together and safe. My brain crashed at the prospect. Safe as what? Away from family, friends, our lives?

We'd have our lives. My mind hop-scotched up and down the idea in a split second. I looked at Harry to gauge if he'd been serious. He must have seen the spark of hope in my expression.

"I'm crazy with worry about you, the children, Hannah, and my parents. I can't let this maniac destroy my family."

Flinging us to the far corners of the country would destroy us too. Maybe Harry planned on England for us. British Intelligence would hide us–the least they could do. If someone met Hannah Jones in Brighton and Harry Smith in London, would they wonder about their resemblance?

If they put us in Seattle, could I attend Mass at Joe's parish? Could I meet him in the confessional or would my presence expose him to danger?

"Gracie," Harry spoke softly in my ear. When had he moved next to me? "Darling, your brain must be on overload. Let's get some sleep and talk in the morning. We have some planning to do."

Marisol stood and stretched. She had decided she'd had enough coffee to get home safely. "I'm going to get going."

Harry followed her to the front door. I heard her say in a lowered voice, "Let me know tomorrow."

I zoomed in on her words as soon as I heard the heavy door shut. "Let her know what?"

I thought Harry would put me off. Instead, he looked at me and cupped his hand under my chin. "Let her know if I'll join Ric in Venezuela or you in obscurity." He pulled me into his arms. For only the second time in our life together I felt him sob. "I've ruined your life."

Chapter Forty-five

Sleep eluded us during the few remaining hours before a decent time to make phone calls. We'd stretched out on top of the coverlet, fully dressed staring up at the ceiling, sometimes leaning up on a side to face each other.

Our conversations were disjointed–at times addressing the present situation. Could I say goodbye to my brothers and close friends or would I have to disappear and let my dad handle the explanation?

In the next moment, we laughed at our first holiday at the seashore in Brighton when we *plighted our trough* as I always called Harry's marriage proposal.

In the moment after the laughter I cried in his arms when he admitted he still considered attempting the mission with Ric. The plan was set, with a drop date of two days from now. A pilot and equipment waited at the ready in Aruba. Harry's earlier calls had been to contacts, sending false papers for Harry and Ric. There was a phone number that would be operative for only six hours day after tomorrow. If Ric didn't get an 'abort' call, he'd initiate his part of the plan. They had a better chance of success with an agent already in place. Contacting him would be dangerous, but necessary for a favorable outcome.

At seven in the morning, I splashed water on my face, trying to push the fatigue from my brain.

Harry tapped at the door. "Shall I make your Highland Grog?"

My stomach twisted and I fought the sudden queasiness that lately popped up at the thought of food. My hands dropped from my face and I stared into the mirror. *Oh my God, I'm pregnant.*

"Gracie?"

I wasn't going to say anything until I knew for certain. Medical specialists had assured us we couldn't have children. More likely stress had caused the symptoms. I would keep my thoughts to myself. Our lives were in turmoil with reality. No sense adding supposition to the mix.

"Gracie. Are you all right?"

I stuck my toothbrush in my mouth and mumbled around it. "Good. Thanks." The contact from the dry bristles made me gag. I listened for him to move away from the door. I stared into the mirror seeing a face filled with fear. Not a good beginning for a pregnancy.

I went back to bed and thought to snuggle down for just a few minutes. The discussion in my head tired me out.

What if he knew you might be pregnant?

Didn't I just say we're not adding supposition to the mix? Didn't I?

Yeah you did, but he'd want to stay with you.

No, he'd want to stay with his child forming in my womb, not just me.

Aren't you splitting hairs–I mean you and the baby are a package deal.

Call me crazy but I'd like for once for him to choose me as the only package.

That's crazy.

Is it? Maybe that's why Lily never told him she was pregnant–she wanted him to choose her and he didn't.

Do you hear yourself? He chose you. Hello!

But would he have continued wooing me if he knew

Lily carried his child? I think not!

More crazy talk. I'm not listening.

You have to, we're a package deal.

"Grace." Harry touched my shoulder. I sat up and swung my legs over the edge of our bed. I saw the Betty Boop alarm clock, a wedding present from one of his friends, on the nightstand. She *lived* on his side. After a few months of her in our lives Harry had taken to patting her plastic derriere for luck each morning. I pretended mock chagrin at his fondling the forties' icon. I smiled to myself, wondering if all her luck had run out.

Harry held out his hand and helped me off the bed. He slipped an arm around me. Soap and his aftershave mingled at my nostrils and I inhaled deeply. "*Hmm.* You smell good."

He leaned closer. I turned my morning mouth away, accepting a light kiss on my cheek. "Your father, Jan, Marisol, Karen, Lily, and Walter will be here at one o'clock. We'll tell them together."

I pulled away from his arm and stared hard at his closed face. No clue in his eyes, the shade of cornflower blue darkened to grey by either his navy polo or his decision.

"Tell them what?"

Harry looked away for a moment, then faced me squarely. Fear, panic, and anguish spilled from his eyes which held no secrets now. "God, Grace. I want you safe. Will and Connor and Hannah, all of you, safe. I don't want to tell them they have to spend the rest of their lives with strangers." He shook his head and walked to the window. He loved that view as much as I did. I didn't move, praying he wouldn't say the words I dreaded.

"I'd rather go after the bastard even if…"

"Even if what? You don't come back, you don't kill

him? Either way I wouldn't have you in my life, and in one case, I still would have to disappear if he's as sick as you say." My voice screeched. I rushed him and pummeled his chest. "You'd be dead. Dead. Dead," I repeated, alternating with punches against his chest. Sobs replaced my shouts.

Harry folded me into his arms. "*Sssh, sssh.*" He rocked back and forth, like he did with Connor when he grew restless or upset.

He'll make a great dad. I took a deep breath and slowed the sobs to the point of being able to swallow the last one. We could get through this.

Not if he's dead. My body stiffened and Harry felt the change. He held me closer, then released me and rubbed my arms. He took my hands in his. "Gracie, you're chilled." He guided me to the chair. "Sit down." Harry picked up the throw from the window seat. "Here, let's wrap you up." He tucked the ends up around my neck and behind my shoulders then leaned close to feel my forehead with his cheek. "You're hot. You should have rested more. Of course how could you–a nutcase tries to kill you, I'm playing cops and robbers, running around in the dark, shooting people, getting shot at, telling you I'm deciding whether to traipse off to kill a drug lord or scurry into nowhere with you." Harry dropped to his knees in front of me. "Of course you're sick. God, Gracie, you should be sick of me."

The room cooled in an instant. I saw Harry's earnest expression through a film, a shimmering glow inches beyond the outline of his body. Harry's voice, slow and thick tumbled, toward me, rolling on the air between us.

Lieutenant Blackmore loomed behind Harry holding a gun at his side. He raised his hand slowly bringing the weapon up close behind Harry's left ear. His finger tightened on the trigger. My entire being focused on the barrel of the gun willing my body to move, to warn Harry, to tackle the spirit threatening my husband.

Suddenly, it wasn't Blackmore standing behind Harry. This man was shorter, darker, his lips curling over yellowed, diseased teeth like an angry dog's snarl.

"No, don't," I screamed and launched out of my chair into Harry's chest toppling him sideways. Harry recovered quickly pulling me into him and rolling both of us up against the side of the bed. He pushed me half under the bed and slid his hand under his pillow.

"Damn," he swore under his breath. His hand pulled back empty. Harry had started locking up his gun in the nightstand when Will moved in with us.

I realized Harry wasn't surrounded by the glowing film and the room wasn't cold.

"Har–"

"*Sssh.* He put his fingers against my lips."

I moved my mouth around them. "There's no one there. Never was," I said quickly, before he could clamp his hand over my mouth.

"What?" He looked at the toppled rocker, at me. "You screamed. I saw your face…" His eyes told me he understood. Harry helped me to my feet and sat me down on the bed. He righted the rocking chair and sat down in it, planting his feet firmly on the floor to avoid movement.

"What in God's name did you see?" He stared at me. I saw an expression I'd never seen before in his eyes. I saw fear; not *for me* but *of me.*

I blinked and stared, but saw only concern and confusion. Had I imagined the fear?

"Gracie, what happened?"

I shook my head slowly. "I don't know. I was sitting looking at you. I saw Lieutenant Blackmore behind you. He had a gun and you were glowing all around, shimmering." I stopped talking realizing how crazy this sounded.

"Go on, what happened?" Harry's low voice coaxed.

"Only it wasn't Blackmore. It was an ugly, mean man who raised a gun and put it against your head here," I touched the spot behind my ear, "and he, he pulled…" I couldn't say it and Harry didn't need to hear it. I had described his execution at the hands of the South American drug lord he planned to seek out and kill.

I took the first steps to his side. "I think Blackmore tried to warn us." I picked up his hand from the rocker arm. "Please, Harry, I know you think this is crazy, but I believe you won't come back this time."

He pulled me around and onto his lap and let the rocker move on its wooden curves. The motion and his arms holding me lightly on his lap lured my head against his chest. I twisted round to study his face. His eyes stared out over my head to a spot on the far wall. Was he attempting to conjure his own prophetic vision, or trying to decide if he should stay with a nutcase, or take his chances in a foreign jungle?

Chapter Forty-six

I woke up, alone, on top of the bed, when the phone rang. I didn't know how many times it had rung and how soon it would switch over to the answering machine so I lunged for the phone on the nightstand.

The caller identified herself as the nurse at my primary care physician's office. She called to tell me the blood test taken at the hospital indicated I was pregnant. "Had I known that?" She went on to suggest I set up an appointment with a GYN/OB and asked if I needed a referral from my primary.

The call Harry and I had waited for so many other times came and went in a moment of routine; no fanfare, no grins of congratulations.

She doesn't know you Gracie. Did you want her to gush? What if you didn't want the baby, her call wouldn't be a joyous one. How's she to know?

Will this be joyous news or burdensome? We're about to change our lives forever, moving away from all the people I counted on sharing my baby's life. Is this the right time?

Babies don't care a bit for timing. You are right about one thing–you're life is about to change forever–you're having a baby!

I felt the corners of my mouth turn up and I swung my legs over the bed and stood.

"You're looking much better. I suspected a bit of a lie-down was what you needed. We're all wound up beyond belief." Harry carried a small tray into the room. "I made you tea and toast. I know you've been off that jam you liked, but I thought you might need some sugar. I've only slathered one piece with jam."

I'd been *off the jam* because it turned my stomach and now I knew why. So many things made sense, the nausea, the mood swings, and the tight clothes; how could I have not guessed?

He put the tray down on the nightstand. "Who called? I couldn't get to it."

I picked up the buttered slice of toast and took a bite to stall for time. "*Hmm*, good. Uh, my doctor's office telling me they received all the test results and all is well."

"Wonderful. No follow up visit? Seems like they should schedule something, you know to be certain."

If I had to continue this conversation my eyes would betray me. I wasn't ready to tell Harry about our impending parenthood. I nodded and mumbled around another bite of toast.

"I'm calling tomorrow to make an appointment. No rush, she said." I looked at Betty Boop to check the time.

"I have time for a long shower before they get here."

I moved toward the bathroom then stopped. "I should feed April and Cash before I clean up."

Harry handed me my cup and pointed me toward the bathroom. "It has been done. Devin is still on call. All the animals are quite content."

All the animals. Would they come with us to wherever we would be hidden?

"Harry, if we go…away can we bring them?"

Harry's sigh tugged at my heart. He felt the burden of being the cause of this catastrophe. "I don't know. Another of so many questions to ask Marisol." He shook his head. "God, Grace, I am so sorry I brought this on us."

"I know. Don't bring worse on us. I'd rather hide with you than bury you."

Harry shook off his melancholy and pointed to the bathroom. "It's now or you face the crowd stinky."

I showered and dressed in cheerful colors. Now when the lavender pants I chose were snug to button I smiled with my secret. I finished the tea and scraped the jam off the toast and devoured the bread. I'd best not start *eating for two* or I'd never lose the baby weight. It felt good to be worrying about something normal.

Oh yeah, normal like how will my family know when the baby is born?

Don't get dramatic. You can mail a birth announcement from a different state.

Sure, drive ten hours to drop mail in an Arkansas post office.

Who says Arkansas would be a ten-hour drive? Maybe it'll be your local postal service.

That would be obscurity.

Chapter Forty-seven

I made a light lunch for us that we pushed around on our plates. Harry lifted the near full plates from the table and scraped the food into the garbage.

"We have two bottles of Luchador left. Let's chill them and drink them with the family."

Harry's favorite wine merchant, Randy Russell, owned a wonderful wine shop in Lisle called Wine Expressions. We were steady customers at the wine tastings and the register.

"A goodbye toast? I don't think I could swallow a drop."

"Not goodbye, well, for now…" Harry rubbed his face with his hands. His usually neatly combed hair showed signs of recent hand combing. The vein at his temple twitched. His nerves, I knew, were stretched with anxiety. "My God, Grace. What have I done to you and your family?"

I reached my arms around his waist and held him close. I had no answer.

He spoke into my hair. "I have to make this right, for all of us."

My heart thumped against my chest, the dull thud muffled against his body.

"They'll be here soon. I have one more call to make. We'll have to pack tonight and be ready in the morning."

He said 'we'll have to pack'. He's coming with me.

Could be the editorial 'we'.

He said 'we'!

Just because two people are packing doesn't mean two people are going to the same place.

I nodded my head against his chest. "I'll chill the wine," I mumbled through a tight throat.

Chapter Forty-eight

My dad arrived first. It took every bit of strength I had not to rush into his arms like I used to as a kid when a bad dream woke me in the night. I tried for the usual light hug, but lingered a little never realizing how I loved his hugs.

I spoke quickly to fill up my head with mundane thoughts.

"Harry has two bottles left of the Shiraz you like. We're going to finish it today. Can you set out some glasses from the bar? I need to check on some laundry."

"The good stuff, huh. Must be one heck of an announcement."

I had my back to my dad and continued up the stairs to my bedroom. He'd have known the purple hue of my eyes meant trouble.

Harry and I had agreed we would wait until everyone sat down. Harry had this bizarre idea to drink a toast first.

I knew three things from the phone calls he'd made. Hannah and his parents were safely tucked away–somewhere. Men trained to protect would soon be on guard outside our house. British Intelligence arranged for two bodyguards to transport us to our new location and identity. Harry had insisted they assign agents he knew. He wasn't taking a chance that Salizar could infiltrate our safe haven team. What I didn't know was if Harry would be with me.

If I decided to tell Harry about our baby I needed to do it now. I wanted him to choose to stay because he wanted to be safe with me and Connor. There was no doubt now we would adopt Connor. He wouldn't be safe with Karen and Claire; poor Connor, losing his mom and now his Sissy. I caught myself rubbing my abdomen in the way I'd seen so many pregnant women do, a natural motion you didn't have to think about. Connor would have another sibling, maybe another Sissy.

In the midst of this terror and confusion I smiled at the thought of the life I carried. I knew I had to tell Harry now. This wasn't a game to see who he chose. This was our baby. I stepped lighter than before as I walked into our bedroom. Harry wasn't there. I walked through the hallway to Will's room.

Harry sat on his son's bed looking at the paraphernalia an almost teenager collects. Posters of Back Street Boys and Beach Boys juxtaposed next to each other; his Boy Scout pants hung carelessly over the back of his desk chair; his bookcase crammed with comics and Goosebumps books.

Marisol's agents profiled the family members at risk under this contract and because of Will's last name he escaped the list. Although Trerra must have known Will was Harry's son, he must not have conveyed the information to his uncle. He probably would have killed Will, but the next assassin wouldn't be targeting him. He would stay in his life with his new family and with Lily. He'd lose the dad he'd only found a year ago.

Harry held the ragtag bear that always sat on Will's bed and usually accompanied him secretly on overnights. He'd left it behind, maybe in his rush to pack or maybe in his rush to adulthood. My heart ached for Harry. He wanted so badly to make up for lost time with Will. I turned away from the door to give him a few more minutes alone with his memories. Now was not the time to offer the news.

Buck up, Harry. Losing one son? Not to worry, I may

have another on the way.

I crept to the head of the stairs, my legs heavy with the awareness of last steps from here to there. How many more times would I walk into my room, down these steps, through my house before tomorrow? I felt I should visit every nook and cranny. Instead I gathered my letters from my bedroom and headed downstairs.

The doorbell rang. I knew my dad would answer. I knew it was safe for him to do so. Marisol thought we had twenty-four to thirty-six hours before news reached Salizar about Trerra's failure. Marisol was working on the assumption he had a spy in her organization, just as she had one in his. Unfortunately cash ruled thicker than blood and she couldn't be sure the information would stay contained longer than a day or so. The timeline for Ric and Harry to go in and eliminate Salizar was crucial.

I heard Harry come out of Will's room. I waited for him on the stairs. We walked down together. Would we be together tomorrow?

Chapter Forty-nine

The knock at the back door had my dad going in two directions. As we entered the living room I saw him scurry through the dining room. Lily came in through the mudroom, while Karen came in the front door. Gertrude, I found out, had stayed back with the twins.

Walter, Marty, and Will arrived last to the family announcement. Marisol and her partner, Jeffers, arrived moments before them.

The chilled wine stood open and "breathing" on the bar cart. Dad lifted enough glasses for the assembled drinkers. Even Will had a wine glass, his destined to hold lemonade.

The time to tell drew upon us and I lost my chance to tell Harry about our baby. I felt a desperate urge to blurt out the news to everyone, to engage their pressure on Harry to stay with me, disappear with me. Instead I stayed silent and reached for the length of yarn tied to my belt loop. The friction from the scratchy strands against my palm felt reassuring.

Harry poured and handed round the glasses, taking the last two for us. He looked into my eyes, willing me to be strong. I accepted my glass from him. He used his free hand to brush the side of my cheek.

"Yuck, lovey stuff," Will wisecracked.

"Will, quiet," his mom admonished.

His face reddened as he realized no one else laughed.

Harry slipped his arm around me and raised his glass.

"To our family and friends whose love is unquestioned

and constant." Harry tipped his glass to his lips and most everyone followed suit. I noticed Marisol and Jeffers refrained from drinking.

"Thank you all for coming so quickly. We are sorry to be so mysterious about the reason, but even more mystery will shroud our lives going forward. Because of my previous line of work I have incurred the wrath of a dangerous and unbalanced drug lord. Ten years ago, I killed his father."

Will's eyes widened and Lily put her arm around his shoulders. Not the most pleasant thing to hear about your dad, but Will had to know that only imminent death would take Harry away from him.

"When I returned to find Lily and Hannah, the son became aware of me. He apparently hadn't known for sure who had been involved in his father's death. My colleagues leaked information pointing to Derek Rhodes, since he was deceased and beyond Salizar's reach.

"In these last few months he has made the connection and issued a warrant of sorts." Harry stopped suddenly and stared at Will. He couldn't make himself say the words in front of his young son. He looked at Lily. Although she couldn't know what was coming, she understood it was bad.

"Will, honey, I left my pills on the counter next to the phone. Please get them for me, I need to take them."

Will's struggle with wanting to help his mom, but wanting to stay and hear more played across his face.

"Go on, son. Get your mum's meds. I'll fill you in privately." Harry's voice tightened.

Jeffers stepped forward. "I'll walk with you." He handed his glass to Marisol and accompanied Will through the mudroom.

Lily's face turned to Harry. "Is he safe?"

Marisol put down both untouched glasses and stepped forward. "He is safe, but not everyone else is at this time."

"Sonofabitch! What in Sam Hill is going on? What have you done?" Dad glared at Harry, who stood quietly, letting his question hang in the air.

Harry looked at him. "I thought my old life would stay in the past. I would have walked away from her, Mike if I'd ever imagined this would happen. When I asked your permission to marry her I vowed to make her happy and keep her safe." Harry's voice cracked. I saw the sheen of tears in his eyes. "I haven't done either well."

Walter moved to Harry's side. Walter had known and protected Harry since my husband's childhood. I knew he must feel helpless to fulfill his own vow.

My father rushed to my side and engulfed me in the hug I'd wanted to give him earlier. Dad's hugs always made whatever imagined injustice or playground scrape I suffered as a child melt into obscurity in the whole scheme of life. He'd rock me from side to side and say, "Gracie girl, this is a tiny speck on the pages of your book of life. Blow it away with one puff." He'd release me and wait until I puffed away the imaginary speck. Sometimes he'd watch my eyes to see if I believed the speck was indeed gone. He'd make me puff until he saw the confidence return to my eyes.

No amount of puffing would clear this speck and he knew it. I felt the fear in his arms as he clutched me to him.

Marty walked to my side and gently tried to move my dad's arms from around me. Dad released me only long enough to put one arm around my shoulders and his other around Marty's waist. Holding on to his kids he asked, "How bad is it?"

To Marisol's credit she explained the *venganza* in a most clinical fashion, talking through the gasps and tears her cold terms brought from those in the room. To Dad's credit, after his initial shock he listened calmly while an FBI agent stood in his daughter's living room handily describing the contract on his daughter, son-in-law, and a little boy who called him *Unka Mi.*

"As the government we cannot engage in a covert strike." She looked at Karen. "Your brother is on the ground in Aruba waiting for the word to go in and rendezvous with his cohort. We have an agent in place who will give them as much help as he can without jeopardizing his cover."

Karen burst into tears. She sat down hard on the couch and covered her face with her hands. She lifted her head and between gulps to calm her sobs she demanded, "Why Ric? What's he got to do with this?" In her next breath she looked at me. I felt like the 800 hundred pound gorilla in the room.

"Who is his cohort?" Her gaze shifted Harry.

Marisol's lips stretched into a thin line. "I don't know for sure," she said softly. "It's possible the mission will be aborted if everyone goes into hiding. Ric is waiting for the call to confirm or abort."

"Harry, he's only just found you. Please, think of Will," Lily pleaded. "He's a little boy who needs his father alive."

"He wouldn't have me around. He couldn't know where I was. What kind of relationship is that?"

Karen snuffled and swallowed her tears. "Ric is the only family I have. Please, I don't want to lose him."

Harry's face drained of color and he stood staring at a point between the two women begging for him to disappear.

I touched his arm. "I'd rather live in hiding than risk your life and Ric's."

Walter's gruff voice filled with emotion. "Can't not the British who you served, help *mit* the taking away of *dat* Salizar?"

"Yeah," my brother chimed in, "They owe you I'd think. You risked your life for their causes."

Harry shook his head. "That was my job and they were my causes too." Harry's voice strengthened. "I knew the risks just as I know the risks now."

My heart hammered against my chest resonating in my ears like an out of control clock.

"Tomorrow, Grace, Connor, and I will accompany two agents to a safe house."

The release of breath from each of us filled the room with a not so soft sigh. My eyes filled with tears and the lump in my throat prevented any speech.

He was choosing to live with me, with us. As soon as everyone leaves I'll tell him my news.

As soon as everyone leaves? You won't see them tomorrow or next week or maybe ever.

How would I say goodbye? I had letters for everyone here and some I'd mail. Would we all stay together, making small talk, holding each other, crying until the tears stopped? Harry's voice pulled me back.

"If there's one thing British Intelligence can do it's confuse and obfuscate. We'll be able to contact you by post using a chain of custody for the letters to disguise their point of origination. We might possibly arrange a visit, not in the very near future, maybe closer to a few months."

Marisol spoke up. "I don't think of relocation as so open. Our witness protection program doesn't allow contact, period. It's the only way to insure safety."

"Nor does British Intelligence, but these chaps are mates of mine from our active status time. They have taken on the task of being our handlers, I think you call them. It's not protocol. It's the only way I'd agree to our going dark to the world." Harry shrugged. "They felt they owed me."

This was wonderful news. I locked eyes with my dad's teary face and tried to smile. I knew I'd see him again and maybe Marty and my other brothers. Maybe not Karen and Claire and my heart ached at the thought. Definitely not Tracy and her boys. Will, what about Will? Of course we'd see him again. All the important people. Ric.

"Ric. What about Ric?" I said it before I knew I spoke.

I'd seen Marisol move to the phone as soon as Harry announced his intention. She appeared to have been on hold, but now snapped into an animated conversation. I couldn't hear her words, but her body language shouted trouble.

Chapter Fifty

Instinctively and without reason I placed my palm over my belly and rubbed gently across the fabric.

Marisol hung up and turned to the room. Her lips drew tight across her face. I noticed a small pulsing on the tight skin of her throat. Her eyes shifted momentarily to my stomach and narrowed as she followed my movement. "Grace, I need a moment."

Harry started to follow me. Marisol held up her hand. "Just Grace for now. I have some news for you too."

Her voice sounded off, her face pinched with fatigue and fear. All at once, I felt queasy and nervous. I needed crackers and a piece of yarn.

I moved closer to her. She spoke quietly, "Are you pregnant?"

My shocked expression, which no one else could see, answered her. "How could you know?"

"I told you last year I saw you with a child. I thought it was Connor, but not today."

"I only found out today."

"Does Harry know?"

"No. I tried to tell him but everyone came and I wanted him to make his choice…" I stopped, realizing what I was going to say sounded so petty and selfish.

Marisol nodded and took one of my hands. "A person wants to feel they head the list. It's natural to want that. But you have to live with where you are on the list."

She squeezed my hand. I wondered if she was making

her peace with her position on Ric's list. She would move up now.

"What about Ric?"

She squeezed her lips together and let go of my hand and released a long breath. Marisol walked past me and entered the living room. The pockets of conversation ended abruptly.

"There is a problem. Somehow the timeline became confused, we're not sure how, not sure if it was intentional. Ric is on his way into the country. We can't stop him. He thinks the mission is on." She faced Harry. "He's expecting you."

Chapter Fifty-one

"No!" The exclamation burst from several people, but not from me.

I stood stunned at how cruel fate could be. I'd saved Harry, convinced him to be with me, but Ric chose jeopardy to save me. How does a timeline get confused? Had Salizar already received particulars about the mission? Would he have thugs waiting for Ric? Would Ric have any chance without the partner he expected?

Harry took me by the elbow and guided me to the couch. The voices, questioning, extolling, demanding, and pleading faded into a murmur. I knew what Harry would say. How could I tell him to ignore Ric? I couldn't, wouldn't. In the moments we sat together I realized how little control we have over our lives. Sure, we pick out cars and paint samples. We don't choose how we are wired, how we rise to trouble or shrink away.

"This isn't my choice, Gracie. It's what has got to be done." He put his arm around me and pulled me close. I leaned my head against his chest. He whispered his thoughts and promises for my ears only.

"I will come back to you, my darling. Only after I decided to give up everything except you did I realize how only you matter in my life. I must do this–he went in for us, I can't leave him."

I nodded into his chest, knowing full well I couldn't say much. I managed a choked, "When?"

I felt him sigh against me. "Now, darling. If he is on

his way in, I have to rendezvous with him by zero two hundred hours."

At two o'clock in the morning, the two men who mean the most to you will be preparing to trek through hostile territory to kill a crazy killer who wants to obliterate you and your family.

"Gracie, I want to talk to Will before I go. Will you wait for me in our room, help me pack, stay with me?"

I nodded, again not trusting my voice.

Harry stood and walked over to Lily. He took her hand. "I'm going to have a few words with Will." She looked close to tears and simply looked down. Harry put his fingers under her chin and lifted it. "You have done an amazing job at raising our son. I am forever grateful for the wonderful young man you've molded. I do regret I wasn't there for him and you."

Tears streamed down Lily's face as she turned away. Harry approached my dad. "Mike, I will make this right."

My dad threw his arms around Harry with a force that rocked him. "I know you will, son." He couldn't say more.

"I am *komming mit* you," Walter said quietly. "I make promise to your parents I was always watching, protecting."

"You have, my dear friend, you have. Your place is here *mit* your *fraulein*. The plan is for two, moving quickly, getting in and out in forty-eight hours. Sorry, old chap, but Gertrude's strudel has slowed you down." Harry's attempt at lightness brought a few smiles to the somber faces around the room.

"You're not in stellar shape, Harry," my brother pointed out. "Nothing to do with Grace's cooking, but you've only recovered from some bad stuff."

I wanted to hug Marty for his concern and punch him for pointing out the obvious. Harry wasn't in the best of shape to handle the physical demands of what he described.

Harry glared at Marty then softened his expression. "Whatever shape I'm in will have to do, won't it."

Harry turned to Marisol. "I know Jeffers has been keeping Will occupied. Can you let him know I'm coming out?"

Marisol lifted the radio to her lips and passed on the information.

Harry left through the mudroom to find his son and explain why he may not see him again. Would Will be proud of his dad's code of honor or angry at the possibility of abandonment, or both.

I stood up anxious now for everyone to leave so I would have more time with Harry. "I'm tired. Can you all come back tomorrow to wait for…" I couldn't talk.

Dad hugged me. "You bet, sweetheart. We'll be back tomorrow morning. Don't worry about anything, the horses, the cats, food. We have it covered."

He lowered his voice. "I'm going to St. Dom's chapel. I'll stay there on my knees all night. We'll get him back. You'll see."

In minutes the room cleared with promises of returning tomorrow. I knew my family; more Morellis would appear on my doorstop, bringing food and comfort while we waited for news. They'd be there with me to support me until we knew if we'd be breathing a sigh of relief that the *venganza* was quashed or if we'd be planning a funeral.

"That's quite a tribe you have there."

Marisol stood alone at the kitchen door. Her head tilted sideways, she looked at me for a long minute. When she spoke she did so slowly and with some effort.

Dear God was there more she wasn't telling us about Ric?

"Harry won't be going in to help Ric. I've made a few calls and his passport isn't valid, in fact his name is on watch list at the airport. He won't be able to get on a plane."

"But Ric is expecting Harry."

"He's expecting a cohort," she corrected. "It was to be Harry, but circumstances have changed. Marty is right, Harry's still not 100% and that's dangerous for Ric. Besides, Harry shouldn't miss the chance to raise his own child from scratch, which will most likely be tougher than this op," Marisol tried to joke.

"I don't understand."

"You and Harry and Connor will be leaving tomorrow. You can't be sure of the outcome and to waste time waiting could mean your lives."

I stared at Marisol trying to wrap my brain around what she was saying. Harry would be with me. Who would be with Ric? She lifted her chin and stared back in a pose of defiance.

"You? You're going?" I gasped in disbelief.

"I'm younger, I'm in shape, I have current training, I speak the language," she paused, "and I want him back even more than you do."

"This won't work. Harry won't let you."

"Harry has no choice. You can tell him what I've done, what I'm planning, or you can let him go to the airport and find out. That's your choice." She walked briskly toward the front door. With her hand on the door lever she turned. Our eyes made contact. I saw an expression of triumph and excitement. She would save her man and in the process save us.

"Good luck, Grace."

How odd she wished me luck. Did she think being a new mom, two times over, and a fugitive from my life would be more daunting than a covert assassination attempt?

"And you, Marisol."

She turned to leave, her hand pushing down on the lever.

"Marisol?" This could be my last chance to make things right for her lifetime.

"It was always Harry for me. When I thought he was dead…even then my heart would never have been totally his."

"I'm happy with the portion of his heart he's given me. Most times nothing is total."

I nodded trying to let her go. "Please be careful. Thank you for doing this. Tell Ric, tell him he should share more of his heart–it does him no good sitting idle." My eyes pinched and tears released.

Marisol's lips curved slightly. "I'll tell him. I have a good feeling about us. I see us beyond this week. I saw that baby in your life." She glanced at my belly. "In that sense I am usually right."

She opened the door and turned one last time. "Lock this behind me." With that terse command she strode down the sidewalk to her car. Jeffers was at the wheel. Within moments they were gone.

I closed the door and slid the deadbolt in place. My thoughts flew to Harry and how he'd react to the drastic change in plans. I didn't have long to wait to find out.

"What did she mean, she saw that baby in your life?"

I jumped at Harry's voice so close behind me. He stood in the hallway from the living room at the door to the mudroom.

Harry led me into the living room. "She's not referring to Connor, is she?"

I faced him and took both his hands in mine and placed

them on my abdomen. His eyes widened in understanding and a look of astonishment filled his face. I held his hands against me and smiled easily, tears streaming down my face.

He lifted his hands abruptly, his expression changing as quickly. Those hands that had gently touched me now strafed his hair with jerky movements. I knew his joy had been short circuited by the mission he'd planned.

"Marisol made a call and put your name and identification on a watch list of some sort at the airport. You won't be able to fly."

"She's taking my place." It wasn't a question. The explosion of anger and angst I expected didn't happen. He stood looking over my head toward the windows. "Do you think me a coward for not rushing after her to make her change her plans? If you can get beyond her gender she is the better choice, the best choice for Kramer's safety and the ultimate success of the mission.

"Your brother was right; I'm a little long in the tooth for these clandestine ops. Kramer, I found out, has been training for his acceptance to the FBI. He's in top shape physically and mentally. It's the mental part that makes or breaks you."

I took his hand again and tugged on it to make him look at me. "You are no coward. You always said the reason you went on the mission ten years ago is because you were trained and in peak condition. The mission and your partner had its best chance with you. Ric and Marisol are the best team. You're not in their league anymore."

Harry slipped his arm around me. "What league am I in now, Gracie?"

"Pre tee-ball league," I said smiling up into his face.

"Soccer."

"Take that up with your father-in-law."

Can it be this easy? We're walking upstairs to our bedroom to pack clothing, keepsakes, a lifetime of memories into suitcases and boxes. In the morning two British agents will escort us to a secret location and we will become who? Who chooses our names, no one asked me?

"Grace, I have to tell Will and Lily I'm not going. Well not going where they think. I'll be back in a jiff."

"I'll make some herbal tea. Maybe I should be cutting down on the caffeine."

Harry headed for the mudroom; I turned my steps to the kitchen. I heard the shot before I'd lifted the kettle to the stovetop.

"Harry!" I turned to sprint to the yard. The pain shot through my side and brought me to my knees.

Oh no, God. Please not the baby.

I slumped against the cabinet and tried to stretch my legs out straight. I clutched at my side. I felt less pain lying down. I let go of my side and looked at my hand and understood. *Venganza.*

Epilogue

Strange noises and smells filled my brain for the three weeks I'd been in a drug induced coma. Thoughts swirled through my brain until I didn't know reality from hallucination.

I'd been rushed to Edwards Hospital, then, once stabilized, transferred to a trauma center in Iowa City, our new home. Harry had been at my side when the doctors weaned me from the drug cocktail keeping me comatose.

Our baby was fine, growing, and thriving according to the latest ultrasound. The bullet had damaged some of my nerves and tissue causing muscle weakness. I went to physical therapy three times a week and Walter worked with me every day.

Walter and Gertrude gave up their lives to follow us into hiding. They'd become so close to Connor it wasn't much of a sacrifice for them to follow him. I needed and would need help for months to come. My prognosis for a full recovery was good.

The shooter had been shot and arrested. Harry had taken to carrying his gun with him. When he heard the shot he'd followed the shooter through the woods, trying to stop him but not kill him. The man had traveled directly to Lily's house. Harry feared Will was the next target and he had opened fire on the running figure catching him in the legs.

News of Trerra's death had reached Salizar faster because of the mole on Marisol's task force. He'd been found out, but only after he had warned Salizar about Ric and Marisol. They failed to reach their target, barely, escaping with their lives.

Their escape had been aided by an unlikely source. Salizar's sister, Mitch Trerra's mother, helped them. Marisol had communicated with her in Spanish about meeting her son and knowing him through his business. She tried to paint him as a nice guy led astray by his uncle's corruptive influence. What mother didn't want to think the best of her child?

Our new home, new life, in the suburbs kept us hidden in plain sight. Every week Harry checked in with our handlers hoping for word of Salizar's death.

Walter and Gertrude took care of Connor and Harry took care of me. We couldn't be positive about Will's safety, so he and Lily had been secreted in another part of the state.

My dad and Jan went through with their wedding. He knew I'd be devastated if I'd been the cause of a postponement and the ceremony provided a good way for the family to come together on a joyous note and not one of grief. The pictures smuggled to me through secure routes gave me a lifeline. Dad had made sure everyone in the family had been photographed. He knew I was recovering and for now he had to be content until he could see me with his own eyes.

We sat on the patio; Harry had Connor on his lap; Elmo sprawled across my lap. In another month he'd be vying for space with my growing belly. I wondered if he could hear the baby's heartbeat.

Harry had smuggled Elmo in his duffle. He made the decision to leave Patches and Trey with April and Cash. The Atwater's took over the care of our animals.

I had the wedding photos spread out on the table watching Harry point out each to Connor. "Grandpa,

Granny Jan, Uncle Marty, Uncle Mike, Aunt Karen…"

Connor squealed with delight and pointed a chubby finger at the photo. *Care*, he drooled, his version of Claire.

My heart ached for all we'd left behind.

Harry knew my pain. He reached out and covered my hand with his. "We will go home someday. If I know anything, I know Kramer will move heaven and earth to bring you back."

Luisa Scala Buehler grew up in the town of Berkeley, Ill., a suburb of Chicago. During her teens, her family–two parents, an older brother, and an uncle–decided to move to Chicago.

Her first exposure to a public library was the small "volunteer" library located in the basement of a nearby grocery store. It was there she discovered Nancy Drew. Luisa realized that this would be her career–not girl detective, but girl mystery writer. Then her family subscribed to the Sunday paper and Luisa found another fascinating role model in the comic pages…Brenda Starr, reporter!

She attended Proviso West High School in Hillside, Ill., where she joined the newspaper staff, but her advisor suggested she try another release for her writing when she continually failed to meet her deadlines. She joined the volunteer docent program at Brookfield Zoo in 1987, where she answered questions from zoo-goers concerning animal habitat behaviors, type of food, and the #1 no animal question, "where is the closest restroom?" An earlier idea, to write children's books, also seemed to fit with her duties at the zoo; eventually she began to write mystery novels.

After submitting her manuscripts for five years without gaining publishing success, she signed a contract in 2002 for her first published book, *The Rosary Bride,* and has been blessed with success ever since. *The Lighthouse Keeper* is her fifth book to date.

Luisa Buehler lives in Lisle, Ill., with her husband Gerry, their son Christopher (Kit), and the family cat, Martin Marmalade. In her spare time, she loves to garden.

CPSIA information can be obtained at www.ICGtesting.com
230426LV00001B/1/P
9 781590 805930